# YOU
# KNOW
# YOU
# WANT
# THIS

# YOU KNOW YOU WANT THIS

## KRISTEN ROUPENIAN

JONATHAN CAPE
LONDON

1 3 5 7 9 10 8 6 4 2

Jonathan Cape, an imprint of Vintage Publishing,
20 Vauxhall Bridge Road,
London SW1V 2SA

Jonathan Cape is part of the Penguin Random House group of companies
whose addresses can be found at global.penguinrandomhouse.com.

Penguin
Random House
UK

First published in the UK by Jonathan Cape in 2019

"Pulchritude" is from Lara Glenum's second book of poetry,
*Maximum Gaga* (Action Books, 2008)

penguin.co.uk/vintage

A CIP catalogue record for this book is available from the British Library

Hardback ISBN 9781787331105
Trade paperback ISBN 9781787331334

Printed and bound in Great Britain by Clays Ltd, Elcograf S.p.A.

Penguin Random House is committed to a sustainable future for our
business, our readers and our planet. This book is made from Forest
Stewardship Council® certified paper.

MIX
Paper from
responsible sources
FSC
www.fsc.org    FSC® C018179

Many thanks to the journals in which these stories first appeared, some in edited form: "Bad Boy" in *Body Parts Magazine*, "Cat Person" in *The New Yorker*, "Scarred" (as "Don't Be Scarred") in *Writer's Digest*, and "The Night Runner" in *Colorado Review*. Thank you as well to the Hopwood Foundation for its support of "The Night Runner" and "The Matchbox Sign."

*For my mother, Carol Roupenian,*
*who taught me to love what scares me*

# CONTENTS

BAD BOY   1

LOOK AT YOUR GAME, GIRL   13

SARDINES   27

THE NIGHT RUNNER   45

THE MIRROR, THE BUCKET,
AND THE OLD THIGH BONE   61

CAT PERSON   77

THE GOOD GUY   99

THE BOY IN THE POOL   149

SCARRED   169

THE MATCHBOX SIGN   181

DEATH WISH   201

BITER   215

*ACKNOWLEDGMENTS*   227

He sez
There is something jerking
in your ribcage

that is not a heart

It is cow-intestine white
& fibrous & gilled

Lara Glenum, "Pulchritude"

# BAD BOY

Our friend came over the other night. He and his terrible girlfriend had finally broken up. This was his third breakup with that particular girlfriend, but he insisted it was going to be the one to stick. He paced around our kitchen, working his way through the ten thousand petty humiliations and torments of their six-month relationship, while we cooed and fretted and bent our faces into sympathetic shapes in his direction. When he went to the bathroom to collect himself, we collapsed against each other, rolling our eyes and pretending to strangle ourselves and shoot ourselves in the head. One of us told the other that listening to our friend complain about the details of his breakup was like listening to an alcoholic whine about being hungover: yes, the suffering was there but good God it was hard to muster sympathy for someone with so little insight into the causes of his own problems. How long was our friend going to continue to date terrible people and then act surprised when they treated him terribly, we asked each other. Then he came out of the bathroom and we mixed him his fourth drink of the evening and told him he was too drunk to drive home but that he was welcome to crash on our couch.

That night, we lay in bed together, talking about our friend. We complained about how small our apartment was, about how we couldn't have sex without him hearing us. Maybe we should do it anyway, we said—it'll be the closest to getting laid he's come in months. (Withholding sex had been one of the manipulative strategies of the terrible girlfriend.) Maybe he'd like it.

The next morning, when we got up for work, our friend was still asleep, his shirt half-unbuttoned. He was surrounded by crumpled beer cans and he'd clearly kept drinking alone long after we'd gone to bed. He looked so pathetic, lying there, that we felt bad about how meanly we'd joked about him the night before. We made extra coffee and fed him breakfast and told him he could stay at our apartment as long as he wanted, but when we got home we were nonetheless surprised to find him on the couch.

We made him get up and into the shower, and then we took him out to dinner, where we refused to let him talk about the breakup. Instead, we were charming. We laughed at all his jokes and ordered a second bottle of wine and gave him life advice. You deserve someone who makes you happy, we said. A healthy relationship with someone who loves you, we continued, and we looked at each other appreciatively before turning the full force of our attention onto him. He was like a sad little dog hungry for friendliness and praise, and it felt good to see him lap it up; we wanted to pat his soft head and scratch him behind his ears and watch him wiggle.

After we left the restaurant, we were having such a good time that we invited our friend up to our apartment with us. Once we were there, he asked if he could crash with us again that night, and when we pushed him, he admitted that he didn't like being in his own apartment by himself right now, because home reminded him of the terrible girlfriend. We said, of course, you can stay as long as you want, we've got a pull-out couch, that's what it's for. But behind his back we gave each other a look, because even though we wanted to be good to him, we were not going to endure a second night without sex—for one thing, we were drunk, and for another, acting so charming all evening had gotten us kind of worked up. So we went to bed, and even the way we said good night to him probably made it clear that we were going to fuck. At first, we tried not to make a lot of noise, but soon it felt like our efforts to be quiet and then giggling and hushing each other were probably calling more attention to what we were doing than just doing it the normal way, so we did what we wanted and we had to admit we were sort of into it, the idea of him out there, listening to us, in the dark.

The next morning, we were a little embarrassed, but we told ourselves, hey, maybe that was what he needed to nudge him out of the nest and back to his own apartment, and it might even motivate him to get a girlfriend who would sleep with him more than once every two months. But that afternoon, he texted us and asked us what we were doing that evening, and soon, he was staying over most nights of the week.

We would feed him dinner, and then the three of us would drive somewhere, us in the front, him always in the back seat. We joked about giving him an allowance, about giving him chores; we joked that we should adjust our phone contracts to add him to our family plan, since we all spent so much time together. Besides, we said, then we could keep a better eye on him and stop him from texting the terrible ex-girlfriend, because even though they were broken up, they were still in touch and he was always on his phone. He would promise to stop, swear that he knew it was bad for him, but then he'd slide right back into texting her again. Mostly, though, we enjoyed spending time with him. We liked fussing over him and taking care of him and scolding him when he did irresponsible things like texting the terrible ex-girlfriend or missing work because he'd stayed up too late the night before.

We kept having sex even though he was staying in the apartment with us. In fact, it was the best sex we'd ever had. It became the kernel of a fantasy we shared, picturing him out there with his ear pressed to the wall, all churned up by jealousy and arousal and shame. We didn't know if that was true—maybe he covered his head with a pillow and tried to ignore us; maybe our walls were more soundproof than we thought—but we pretended, between ourselves, and we would dare each other to leave the bedroom while we were still all flushed and breathless, to get a drink of water from the refrigerator and see if he was awake. If he was (he always was) we would exchange a few casual words with him and then rush back to bed to laugh about it and fuck again even more urgently the second time around.

We got such a charge from the game that we began upping the stakes, coming out half-dressed, or wrapped in towels, leaving the door open a crack, or a little more. In the morning after a particularly raucous night, we would tease him by asking him if he slept well, or what he'd dreamed about, and he would look at the ground and say, I don't remember.

This idea he wanted to join us in bed was only a fantasy, but strangely, after a while we started feeling a little bit annoyed at our friend for acting so coy. We knew that if something were going to happen, we would have to make the first move. We outnumbered him, first of all, and second, it was our apartment, and third, that was the way it worked between us: we bossed him around and he did what we asked. But still, we allowed ourselves to be irritable with him, to pick on him a bit, to blame him for our frustrated desires and to tease him a little more cruelly than we had before.

When are you going to get a new girlfriend, we asked him. God, it's been so long for you, you must be losing your mind. You're not getting yourself off on our couch, are you? You better not be getting yourself off on our couch. Before we went to bed, we would stand with our arms folded, like we were mad at him, and say, you better behave yourself out here, this is a nice couch, we don't want to see any stains on it tomorrow morning. We would even allude to the joke, obliquely, in front of other people, pretty girls. Tell her, we'd say. Tell her about the couch and how much you love it, you love it there, right? And he would squirm and nod and say, yeah, I do.

Then a night came when we all got drunk, really drunk, and we began hitting the joke even harder, insisting that he admit it: come on, you do it all the time, right, you're out here going crazy, listening to us, you pervert, you think we don't know? And then we froze for a second because that was the first time we'd said out loud that we knew he could hear us, and we hadn't quite meant to give it away. He didn't say anything, though, so we tore into him even harder—we can hear you, we said, waving our beers at him, we can hear you breathing heavy and the couch squeaking, you're probably at the door half the time, watching us, I mean, it's fine, we don't mind, we know you're desperate, but God, stop lying about it, please. Then we laughed, too loudly, and did another round of shots, and then a new joke started, and the joke was that since he'd already watched us, dozens of times, it was only fair to let us watch him. He should show us, he should show us what he did on this couch, *our* couch, when we weren't around. For what felt like hours, we mocked him and prodded him and teased him and he got more and more flustered but he didn't leave, he stayed pinned to his seat on the couch and when he finally began unzipping his jeans we felt a rush that was like nothing else. We watched him for as long as we could stand it and then we stumbled into our room and did it with the door open, but we didn't invite him to come any closer, that first time; we wanted him to watch us from the outside, looking in.

The next morning was delicate, but we made our way through it by proclaiming how drunk we'd been, God, how completely obliterated. He left after breakfast and disappeared for three days, but on the fourth night, we texted him and we all went to a movie, and on the fifth night he came over. We didn't mention the joke, or what had happened between us, but simply to all be drinking together, alone, seemed like an agreement that it would happen again. We drank steadily, seriously, and every hour that passed increased the tension, but also our certainty that he was willing, until at last we said, Go into our room and wait for us. When he did, we took a long time finishing our drinks, savoring them, before we set them down and went in after him.

We made up rules about what he could and couldn't do, what he could and couldn't touch. Mostly he couldn't do anything; mostly he watched, and sometimes he wasn't even allowed to do that. We were tyrants; we got most of our pleasure from making the rules and changing them and seeing him respond. At first, what happened during these nights was a strange, unspoken thing, a bubble clinging precariously to the edge of real life, but then, about a week after it started, we made the first rule for him to follow during the day, and suddenly the world cracked open and overflowed with possibility.

In the beginning, the things we told him to do were the things we'd been telling him all along: to get up, to take a shower, to shave his face, to stop texting that terrible girl. But now, each instruction was accompanied by an electric crackle, a shimmer in the air. We added more: He should go shopping and buy nicer clothes, which we picked out. He should get a haircut. He should cook us breakfast. He should clean up the area around the couch where he slept. We made him a schedule, sliced it up into finer and finer increments, until he was sleeping, eating, pissing, only when we told him to. It seems cruel, laid out like that, and maybe it was, but he gave in without complaint, and for a while, he flourished under our care.

We loved it, his eagerness to please, and then, slowly, it started to get under our skin. Sexually, it was frustrating, his unerring instinct toward obedience; once we settled into this new pattern there was none of the friction or uncertainty of that first dizzying night. Soon, the teasing started up again; the jokes about us being like his parents, about how babyish he was, about what he was allowed to do or not do on the couch. We began making rules that were impossible to follow and instituting little punishments when he broke them; bad boy, we'd tease him. Look at what you've done. That kept us occupied for a while. We were devilishly creative about the punishments, and then they, too, began to escalate.

We caught him texting that terrible girl, and when we confiscated his phone, we discovered he'd been talking to her all along, after he'd promised—sworn!—that they were over. There was nothing funny about how angry we felt then, how personally betrayed. We sat him down at the table, across from us. Look, we said, you don't have to stay with us, we're not keeping you here, go back to your place if you want, seriously, we don't fucking care.

I'm sorry, he said, I know she's bad for me, that's not what I want. He was crying. I'm sorry, he said again, please don't make me go.

Fine, we said, but what we did with him that night was too much even for us, and the next morning we were disgusted with ourselves and the sight of him made us feel a little sick. We told him to go home and we'd let him know when we wanted to talk to him again.

As soon he was gone, though, we got so bored we could barely stand it. We white-knuckled it through two days, but without him around to watch us, we felt so dull and pointless it was almost as though we didn't exist. We spent most of our time talking about him, speculating about what was wrong with him, about all the ways he was broken, and then we promised ourselves that if we were going to do this, whatever this was, we'd do it respectably, with house meetings and safe words and polyamorous meet-ups. And on the third day we told him to come over again. We had nothing but good intentions, but we were all so hideously polite and uncomfortable with each other that in the end the only way to purge the tension was to go into the bedroom for a repeat of all the things that had so disgusted us three days before.

We only got worse after that. He was like some slippery thing we had caught in our fists, and the harder we squeezed the more of it bubbled up through our fingers. We were chasing something inside of him that revolted us, but we were driven mad as dogs by the scent. We experimented—with pain and bruises, chains and toys—and afterward, we'd collapse in a tangle of damp limbs, all jumbled together like the trash that washes up on a beach after a storm. There was a kind of peacefulness in those moments, the room quiet except for our slowing, overlapping breath. But then we'd banish him so we could be alone, and before long the need to take him apart would start building up in us again. No matter what we did, he wouldn't stop us. No matter what we told him to do, he would never, ever say no.

To protect ourselves we pushed him as far into the corner of our lives as we could. We stopped going out with him, stopped having dinner with him, stopped talking to him. We returned his phone calls and summoned him only for sex, brutal three-, four-, five-hour sessions before we'd send him home again. We demanded he be available to us, always, and we pushed him back and forth like a yo-yo: go, come, come, go. None of our other friends had heard from us in ages; work was a place we went to space out and nap. When he wasn't in the house, we stared at each other, utterly drained, the same washed-out pornographic movie playing on an endless loop in our heads.

Until the day came when he stopped answering our texts right away. First came a five-minute delay, then ten, then an hour, and then, finally, *I'm not sure I can do this tonight, sorry, I'm feeling really confused right now.*

We lost it, then. We lost our fucking shit. We stormed around the apartment and sobbed and smashed glasses and screamed *what is he thinking what the fuck he can't do this to us.* We couldn't go back to the way it was before, the two of us, bland vanilla sex in the bedroom with nobody watching, nothing to gnaw on and tear at except for each other. We worked ourselves up into a frenzy and called him twenty times but he didn't pick up and at last we decided: no, it's not acceptable, we're going over there, he can't hide from us, we are going to figure out what the fuck is going on. We were furious, but mixed in with the anger was a rowdy excitement, the thrill, almost, of the hunt: the knowledge that something explosive and irrevocable was about to go down.

We saw his car parked in front of his building, and the light in his room was on. From the street, we called him again but again he didn't answer, and since we had an extra copy of his key from the days when we watered each other's plants and got each other's mail, we let ourselves inside.

There they were, in the bedroom, our friend and the terrible girl. They were naked, and he was on top of her, pumping away. It looked so ridiculously simple after everything we'd gone through that our first reaction was to laugh.

She saw us before he did and gave a little squeak of surprise.

He rolled over and his mouth opened but no sound came out. That terrified face he made soothed us a little, but it was a drop of water on a conflagration. The girlfriend scrambled to cover herself, and her shocked bleating transformed itself into a torrent of accusations. What the hell are you doing, she shrieked, what the fuck is this, what are you doing here, you are both so fucking twisted, he's told me all about it, the stuff you do, it's so messed up, get the fuck out of here, you don't belong here, you freaks, go, go, go.

Shut up, we said, but she ignored us.

Please, our friend begged her. Please, stop. I can't think. Please.

But she wouldn't. She kept talking, saying things about him, about us, about everything that had happened. Even as he'd been talking about her to us, he'd been talking about us to her; and now she knew everything, including the things we were too ashamed to talk about even with each other. We'd thought we'd exposed every part of him, and yet he'd been lying to us, hiding this from us, all this time, and in the end, we were the ones who were exposed.

Make her stop, we screamed, feeling a kind of panic rise up; make her stop saying that, shut her up, shut her up now. We clenched our fists and stared him down, and he trembled, his eyes watery, and then the anger that had consumed us burned itself out, and something clicked into place.

Make her stop, we said again—

And he did.

He fell on her with the full weight of his body, and they wrestled, flailing and scratching, until the bed shook and the bedside lamp wobbled on its table, and then they steadied and reached an equilibrium, his chest against her back, his arm wrenched across her neck, her face buried in the mattress.

Good, we said. Now, go on. Keep doing what you were doing.

Don't let us interrupt you. You want this, right? You know you want this. So go on. Finish it. Finish what you started.

He swallowed, looking down at the terrible girl beneath him, who had stopped struggling and gone still, her hair a tangled nest of matted gold.

Please don't make me, he said.

At last: that small nub of resistance. But it was anticlimactic, in the end, because he was so abject, lying there, so small, and we, we filled the whole world. We could have walked away then, having found it, knowing we could break it, break him—but we didn't. We stayed, and he did what we told him. Soon, the terrible girl's skin was parchment-white except for a stamp of mottled bruising that spread across her thighs, and she didn't move except as he moved her, and the tight knot of her hand came loose and her pale fingers unfurled. Yet he kept going; as the room darkened and the light came in again and the air thickened with smells, we kept him there, and he did what we told him to do. By the time we told him to stop, her eyes were blue marbles, and her dried lips had pulled high up over her teeth. He rolled off her and moaned and tried to burrow away from her, away from us, but we rested our hands on his shoulders and smoothed his sweaty hair, stroked the tears off his cheeks. We kissed him, and we wrapped his arms around her and we pressed his face to her face. Bad boy, we said softly as we left him.

Look at what you've done.

# LOOK AT YOUR GAME, GIRL

Jessica was twelve years old in September 1993—twenty-four years after the Manson murders, five years after Hillel Slovak died of a heroin overdose, seven months before Kurt Cobain shot himself in the head, and three weeks before a man with a knife kidnapped Polly Klaas at a sleepover in Petaluma, California.

Jessica's family had moved from San Jose, where she had been the most popular girl in her sixth-grade class, out to Santa Rosa, where she orbited uneasily around several groups of friends: her popular friends, who neglected her; her band friends, who were nice but boring; and the ones she secretly thought of as her bad friends, who were the most fascinating but also the nastiest, their jokes digging like little nails into her skin. She could spend time with the mean friends only in short, thrilling bursts before she'd start feeling exhausted and sore, and then she'd have to retreat into the comfort of her band friends to recover.

Jessica's family lived in a bright yellow Victorian in Lomita Heights, and every day she would come home from field hockey practice, empty her homework onto her bed, and refill her backpack with her Discman, her black folder of CDs, the books she'd checked out from the library, and an apple and three slices of cheese for a snack. Then she would run the three blocks from her house to the park where the skateboarders hung out. When she got to the park, she sat at the bottom of the twisting slide and selected the music she wanted to listen to and the book she wanted to read. She owned seventeen CDs but she only listened to three: *Blood Sugar Sex Magik*, *Use Your Illusion I*, and *Nevermind*. The books were mostly broken-spined paperbacks from the science fiction and fantasy shelf, about boys coming into their powers.

The skateboarders at the park were older than she was, thirteen or fourteen maybe, and they shouted at each other and rode their skateboards down the concrete railing, making a terrible scraping sound. Sometimes they pulled their shirts up to wipe the sweat off their faces, revealing flashes of flat brown stomach, and every once in a while, one of them caught his skateboard on the rail and went flying forward on his hands and knees, leaving a quartet of bright red streaks on the pavement. None of them ever spoke to her. She would watch them for an hour, listen to her music, pretend to read her book, and go home.

The first time she saw him, she was in the middle of opening a new Guns N' Roses CD. She had finished sliding her fingernail along the cellophane wrapper and was about to tear through the plastic with her teeth when she caught him staring at her from the other side of the playground. She thought he was one of the skateboarders. He was about their height, with the same thin, slippery build, but his hair was longer, down past his shoulders, and as he moved to the side, so that he was no longer silhouetted against the late-afternoon sun, she realized that he was in his twenties at least—a young but full-grown man. When he saw her looking at him, he winked, pointed his thumb and finger at her like a gun, and fired.

Three days later, she was listening to her new album when the man came out of nowhere and sat down, cross-legged, on the gravel in front of her slide. "Hey, girl," he said. "What are you listening to?"

She was too surprised to talk, so she popped her CD player open and showed him the disc.

"Oh, right on. You like him?"

He should have said, *You like them*, because Guns N' Roses was a band, not just one singer, but she nodded.

The man's eyes were flat and blue and they disappeared into the folds of his face when he laughed. "Yeah," he said. "I bet you do."

The way he said this made her think maybe he did know—not how she felt about the band, but how she felt about Axl: about the way his ripped T-shirts clung to his shoulders, and his silky sheet of reddish-gold hair.

"He has a nice voice," she said.

The man frowned, thinking this over. "That he does," he said. Then he asked, "How's the album?"

"It's okay," she said. "It's mostly covers of songs by other people."

"Is that a bad thing, do you think?"

She shrugged. He looked as though he were waiting for more, but she didn't have anything to add. She opened her mouth to say something like, *Aren't you too old to be talking to me*, or, *Don't you know this place is for kids?* but instead she heard herself say, "There's a secret track on it."

He lifted his eyebrows. "Oh really?"

"Yeah."

She waited for him to ask if he could hear it, or even what a secret track was, but he didn't. He just kept sitting there in a way that made her feel foolish. She put her headphones back on, skipped to the last song, and fast-forwarded through the silence until the sound began again. She offered the headphones to him, and he nodded. As she passed them over, his fingertips brushed against hers. She jerked her hand away, as though from an electric shock, and he gave her a sad half-smile. He pulled the headphones tightly over his ears and they disappeared into his messy hair.

"Are you ready?" she asked.

"Hit me."

She pressed play. He closed his eyes, cupped his hands against the headphones, and started to sway. He licked his lips and half-mouthed the words, moving his fingers in the air as though he were pressing chords onto the neck of a guitar. It was embarrassing, how intensely he got into the music, and after a while, she found she couldn't look at his face, so she looked at his feet. He was barefoot, and the soft spaces between his toes were crusted with dirt. His toenails were yellow and long.

When the song was over, he handed the headphones back to her, tapped her Discman twice, and said, "I like the original better."

He was watching her as he said this, and when she didn't answer right away, he pounced. "You know what I'm talking about, right?"

"It's not in the liner notes," she admitted.

"So you've never heard it? The original version of that song?"

She shook her head.

"Oh, girl," he said, drawing out the word. "Oh, girl, you're missing out."

She started putting her things away.

"Don't be mad," he said.

"I'm not mad."

"I think you are. I think you're mad at me."

"I'm not. I have to go."

"Go, go." He waved his hands at her. "I'm sorry I made you angry.

I'll make it up to you, I promise. Next time I see you, I'll bring you a present."

"I don't want a present."

"You'll want this one," he said.

She didn't see him for the rest of that week. Over the weekend, she went to her mean friend Courtney's house and drank for the first time, three stinging gulps of vodka and orange juice that made her limbs feel unbearably heavy. The next Wednesday, he reappeared, holding something in his hand.

"I have that present for you," he said.

"I don't want it."

He bobbed his head, as though her rudeness pleased him. He turned his palm outward to show her that he was carrying a cassette tape. Through its clear plastic case, she could see a handwritten playlist done in dense, dark ink.

"I can't listen to that," she said. "I don't have a tape player."

"Not here you don't," he said. "But maybe at home?"

"Not at home, either."

"I'll bring you one, then."

His shirt was dirtier than it had been the last time she'd seen him, and he'd drawn his hair back into a sloppy ponytail tied up with a tattered brown shoelace. She wondered where he'd gotten the shoelace, since he wasn't wearing shoes. Maybe he was homeless.

"Don't do that," she said. "Don't bring me anything."

He laughed. His eyes were very, very blue. "I'll bring it to you tomorrow," he said.

She thought about staying home, but then she thought, why should I, it's my park, too. Besides, the park was crowded during the daytime;

17

if he tried anything, she would yell for help and all the skateboarders would come to her rescue. She didn't think he would try anything, not really. So she went, but although she stayed on the slide until nearly six thirty, he didn't show up.

Another week went by before he came to her again. "Sorry," he said. "I told you I would find you a tape player, but it took me longer than I thought." He was holding a battered yellow Walkman that looked as though it had been fished out of the garbage. Most of the rubber buttons were missing, and the bottom corner had been dipped in something sticky and red.

"I don't want to listen to anything on that," she said. "It's disgusting."

He sat down again in front of her slide. "I'll need to borrow your headphones," he said. "I couldn't find any."

"Who are you?" she asked. "Why are you talking to me?"

He grinned. His teeth were straight and white. "Who are *you?*" he asked. "Why are you talking to *me?*"

She rolled her eyes. Her headphones were in her lap and he took them and plugged them into the Walkman. He dug into his pocket for the cassette tape Jessica had refused to take from him the week before, then opened the case and slid it into the tray.

"Are you ready?" he asked.

"No," she said. "I told you, I don't want to listen to your stupid tape."

"Yes, you do," he said. "You just don't know it yet." He reached up and slid the headphones over her ears. She could smell his body odor, a mix of cigarette smoke and sweat and sour breath. She was about to snatch the headphones off when she heard a dusty crackling, like the static at the start of a record, and then a man singing, accompanied by rough strokes of acoustic guitar. His voice was high and melancholy and just a little off-key. It reminded her of the way she'd felt after she'd drunk the vodka, as though an entire planet were pressing on top of her, holding her down.

When the song finished, she yanked the headphones off, leaving them dangling around her neck.

"Was that you?" she asked. "Was that you singing?"

The man looked delighted. "Girl, that's not me. That's Charlie."

"Who?"

"Charlie. Charles Manson. Don't you know Charlie?"

"He's a singer?"

"He was. Right up until he killed a whole lot of people, out in Benedict Canyon."

She glared at him. "Are you trying to scare me?"

"Never," he said. He put his hands on her shoulders. "Charlie was a singer and he could have been a star. All the girls worshipped him. They loved him even more than you love Axl, and he loved them back the same. They followed him everywhere, Mary and Susan and Linda and the rest. But then they killed that woman and her baby and a lot of other people and now he's locked up and they're locked up too and the whole family is scattered but they never stopped loving each other, not for one single minute, not for one single day, and that's what all those songs are about."

"That is really messed up," she said, twisting away from him. "I don't know what you're talking about but I think you should get out of here."

"But you liked that song," he said. His voice had become boyish, almost pleading. "I knew you would. That's why I brought it to you."

"I didn't know it was by a murderer!"

"I'm sorry," he said. "You're right. I shouldn't have told you about Charlie. I didn't mean to scare you, I promise."

She looked at him, confused. She could see that his arms were tanned and strong, with thick black hair curling on them, but his eyelashes were a different color—reddish gold, like Axl's.

"You can borrow the tape if you want," he said, as he stood up to go. "Listen to all the songs. I think 'Look at Your Game, Girl' is the best, but I like 'Cease to Exist,' too, and 'Sick City.' Maybe you'll agree with me. Or maybe you won't. That's okay. All the songs are great, really." He popped open the player and put the cassette back in its case, then handed it to her, staring at the ground as though he were too embarrassed to look at her face.

She took the tape and put it in her bag. "Thanks," she said.

"You'll listen to it?"

"Sure."

"That's great! Maybe you'll be able to find a tape player somewhere. I'd give you this one if I could, but I can't. I'm sorry."

"That's okay. I'll figure it out."

She thought he was about to leave, but then he crouched over her and cupped her face with his hands. His hands were huge and warm and they made her face feel tiny, like a doll's face. She thought he was going to kiss her, but he stroked his thumb across her mouth. She opened her lips and his thumb slid between them. She felt the rough ridges of his fingerprint pushing down on her tongue, and she tasted the acrid dirt under his nail. He said, "Of course, you'll have to give it back to me. The tape, I mean. You'll give it back to me, won't you? You promise?"

Her answer was muffled by his hand.

"When?" he asked. "Tonight?"

She shook her head. He slid his thumb free, and she could see her spit shining on it. "I can't!" she said breathlessly. "I can't tonight."

"Why not?"

"My friend—my friend is having a sleepover. I have to go."

He laughed as though this were the funniest thing he'd ever heard. "I don't give a fuck about your friend," he said. "Meet me here, after you've listened to the tape, and tell me which one is your favorite."

"I told you, I can't!"

"Oh, girl," he said. He ruffled her hair. "Of course you can. Should we say ten o'clock? Or no, how about midnight?"

"I'm not coming here at midnight. I'm twelve! Are you crazy?"

"Midnight it is, then," he said, chucking her under the chin. "See you soon."

Of course she wasn't going to go out and meet some dirty stranger in the park at midnight. The whole idea was stupid; it was stupid to even let it cross her mind. She couldn't stop thinking of him as Charlie, even though she knew that wasn't his name, and she kept thinking about Charlie's thumb, about how bony and filthy it had been, and how his nail had scratched at the spongy bit of skin where her throat met the roof of her mouth. She kept running into the bathroom to open wide and make sure she wasn't bleeding. She should have bitten him. She should have bitten his horrible thumb right off his hand, so he'd have shrieked and yanked his hand out of her mouth and been left with nothing but a torn, bloody stump gushing all over the playground.

Of course she wasn't going to meet awful creepy Charlie at the park at midnight, and yet when her band friends called her to ask her to bring her copy of *Dirty Dancing* to the sleepover, she said she couldn't come over after all, because she had a stomachache.

The thought of listening to her band friends giggle and hug their teddy bears and play Light as a Feather, Stiff as a Board made her want to kick someone, but also her stomach did sort of hurt. Afterward, though, she thought maybe she should have gone to the sleepover, because watching her mom and dad and little brother sitting around the kitchen table, eating lasagna, made her even angrier.

"Mom. Dad," she said. "I'm just wondering. Have either of you heard of Charles Manson?"

Mom and Dad had heard of Charles Manson, but they didn't want to talk about him at the dinner table. Jessica thought about calling Courtney and Shannon to see what they were up to, but then she imagined them wanting to sneak out to smoke cigarettes, and the last place she wanted to be was outside, at night, where Charlie might find her. Probably she was better off just staying at home. Home was the safest place for her, because Charlie didn't know where she lived, and even if he had followed her home at some point, which he almost definitely hadn't, they had a super-top-level security system that her dad had installed when they moved in, not to mention their dog, Bosco, who was a German shepherd mix and didn't like anyone he hadn't met when he was a puppy. She was safe. She was fine. No way was she going out to meet Charlie in the park at midnight and she was absolutely fine.

After dinner, her mother put on a movie, and as the clock ticked past ten o'clock, Jessica thought about the first time she'd seen Charlie, and about how she'd thought he was a skateboarder, and all the questions he'd asked her about the Guns N' Roses album, and how much he'd liked the music. She thought about him swaying to the song she'd played for him, cupping her headphones against his ears, and about how she'd felt in those seconds when he'd first touched her face, and about how his eyes were so blue. She thought about the cassette tape, still buried deep in her bag, and she wondered what would happen if he came to get it from her. She thought about what would happen if she did go out to the park, and gave him his cassette tape back, and told him what her favorite song was, and let him take her wherever he wanted to go.

Her mom, dad, and brother fell asleep on the couch before the movie was over. This was a thing that happened not infrequently at their house on movie night, and usually it annoyed the crap out of her, but tonight, she thought she might cry. She looked at her mom, with her ridiculous feathery haircut that made her look like a scared old bird, and her dad, snoring through his mustache, and her brother in his Teenage Mutant Ninja Turtles pajamas. What would they think if they knew she'd been approached by some nasty-looking guy, a guy who'd shoved his filthy thumb in her mouth and thought the Manson murders were the best thing ever? Her mom and dad would be so upset. They would be *so scared*. The thought made her feel brave, and when the movie ended, instead of waking them up and telling them to go to bed already, she went to her room and got her pillow and her blanket and brought them back to the couch. She kept watch over her mother and her father and her brother and herself until midnight had safely passed, and when the clock had finished chiming, she pulled the blanket up to her chin and ended her vigil by chanting to herself, *Fuck you, Charlie, fuck you, fuck you, fuck you.*

The next night, her family was watching the news when the first story came on, about the little girl who was Jessica's age and had the same hair and freckles as Jessica, and who had been taken out of her bedroom during a sleepover by a man with a knife, a man whose face in the wanted poster was a scarily familiar thing.

23

It took nearly an hour for Jessica's parents to get the story out of her, and for them to separate out the relevant details from her hysterical sobbing about Axl Rose and Charles Manson, but when they did finally understand what she was trying to tell them about *man* and *park* and *sleepover*, they called the police. It took them another two hours to get through to someone at the station, because Polly's kidnapping was quickly turning into the most notorious crime that had ever taken place in Sonoma County, and the calls from the crackpots and the pranksters and the reporters and the psychics were already flooding in.

Forty-eight hours later, Jessica was visited at home by a pair of lady police officers, and in this interview, the police learned, among other things, that while Jessica didn't know the drifter's real name, he had given her a cassette tape, which he'd touched with his dirty hands, and he'd put that cassette in a case, and given it to her, and that cassette was still sitting at the bottom of her schoolbag. They went to their police car and got out their white rubber gloves and their tweezers and their evidence collection bag, and then they took the tape away from her, thanked her gravely, and told her parents they would be in touch soon.

Months went by, during which more than four thousand people swarmed over every inch of Sonoma County, calling Polly's name, and a black-and-white version of Polly's school photo was papered onto every wall and tree and telephone pole in the state of California. For a little while, it seemed like all anyone in the entire country could talk about was what had happened to Polly, and Jessica was certain that soon the police would return and confirm her culpability, expose her to the world as the girl who had first crossed paths with the kidnapper and so invited in evil. But when the police did finally find Polly, in a shallow grave off of Highway 101, it turned out the man who had killed her was an old man whose resemblance to Charlie in the poster had been nothing but a trick of the imagination, or the light.

Nearly a year later, a manila envelope arrived at Jessica's house, bearing the return address of the Petaluma police station. While Jessica was certain that the envelope contained the tape Charlie had given her, her parents seized it before she could look at it, and she never saw the tape, or the envelope, again.

By the time she turned fourteen, Jessica understood she had been wrong, that Charlie had not gone after her and taken Polly in her place, that the timing of the two events was nothing but a coincidence. Nonetheless, she continued to believe, for the rest of what remained of her childhood, that what had happened to Polly and what had happened to her must somehow be connected—if not as a matter of practical fact, then by some gravitational pull that flowed deep under the surface of things.

After she went away to college, Jessica came to believe that this early impulse to link her own experience to Polly's had arisen from a childish self-absorption, the impulse to see herself as the center point around which the rest of the universe revolved. As Jessica then saw it, the man who had killed Polly was a supernova, a great and devastating force of harm, while Charlie was an insignificant dwarf star. From where she had stood when she was younger, the small and close and the huge and far away may have appeared, briefly, to be equally luminous—but that was an illusion, nothing more.

In the end, Jessica told herself, she had gotten off easy. After all, the only damage Charlie had inflicted on her was a small scratch on the back of her throat that she may or may not have imagined. Compared with what had happened to Polly—compared with the infinite number of bad things that had happened in the universe—her brush with evil was just a tiny pinprick of light, nearly imperceptible against a backdrop of whirling constellations made up of other, brighter stars.

And yet, long after she had married, and had children of her own, and moved far away from California, Jessica still had trouble falling asleep until after midnight had passed by. As her twin daughters slept peacefully in the bedroom next to hers, she would stand at her window, peering out at the vast, terrible, light-punctured night, and catch herself wondering if Charlie was still out there at the park, waiting for her to arrive.

# SARDINES

This is Marla's first wine afternoon with the moms since The Incident. Tilly is playing outside with the other little girls, all hurt apparently forgotten, but Marla is nursing her grievance along with her Merlot. She can feel it scratching at her, her anger, wedged in the space where the two halves of her rib cage meet.

"We're *so* glad you and Tilly came this afternoon," Carol says, cupping her streaky wineglass in two hands. Her nails are short and stubby, clipped just above the quick.

"I missed you guys," Marla says. "I really did."

"Oh, of course, of course," Babs says, her eyes watery and pink. "But we all understand why you had to take a break."

There is a moment of silence during which they all mournfully acknowledge the seriousness of The Incident.

"God, those fucking *sluts*," Kezia exclaims at last. "I swear, if I hadn't squeezed Mitzi's basketball of a head out of my own goddamned cunt, I would have murdered her for what she did to Tilly." She waves her glass at Carol, whose daughter is adopted. "No offense."

"The point is, we're really sorry," Babs says, blotting at her eyes with her drapey linen sleeve. "I had nightmares about it. We all did."

"That's sweet of you," says Marla. She, too, has been plagued by a recurring dream—Tilly in a yellow field, twirling and sobbing and tugging at her hair. Marla herself has no presence in the dream; she is simply a camera that pulls back to reveal a vast expanse of nothingness: the field, the country, the continent, the planet containing nothing but Tilly, alone, alone, alone.

"How are you doing with all this, honey?" Carol asks.

Good question, and the answer is: not great. In the chaos immediately following The Incident, after reasoning, arguing, shouting, and shaking had done nothing to snap Tilly out of her crying fit, Carol—pacifist, medical-marijuana-card-carrying, Earth Mother Carol—had slapped Tilly across the face. The force of the blow had bounced the glasses right off Tilly's nose, and Marla, who has never struck her daughter, nor even considered such a thing, had clapped a hand across her mouth to suppress a snicker. Some of the messier aspects of parenthood are impossible to anticipate until you crash right into them. Discovering that, in certain circumstances, when someone smacks your daughter you respond with crazed laughter has proven to be a new and unwelcome entry on that list.

"Tilly seems okay and that's what matters," Marla says, realizing she's been staring into space. "If she can roll with it, I should, too. You know?"

"Kids are real resilient," says Babs, and all the women bob their heads. Bullshit, Marla thinks. Maybe some kids are resilient. But are all of them? Is Tilly? Resilience—the ability to brush off pain—is something Marla herself has only fitfully and imperfectly grown into, over time. The petty miseries of her own early childhood are some of her most vivid memories, even now.

"I guess she turned out to be a tough little shit in the end, your Matilda," says Kezia. "Mitzi says the two of them have started playing some game on the bus?"

Marla yields to a temptation she's been struggling against for the past ten minutes and sneaks a glance out the window to where the girls are gathered. They sit sprawled across each other in the sunshine, a pastel tangle of polka-dotted headbands, frilly socks, bright hair. "I don't think they're actually playing the game on the bus?" Marla says. "They're only planning it? Or talking about it? I don't know the details. It's something Tilly picked up at her dad's."

"You make it sound like an STD!" Babs says, and just as the ickier implications of the joke occur to everyone, there is a ripple of soft movement on the lawn.

"Oh," Marla says. "I think they're starting."

She drifts over to the window, letting her wineglass clatter in the empty sink. It's past five, and the late-afternoon air has grown honeyed, gold and slow. On the freshly mown lawn, all the girls are standing up, brushing strands of cut grass off their knees, their hands.

"I'm sorry you think I'm being a dum-dum, Till-Bill," Marla says. "But could you maybe explain it in a different way? What exactly do you mean, the opposite of Hide-and-Seek?"

In the car's rearview mirror, Marla can see Tilly twitching her limbs in agony, like a frog forced by electricity to dance. "I don't know what else to say! It's just like Hide-and-Seek! But the opposite! You know?"

Marla grits her teeth and counts down from five. "No, I don't know, Punkin. You mean, nobody hides? Or you don't look for them?"

"*Please* stop making me explain it, please!" Tilly is literally pulling out her hair in frustration: she's got two thick handfuls wrapped around her fingers and is yanking it viciously out to the sides of her head, like wings. *Trichotillomania*, their therapist has labeled the behavior. Marla has been instructed not to make a big deal of it, but instead to gently redirect.

"Okay," she says. "Your birthday is coming up next month! Are you excited?"

"I want the party to be at Dad's house," Tilly says. She begins kicking a staccato pattern on the back of Marla's seat.

"I'll see what we can do about that, Babygirl," Marla tells her, stomping down on the gas as she blows through a yellow light.

Tilly has a secret.

In her head, Marla enumerates the evidence: the flat fishy gleam in Tilly's mudbrown eyes. The giddiness of her laughter. The way she alternates between logorrhea and stubborn silence whenever Marla asks her about a certain game.

Marla is not the only one whose suspicions have been aroused: all the moms are united in their distaste for the way their daughters have started to behave. The game has enmeshed all of the girls in a taut web of constant texts, passed notes, IMs. "What could there possibly be to babble on so much about?" Babs asks Marla over the phone. This seems like a silly question, as in Marla's experience ten-year-old girls can talk nonstop about anything, forever. But Marla, too, finds it hard to comprehend the avid fervor the game has inspired.

Collective investigation on the part of the moms has uncovered the game's name, Sardines, and a rough outline of the rules, which are innocuous as far as any of them can tell. Yet the way Tilly has been acting reminds Marla of nothing so much as the week her daughter discovered what would happen when she typed *boobs* into the browser of the family computer—the overeager way she would hurry into the den after school, calling out in a trilling, syrupy voice, "Oh, nothing!" whenever Marla asked her what she was up to in there.

Marla would prefer to blame the other girls—vicious, clique-y little beasts, they are—but in fact Tilly herself seems to be the ringleader. That, too, is strange, because Tilly has always been a little bit excluded, either picked on or left out. Although all the other moms are too polite to say so, the game's apparent ability to rescue Tilly from her position at the bottom of the social hierarchy is a large part of its unsavory aura. It's unnatural, Marla thinks blearily one night, right before she falls asleep.

Something *unnatural* is going on.

Tilly's dad agrees to host the party, which means he has agreed for it to be at his house, as long as Marla does the organizing and runs the thing. He has *not* agreed to Marla's request that he tell his live-in girlfriend to vacate the premises for the afternoon, and therefore, in order to fulfill Tilly's birthday wishes, Marla will have to spend four straight hours distributing party favors alongside the twenty-three-year-old whom she once found fucking her husband on the family's living room couch.

Does this put Marla a little bit on edge? Does it make her a little bit impatient with Tilly's refusal to drop a single hint about what she would like to do at the party other than play Sardines?

*What kind of cake do you want at the party, Tilly? Chocolate? Strawberry? Funfetti?*

*Whatever.*

*Other than the neighborhood girls, is there anyone in particular you want to invite?*

*Not really.*

31

*Should we have a theme this year? Pirates, maybe? Or clowns?*

*Nah. Sounds boring.*

*What kind of games should we play?*

*Duh. Sardines.*

*Okay, sure, but what else? Do you want a piñata? A scavenger hunt? Capture the Flag?*

*MAMA, WOULD YOU PLEASE STOP BEING DUMB, I SAID SARDINES.*

Why yes, it does get under Marla's skin. Yes, as a matter of fact, it does.

The other moms will all be in attendance at the party, and at first Marla is glad for their support. Her troops will outnumber those of her enemy! She won't have to enter the lion's den alone! But on the morning of Tilly's birthday, Marla lies miserably in bed, wishing she hadn't asked any of them to come.

After discovering Steve and his little girlfriend in flagrante, Marla had sketched out dozens of schemes for revenge—swapping the lube in the girlfriend's bedroom drawer with superglue, tying her down and tattooing SLUT across her face. And yet somehow, day by day and drip by drip, all her fearless fury has dwindled down to this: she will spend a day smiling tightly and choking down her rage as her nemesis parades around victorious—unhumiliated, unsuperglued, untattooed. How could Marla have let this happen? How could she have resigned herself so meekly to defeat?

The snoozed phone alarm starts chirping, and Marla shoves it under her pillow to shut it up. A minute later, Tilly skips into the bedroom, a preening flamingo in her bright pink birthday dress.

"Mama!" she says sweetly. "Mama, you sleepyhead! I *told* you I wanted birthday waffles! Did you forget?"

The first time Marla had dropped Tilly off at Steve's new house, she'd felt sick: the rambling colonial was the kind of house worth buying only if you planned on someday filling it with kids. But she's got to admit it's the perfect place for a birthday party—high-ceilinged, full of funny little rooms, and surrounded by a smooth green lawn that tumbles down a hill into an expanse of unkempt, brush-filled woods. She parks the car and pops the trunk, unloading bags of party supplies as Tilly scampers up the driveway to her dad.

Marla's survival plan for the day involves pretending that The Girl-friend doesn't entirely exist. She engages in elaborate conversational acrobatics in order to avoid mentioning her by name, never looks at The Girlfriend directly but instead plants her gaze slightly to the left of her face. (She also has a small tube of superglue in her pocket. Superglue with a strikingly similar consistency to Steve's favorite brand of flavored lube. She probably won't use it. Almost *certainly* not. But still.)

Marla does all the decorating—after one half-hearted attempt at stringing a birthday banner across the doorway, Tilly disappears into the woods. She doesn't return until after the first of the guests have arrived, her white tights spattered up the calves with mud.

At the birthday girl's insistence, they open presents first. Tilly sits cross-legged on the couch and plows robotically through the stack of gifts, ripping the sparkly paper off in fistfuls and dumping each toy into a pile at her feet. Marla reminds her, "Say thank you, Tilly," and Tilly echoes, "Thank you, Tilly," in a grating monotone.

Next up is cake and ice cream. The night before, eager to retreat into her improvised shelter of wine and Netflix, Marla hadn't waited long enough for the cake to cool. As a result, the canned frosting she smeared over the Duncan Hines pudding cake has gone melty, turning the blue piped lettering of HAPPY BDAY TILLY into an illegible smudge. An attempt to use the flat edge of a knife to turn the words into an arty marbled swirl only makes everything worse.

Marla is in the kitchen, staring down at the mess she has created, when someone comes up behind her and a pair of short-nailed hands curl around her waist. "Hey, love," Carol says. "The natives are getting restless. How you holding up?"

"Look at this!" Marla cries, nearly stabbing Carol in the eye with the frosting-encrusted butter knife. "It's a disaster!"

"Oh, it's not that bad," says Carol. She pauses. "Admittedly, it's not that great. But Tilly can suck it up. And look, I stopped for groceries on the way over here," Carol says. "I just had a sense." She opens an oversized Whole Foods canvas tote bag and places a can of dark chocolate frosting on the kitchen counter.

Marla, contemplating it, sinks deeper into despair. What in the everloving fuck?

"Here," Carol says, gently taking the knife from Marla and opening the can. "We can just . . . right?"

Marla nods. From the other room comes the sound of Tilly screeching: *Stop touching that! It's mine!* but she can't bring herself to deal with it. Not yet.

"I got this," she says, grabbing the knife back from Carol. "Can you go see what they're spazzing out about in there?"

After slapping on the extra layer of frosting, Marla pokes eleven regular birthday candles around the periphery of the cake. In the center, for good luck, she inserts a final candle—a novelty toy she found in the bargain bin at the grocery store. The candle is shaped like a fat, yellow-petaled flower bud, and when Marla touches the flame of her lighter to the wick, it unfolds jerkily and starts to spin.

"Okay!" she calls out. "Cake time!"

She hefts the cake platter in both hands and backs out the kitchen door.

The guests have assembled around the dining room table, all crowned with pointy birthday hats except for Tilly, who wears a silver polka-dotted bow stuck in the middle of her head. When Marla enters with the cake, the novelty candle hissing and sparking like a tiny firework, an astounded Tilly claps her hands to her face. "It's *beautiful*!" she cries. The guests launch into the opening lines of "Happy Birthday" at the moment that the novelty candle begins chirping out the notes of an unfamiliar tune. Everyone stops, confused, as the candle toodles on—deedledeedledeedledah—until finally Kezia bellows: "Happy Birthday to YOU!" and they all shout down the candle and march through the birthday song.

When they've finished, Tilly blows out the regular candles with one explosive, only slightly spitty *sssssssshhhhhh*, but no matter how much she blows on it, the novelty candle will not go out, nor will it stop playing its infuriating song, so eventually, in order to prevent the cake from being entirely drenched in Tilly's spit, Marla takes the candle back into the kitchen and runs it under the sink, which extinguishes the flame but doesn't shut it up. She throws it on the floor and stomps on it but it *keeps fucking playing* and even after she shoves it deep into the garbage, she can still hear it tinkling faintly, stubbornly—deedledeedledeedle*DAH*!

"Mama," Tilly asks when Marla returns to the dining room. "Even though I didn't blow out the good-luck candle, did I still get my birthday wish?"

"I think so," Marla says. "That thing was a piece of junk."

"Good," says Tilly. She mushes her ice cream into her cake with her fork and takes a giant bite. "Wanna know something?"

"Of course, sweetheart," says Marla absently. Steve is cooing at The Girlfriend, bouncing her on his knee and petting her curly hair. If the two of them start making out, Marla swears to God, she will shove the cake knife straight through The Girlfriend's throat.

"I think you'll like what I wished for, Mama." Tilly sucks the frosting off her fingers, wriggles happily, and adds, "I wished for something *mean*."

Here are the rules of Sardines, which can be found in any book of children's games: Everyone closes their eyes, except for one person, who is the Hider. While everyone else counts down from one hundred, the Hider goes and hides. After they've finished counting, the first person to find the Hider hides with them. The next person to find the Hider hides alongside the other two. And so on and so on until everyone except for one person is crammed into the same hiding place, squished as tightly together as a pack of sardines.

Here are Tilly's special birthday rules:

Tilly gets to pick the Hider.

You can't hide in the house.

Everybody has to play.

Tilly leads the guests outside, climbs up on a lawn chair, and looks down at them. Marla thinks she's acting with the benevolent condescension of a queen. "Now I'm going to pick the Hider," she says. She lifts her finger and lets it drift, a daydreamy expression on her face. Her finger bobs briefly over Kezia, Carol, and Steve. Then it jerks and dips.

"You," she declares, pointing at The Girlfriend. "You're the Hider. That means you have to go and hide."

Everybody bows their heads as Tilly counts backward from one hundred. From beneath half-lowered lids, Marla watches as The Girlfriend stands frozen, looking panicked, until the countdown reaches eighty, at which point she sprints off down the hill.

"*3-2-1 WE'RE COMING!*" Tilly screams, and everybody scatters.

Marla creeps around the porch. Once she is sure that no one's watching, she ducks through the back door into the house. Sorry, Till-Bill, but no way in hell is she going to run the risk of finding The Girlfriend and having to curl up next to her in some grimy hole in the woods. (She also takes the opportunity to do some sneaking. Some seeking. And some swapping. Hey, it's just a prank. A harmless joke. Just a small taste of sticky-sweet revenge.)

Steve isn't a big wine drinker, but The Girlfriend must be, because during her expedition, Marla discovers a cabinet full of Two-Buck Chuck. She grabs a bottle of Sauvignon Blanc, considers hunting for ice cubes, and decides she's lazy enough to drink it warm. Once she's finished exploring, she kicks off her shoes, puts up her feet, and settles down on the couch with the remains of the cake.

Marla is halfway through the wine when she looks up and sees her daughter in the doorway. Tilly's arms hang heavily by her sides, and the afternoon sun is reflecting off her glasses, rendering them eerily opaque.

"Jesus, Till, you scared me!" Marla cries. "How long have you been standing there?"

"What are you doing in here, Mama?" Tilly asks. "Didn't you hear me when I said everybody had to play?"

"I did. I'm sorry. I'll come join in a second. I just . . . needed a little bit of a break."

Tilly shuffles farther into the room, a dazed expression on her face. She entwines her hand in Marla's and presses her damp forehead against Marla's neck. "Mama," she says. "I was wondering. Do you like Layla and Mitzi and Francine?"

Hypnotized by the sensation of Tilly's cold fingers drawing circles on her palm, Marla almost blurts out, *Who are they?* before coming back to Earth. "Actually, Till, not really. I know they're your friends, but I think they're kind of cliquish."

"What's *cliquish*?"

"The way they always stick together. I think it's kind of mean."

"What about their mamas? Do you like them?"

Marla sighs and frees her hand, then licks her thumb to rub a flake of chocolate frosting off of Tilly's chin. "I don't know. They're fine. There's nothing wrong with them. But if I had to choose, right now, I guess I'd say no I don't."

"And what about Dad and—"

Before Marla can say anything, Tilly answers for her. "I know. You hate them, right?"

Tilly's adult nose—Steve's nose—arrived on her face a few months ago, knocking all her other features out of whack. She's got a greasy sprinkle of new acne sprouting along her half-plucked hairline, and a puffy brown mole has popped up on the side of her neck. She sweats through her deodorant by midafternoon, even the Men's Sports Prescription Strength Marla left last week, without comment, on her bed. At random times of day, her breath turns dank and meaty, and Marla finds herself opening the car window, without comment. Her breasts appear to be growing at two slightly different rates, so none of the training bras Marla buys her ever fit. The further Tilly lurches into gruesome adolescence, the more she insists on acting like a baby, trying to recapture a cuteness she never possessed. Maddening, tic-ridden, love-hungry Tilly; beloved Tilly, who, despite Marla's best efforts to protect her, at times seems not only destined but determined to be chewed up by the world's sharp teeth.

Marla knows the kind of thing she's supposed to say—*Of course not, baby* or *Hate is not the nicest word* or *I will always love your dad because he gave me you,* but all the necessary platitudes shrivel on her tongue. So instead, she says nothing, and Tilly nods. "You make a lot of mistakes, but you're still a good mama," she says. She hugs Marla fiercely, plants a sloppy kiss right in her ear, and scoops up a handful of cake.

"Tilly?" Marla calls out as her daughter leaves the room.

"Yeah?"

"What did you wish for, earlier?"

Tilly's cake-ringed grin is glisteningly lovely. "Oh, Mama. Pretty soon you'll see."

Leave Tilly to her plotting. Leave Marla to her wine. Imagine yourself, instead, as The Girlfriend. Here at your boyfriend's daughter's birthday party. Hosted by your boyfriend's daughter's mother. Attended by your boyfriend's daughter's mother's friends. Who have all come parading into your home, hell-bent on proving how much they dislike you. And it is your home! It's not like you're some party crasher. You live here! The mother, refusing to say your name or look straight at you. Your boyfriend, embarrassed, squirming out from underneath your touch. And the daughter, jabbing her pointy finger in your face. *You. You're the Hider.* How can those words not ring in your ears like an accusation? How can you help but feel, as you flee down the hill in your clunky espadrilles, at least a little bit like—prey?

To hide too well is to extend your misery. Only when the game is over can the party end. But to hide too poorly—to duck under the picnic table, to crouch behind the first big tree that you see—is to fail at your assigned role. *You're the Hider. That means you have to go and hide*. To be found too soon is to annoy Tilly, to let down Steve, to give the mothers one more excuse to judge. And that is why you leave the sunlit lawn and enter the dark forest, the low brush scratching at your ankles, the bare thorns catching at your skirt.

Over a hill and down again, across a small dried riverbed, through an opening in the trees. You find a ring of stumps high enough to shield you, as long as you curl up and pull your knees against your chest. Quiet. Birdsong. Scent of crushed pine needles and rotting leaves.

It's peaceful here, you tell yourself. Listening to the sound of your ragged breath slowly softening, becoming even. Daydreaming about what you'll do when the party's over.

Waiting to be found.


Marla closes her eyes and opens them again, and when she does, she wakes into her dream. The dream in which everyone has disappeared except for Tilly. How much time has passed? An hour, a day, an epoch? Impossible to say. It's early evening, she knows that much. The sun has burst into red flame on the far side of the forest, and all the shadows are running wild. Tangled, deepest black. Stretching every which way.

The light-struck windows of the house have gone as blank as Tilly's glasses. The birthday banner dangles from the door, an unfurling tongue. Marla ventures outside, where the birthday girl, crowned by a silver ribbon, is standing—waiting?—floating?—down where the lawn meets the woods.


Sardines is a game of overlapping bodies. Arms wedged up against hip bones, butts plopping into laps. One person's hair sticks between your teeth; another person's finger jams into your ear. Whose leg is whose? Whose fart was that? Who's *moving*? Who's *talking*? Stop squirming! Get your foot out of my crotch! Get your nose out of my armpit! Stop elbowing me in the boob, Francine! My elbow's nowhere near your stupid boob, you jerk, that's Layla's kneecap. No, it's not! Shut up! Shhhhh, girls, Tilly's coming! Oh no, my hand is sticking out. We can't fit! It's way too cramped! No, we can do it. Get closer. Get closer. Get closer until every single piece of you is touching a part of someone else. Push and squish and smoosh and squash and squeeze.

Tilly drifts in among the trees and Marla follows her, her footsteps muffled by a bed of pine needles, the soft mulch of arboreal decay. The vaginal lips of a pink lady's slipper peep out from behind some bushes; a rubber shred of burst balloon, studded by a plump red navel knot, dangles from a tree branch, and the corpse of a crushed mushroom gleams sad and cold and pale.

Wait.

Before the finding starts.

There's one last thing you need to know.

Tilly's good-luck candle grants wishes.

It grants wishes to the lonely. The awkward. The insulted. The smelly. To the angry, the tortured, the hate-filled, the powerless. To daughters and mothers. To mothers and daughters. To Marlas and Tillies. To Tillies and Marlas. To Tarlas and Millies, to tothers and marlies. To maughters and dothers. To Marlyandarlaandollyandlaughterandlillyandothers.

In the woods, by the pit, in the darkness, together, mother and daughter, Tilly and Marla, hear no noise but the wind in the leaves, heartbeats and breath.

*Shhhh!*

Listen.

These are the sounds of wishes being granted—

(Mean wishes. Bad ones.)

Screaming. Lots and lots of screaming—

But muffled. Like someone is screaming into a pillow.

Or maybe into something a little more elastic.

Like a rubber balloon.

Like bubble gum.

Like skin.

Surprise! It turns out that with the help of just a little birthday magic, hatred can be captured like a ray of sunlight. Hatred can be magnified, refracted, *aimed*. And a group of party guests who are clustered together like ants on a sidewalk (like sardines in a can) find themselves bathed in the rays of a mysterious force, one that is no less powerful for the fact that it's unseen.

The guests' smooth collective skin grows warm, then hot, then hotter.

Their bright hair begins to smolder. And then to smoke, and char.

Their trembling, pulsing, pumping, wheezing bodies begin to sweat. Then scorch. Then singe. Then cook. Then burst. Then melt. And then to *fuse*.

Their overlapping bodies become one body. Their many brains become one confused and panicked brain. Instead of many separate people they become one seething mass, a terrified and maddened organism, a puddle of sentient, erupting flesh, a dozen-eyed and many-limbed *thing*.

At the top of a hill, under garish moonlight, Marla and Tilly hold each other tightly, as, beneath them, Tilly's birthday monster jerks and shakes and gnashes its teeth; howls, and tries to tear itself apart, and screams.

*I'm scared I don't know what's happening I want my mommy my baby who are you what are you doing in my head in my body I'm not you're in mine are you no is my mommy no I'm Francine no I'm Carol no Kezia baby it's Mommy how can this please make it stop no I'm Steve I am Stacey I'm Mitzi I'm Layla I don't understand I'm so scared I don't like this please somebody help me I can't move I can't stop moving oh God it's where did that come from why can't I see I can see everything what are these noises who is this what is this what am I who did this it hurts please make it stop it hurts me oh baby I'm sorry who is this what are you are me . . .*

Dumbstruck, Tilly stares at the monster. Her eyes are glowing as though her skull is crammed full of a thousand birthday candles, and a trickle of drool is running down her chin.

Amidst the writhing limbs and shrieking heads, The Girlfriend's face briefly distinguishes itself from the others. She is wild-eyed and mud-streaked, her pert nose is crushed and bloody, and there's a jagged gap where half of her front tooth used to be.

Tilly's birthday party has become her birthday present—a monster that twitches and throbs and gurgles instead of making fun of people. A monster that drools and spasms and suffers and does not tease. A monster that wails and gibbers instead of cheating and divorcing; that writhes and shrieks and flails in agony instead of leaving the people it's supposed to love and care for all alone.

"Mama?" Tilly whispers, astounded, to her mother. "Do you think birthday wishes can ever be *un*wished? Like maybe next year on my birthday? Or maybe even now?"

"I don't know, baby," Marla says.

"Do you think I *should* unwish it?" She looks imploringly up at her mother. "Do you want me to?"

Marla tries to answer but finds the words are sticking in her throat. She thinks it over as Tilly waits, as the monster at their feet howls and yawps and begs for mercy, and as—beneath gobs of melted ice cream, tattered party streamers, and crumbs of soggy cake—the yellow candle spins, and sparks, and chirps: *deedledeedledeedleDAH!*

# THE NIGHT RUNNER

The Class Six girls were bad, and everyone knew it. All the teachers at Butula Girls' Primary School had a Class Six story—the time the girls had locked a female instructor in the boys' toilet overnight; the time they'd led the school in a sit-down strike after being fed githeri for ten days in a row; the incident with the goat in the supply closet. After they learned that the American Peace Corps volunteer, Aaron, had been assigned to Class Six, all the teachers gave him sympathetic looks when they passed him in the hallway, and one of the younger ones felt so sorry for him that as she was talking with her colleagues about his dilemma in the lunchroom, she burst into tears.

But when Aaron begged the teacher for hints about how to deal with the girls, she could only say, with a fatalistic sigh, "There is no dealing with those ones. The devil is in them, and there is nothing to be done except—" She whipped her hand through the air to demon-strate.

*Thwack.*

Everyone at school had served their time with Class Six. Of all their put-upon teachers, though, only Aaron was afraid to drag them outside and apply a switch to the tender backs of their calves. As a result, he could not even turn around to write on the chalkboard (*The HIV virus is transmitted//are transmitted in the following ways . . .*) without the girls' endless bubbling mockery boiling over into full-fledged chaos.

The girls mimicked his voice when he spoke, squeaking at him in high-pitched, nasal tones. They flicked things at him: not only chalk, but bits of spit-sodden paper, corn kernels, bobby pins, and flaky greenish balls made up of snot. Once, after he'd handed back a set of exercises, Roda Kudondo sauntered up to his desk and shoved her notebook in his face, mumbling in a slurred mishmash she intended as an imitation of his Texan drawl. The class exploded in laughter, and Aaron, not understanding, ordered her to sit down. But she only repeated what she'd said and jammed her index finger deep in her mouth, poking the inside of her cheek so that her face bulged out. She was propositioning him, and the joke of her offer to take him back behind the classroom and suck him off in return for a higher mark left him red-faced and stunned, while she strolled back to her desk amidst cheers.

Then, one humid afternoon in December, Linnet Oduori trailed Aaron out of the school gates and back to his house, meowing like a cat all the way. Linnet was the smallest girl in Class Six, as pretty and fine-boned as the bird after which she'd been named. Until then, Aaron had made her into a kind of pet, praising her at every opportunity and holding her mediocre work up as an example to the others—a lazy, unearned favoritism for which, that afternoon, she extracted her strange but effective revenge.

"It is because of your eyes," Aaron's friend Grace informed him that evening, when he described what Linnet had done to him, and how the other children they'd passed on the road had all enthusiastically joined in, until he was surrounded by a pack of children all crying out *meow, meow* in high, teasing voices. "Your eyes resemble a cat's because of their color," she continued, as though this were an obvious fact.

Aaron thought Grace's eyes looked more catlike than his own, which were only an unremarkable blue. Grace was a local Luhya girl, and she had brown eyes, of course, but they curved up witchily at the corners and bulged out a little, so that when he looked at her from the side, he could see the clear meniscus of her pupil, like a thimbleful of water about to overflow.

Grace had adopted Aaron during his first week in the village, arriving at his doorstep one evening bearing a warm Coke and a scorched chapati as an offering. With the slick rash of pimples across her forehead, her dark-gummed, gappy smile, and her air of free-floating disdain, Grace would have blended easily among the girls of Class Six, though she was nineteen, older than any of them. Early on, she'd asked Aaron where exactly in America he was from, and when he had answered, she'd said coolly, "Me, I thought all Texans were large, cowboy-type people, but you are not large. You are only . . . ordinary-sized." Grace had attended Butula some years before, and she responded to his stories of the goings-on at the school with a stubborn refusal to believe he could tell her anything she didn't already know.

As soon as night fell, Grace would stalk inside Aaron's cramped, sour-smelling house, conveying with every shallow breath that she was here on sufferance, and that spending time in such a hovel was beneath them both. Once, she'd come right out and asked him, "Why did you come all the way from Texas to live in this small-small house? Don't you know that even the cook at that school has a nicer house than this?"

Aaron had informed her that he was a volunteer, that the house had been provided by the school, and that therefore there was nothing he could do about it, though in fact he'd complained vociferously about his living situation to his Peace Corps supervisors as soon as he'd arrived. Indeed, when he'd crossed the threshold for the first time, a smattering of dusty bat droppings had rained down on him from the doorframe, and later he'd found the desiccated corpse of one of the culprits, itself resembling nothing so much as a baked brown turd, trapped inside the disconnected stove.

Despite her obvious distaste for their surroundings, Grace often stayed at his house past midnight, sucking her knuckles and eyeing him across the lantern-lit table. Aaron suspected she would eventually proposition him, and he spent a lot of time thinking about how he would respond, but so far she hadn't yet done so; at the end of the evening, she would only stand, yawn, and casually rearrange the bra strap that had slipped out from beneath the shoulder of her dress.

The night of the meowing incident, though, Aaron accompanied Grace to the edge of his compound and lingered. Impulsively, he reached for her, but instead of yielding, she lifted his hand off her waist, placed it back at his side, and laughed in his face.

"Very bad," she teased, wagging her finger under his nose.

Now Aaron had this embarrassment to add to the litany of humiliation that kept him lying awake at night, staring at the ceiling and dreading the arrival of morning.

Not long after he finally fell asleep, Aaron was awoken by a knocking at his door. His lantern had gone out, so he blindly untangled himself from his mosquito net and stumbled through the darkness to the front of the house. "I'm coming!" he called, but the knocking continued unabated. His visitor was so insistent that he wondered if there had been some kind of emergency, a terrorist attack or a rebel invasion, and people from the Peace Corps had arrived to helicopter him to safety. The possibility was both scary and a little bit thrilling, but when he finally unbolted the door, no one was there.

Confused, he ventured out into the compound. The night air smelled of charcoal and manure, and its chill sent gooseflesh prickling down his skin. The last knock had come only seconds before he'd opened the door; it seemed impossible that a person would have had time to run. But in the moon's dim light, he could see that the yard was empty, the gate barred, and everything around him still.

"Hello?" he called out, but heard nothing in return save his own heaving breath.

He went back inside, rebolted the door, and rearranged his mosquito net, tucking it carefully under the corners of his mattress—but as soon as he was beneath the covers, the knocking began again. Three times, he flung open the door and saw nothing. Once, he snuck out the back and tried to creep around the house to catch his tormenter in the act, but as soon as he stepped outside, the knocking subsided into silence. He returned to his house and sat with his back wedged up against the wall as he tried to keep himself from succumbing to panic. That was when the knocking began once more, the hammering on his metal door deafeningly loud. "Go away!" he screamed, his hands pressed to his ears. "Go away! *Toka hapa!* Go away!" But—madly, impossibly, mind-numbingly—the knocking kept up all night long.

At dawn, when his eyes were burning and his thoughts twitchy from lack of sleep, the door at last went quiet. Thinking his harasser might have left some clues that would be discernible in daylight, Aaron stumbled outside, only to confront a steaming pile of shit coiled snugly in the center of his porch.

The fresh intimate stink of it made him gag. He flung his arm across his nose, ran back inside, and slammed the door shut, but even

so, he was sure he could smell it. Later, he drank two bottles of warm
Tusker beer for courage and gathered the feces between the pages of
a newspaper, its slithering warmth radiating through the thin pages.
Then he ran through his yard with his arms outstretched and flung
the crumpled ball over the wall and into the street.

Aaron knew that if he didn't go to school that day, he would lose any
chance he had of ever gaining control of Class Six, but he couldn't make
himself do it. He lay on his couch, sweating, his face covered with blan-
kets, and tried to identify the most likely suspect for the night's attack.
Delicate, meowing Linnet? Vulgar Roda Kudondo? Or someone less
obvious, like pretty Mercy Akinyi, who'd once turned in an exam sheet
that consisted of nothing but the words *I love Moses Ojou* over and over
again? Maybe it was Milcent Nabwire, who, last week, had raised her
hand during a lesson and asked, *"Mwalimu*, is it—is it—is it true that—
that *wazungu*—is it true that . . ."* and then, in a great stuttering burst:
*"Mwalimu, ni kweli wazungu hutomba wanyama?"* In an attempt to mask the
slowness of his ability to translate, he'd pretended to consider the question
carefully, frowning and furrowing his brow so that only when he finally
unlocked her meaning (*Teacher, is it true that white people fuck animals?*) did
he realize how perfectly he'd set himself up to be the butt of her joke.

Or perhaps it was Anastenzia Odenyo, one of his class's many or-
phans, who served as the head of household for five younger siblings.
She came to school so rarely he had trouble remembering her face,
although he would sometimes pass her in the village, looking tired and
harassed, a basket of shopping balanced on her head, a child clinging
to her hip. He'd once offered to pay for the handful of onions she was
buying at the market, telling her he hoped she'd be able to return to
school someday soon. She'd accepted the handful of shillings he'd
given her, then pointed to his iPod and said something in Swahili he
didn't understand.

"To hear music," she'd said in English, each word enunciated carefully. "I like to listen to music." Requests for his belongings were common but always awkward for him.

"No, Anastenzia," he told her. "I'm sorry."

"Okay," she said. She shushed the child she was carrying, who'd begun to cry. "Maybe later. Thank you for onions, *Mwalimu*. Goodbye." He'd been halfway home before the sickening possibility occurred to him that she might not have been asking for the iPod as a gift, but simply to listen to a song.

Yes, it could have been Linnet or Roda or Mercy or Milcent or Anastenzia . . . but it could also have been Stella Khasenye or Saraphene Wechuli or Veronica Barasa or Anjeline Atieno or Brigit Taabu or Purity Anyango or Violeta Adhiambo. The truth was, it could have been any of them, because they all loathed him, every single one.

The Headmaster came by the house in the midafternoon, and Aaron said he was sick. The Headmaster warned Aaron of the dangers of malaria and offered to send one of the children to bring him some Panadol, but Aaron declined politely and crawled back to bed. Later, Grace arrived at her usual time, and, lonely and shaky, he invited her in. "What is wrong with you?" she demanded as soon as she saw him. He told her an abbreviated version of the night's ordeal, though he couldn't bring himself to admit that someone had taken a shit on his porch. Like Roda's vulgar proposition, its insolence somehow shamed him, the victim of the act, more than it did the transgressor. He expected that Grace wouldn't believe him when he told her the knocking had kept up until sunrise—he had trouble believing it himself—but when he finished his story, bracing himself for ridicule, she only nodded and said sagely, "Ah. It is a night runner."

"A night runner?" he echoed.

"They did not teach you about night runners at your Peace Corps school?"

Early on, Aaron had mentioned the eight weeks of Peace Corps training he'd completed before arriving in Butula, and ever since, he'd had the sense that Grace believed he'd spent months in a classroom, being taught every possible detail about Kenyan life, from the right way to greet a grandparent to how to properly slice up a mango. She acted astonished at even his smallest mistakes, and sometimes appeared truly offended by the extent to which these imaginary teachers had failed him.

"Night runners are a very common thing among us Luhya people," she told him. "They cause too much trouble by running around naked anyhowly." Perhaps inspired by Aaron's boggled expression, she lowered her voice into a masculine range, furrowed her eyebrows, and elevated her explanation into performance. "They come around, *boom boom boom*, making noises like this"—she demonstrated by pummeling her fists against the air—"and they will rub their *ninis* against your wall"—she poked out her ass and pointed—"and if you are very unlucky, they will leave you a little present." She giggled and concluded emphatically, "Yes! That is the night runner."

For the rest of the evening, Aaron tried to get Grace to confess she was making this up. She'd told him wild stories of the supernatural before—one about a man who'd been cursed so that every time he urinated he crowed like a rooster; one about a witch who'd cast a spell on an adulterous couple so that they got stuck together while having sex and had to be brought to the hospital to be surgically taken apart—but always in a way that seemed like a tease, as though she knew he wouldn't believe her and was daring him to defy her. Of the reality of the night runners, however, she seemed utterly convinced. No, they were not spirits, they were actual people, driven to run by a kind of demonic mental disease. Their identities were secret, because if the community found out you were a night runner—whoa, you were in for it then! Once, three towns over, a night runner had been caught and almost lynched before it was discovered that during the daytime she was the well-respected wife of a pastor.

His skepticism slowly eroding in the face of her conviction, Aaron asked how one went about ridding oneself of a night runner's harassment. Grace began telling a convoluted story about how the best night runners did their work in pairs, and the elaborate joint rituals they performed to keep themselves from being caught, but then she interrupted herself and shook her head in despair. "No! The real problem is, these night runners are too difficult to stop, because when you chase them, they can become something like a cat or a bird or even a leopard, so how can a person catch up?"

"Grace!" Aaron cried as she burst into snorting laughter. "You're not funny!"

Grace slapped her hand on the table and shouted, "Wrong! I am funny. Your problem is you are too serious. 'Oh no, a child is meowing at me!' 'Oh no, someone is knocking on my door in the night!' There are worse things in this world than being meowed at. So you have your troubles—that means a person can't laugh?"

"I just think you could be a little more sympathetic," Aaron said morosely, as he drank down the rest of his Coke.

The next morning, fortified by a good eight hours' sleep, Aaron decided to venture onto campus. Instead of going to his classroom, though, he presented himself at the Headmaster's office. The Headmaster's feet were propped up on his desk, the bottom of one of his shoes blackened with a smear of chewing gum. "*Mwalimu*, Aaron!" the Headmaster exclaimed. "How is your malaria doing today?"

"It wasn't malaria," Aaron said. "And I'm a lot better. But I need to talk to you about the Class Six girls. Their behavior is out of control."

As the Headmaster listened, rocking back in his chair, Aaron launched into a litany of Class Six offenses. They threw things at him. They imitated him. They asked vulgar questions. They refused to do their assignments. They failed to treat him with the proper respect. When Aaron recounted the story of Linnet's meowing, the Headmaster began to frown, but when he described the assault on his house, the Headmaster dropped the front legs of his chair to the floor with a clatter.

"No!" the Headmaster declared. "This is too serious. With harassment like this, how can you sleep? Someone coming to your door, banging, banging, banging, all the night long!"

Aaron was about to agree, but before he could say anything, the Headmaster continued, "This is not just a nuisance, no! It is a real problem in our community, this nasty habit of night running!"

Aaron slumped back in his seat as the Headmaster burst into a wide smile, showing off a mouth full of damp, shiny teeth. He clasped Aaron on the shoulder. "My friend. If you want your class to have discipline, you must discipline them! The next time a small-small girl meows at you—pah!" He whipped his newspaper through the air. "Do so, and I think you will not be visited by this night runner again."

Defeated, Aaron returned to his classroom. On any other day, the girls would have gone wild in his absence, but today they sat primly at their desks, their ankles pressed together, their hands clasped in front of them. A hundred eyes tracked him as he crossed to the front of the room. As he cleared his throat and prepared to speak, he allowed himself a moment of hope. *Maybe it's over. Maybe they finally realize they've gone too far.*

"Good afternoon, girls," Aaron prompted the class.

The sound of shuffling feet and squeaking desks filled the air as Class Six rose, as one, to greet him.

*"MEOW!"*

In the ensuing hysteria, Aaron grabbed the arm of the girl closest to him: Mercy Akinyi, the one who loved Moses Ojou. Mercy shrieked and dug her fingers into his hand, but he yanked her forward, forcing her toward the door. They were almost at the courtyard before the rest of the girls realized what was happening, and when they did, they followed en masse, enveloping him in a shrieking maelstrom. Spit and paper and shoes flew around him, but Aaron focused only on keeping control of his one writhing charge.

Drawn by the commotion, the rest of the schoolchildren flooded outside, their curious teachers making no effort to stop them. With the entire school looking on, Aaron frog-marched Mercy into the middle of the yard and then, as was the custom, lifted her hands above her head and placed them on the flagpole. Mercy's blue-and-white plaid skirt rose over the backs of her knees, exposing her smooth brown legs. Beneath them, dozens of thin sticks littered the grass, remnants of earlier beatings. Aaron snatched one up and pressed it against Mercy's leg. A plump calf muscle twitched beneath her skin.

Aaron's stomach had gone oily and cold. He thought he might lose control of his bowels, but he raised the stick to strike. As he did, Mercy cocked her head and smiled faintly at him.

*"Meow,"* she whispered.

He couldn't do it. He threw the stick on the ground and walked home.

Grace didn't come that evening, but the night runner did. The next morning, Aaron opened his door and was briefly surprised to see an unsoiled porch, until the stench hit him and he turned to see the clumped brown streak smeared at hip height in an unbroken circle around the white walls of his house.

Aaron went inside and called his Peace Corps supervisor. He said that he had been the target of harassment in his village, that he no longer felt as though he had anything to offer his community, and that he wanted to go home. He expected her to try to talk him out of it, to reassure him that what he was doing was valuable, but she did not. The Peace Corps had left him almost entirely alone at his site, but as soon as he wanted to leave, it was as though he'd pulled a lever and activated the workings of a complex machine. His supervisor asked him only if he felt unsafe in the village, or if he was considering doing harm to himself. When he said no, she told him to come into the office the next day to begin filling out his separation paperwork, and that was that. It could not have been easier. He was done.

When he got off the phone, Aaron filled a bucket with warm, sudsy water. He knotted up an old T-shirt, went outside, then got down on his knees and scrubbed his walls until they shone. He felt no disgust or revulsion, just a kind of deadened disdain. It was a choice they'd made, to drive him out. Like beating children was a choice. Like having unprotected sex was a choice. *They chose this*, he said to himself, and the words were like blood in his mouth.

As the sun set on his last day in the village, Aaron walked into town for the final time and bought himself a chapati and a Coke, and then, after some thought, a second chapati and Coke for Grace. He wondered what she would say when she found out he was leaving and he heard her shocked voice again in his head: *They did not teach you about night runners at your Peace Corps school?*

*No, Grace*, he thought. *They didn't teach me anything I needed to know.*

That night, there was no Grace, and at first no night runner, only a suffocating heat that crawled into the house and stubbornly refused to leave. Struggling to breathe but afraid to open the windows, Aaron stripped to his underwear, dabbing his soaked forehead with a tissue as he squatted on his mattress. On his lap, he held a tool that he'd taken from the shed in his compound, one of the long, flat blades that people around here called "grass cutters." He'd told his supervisor the truth—he did not feel unsafe in the village. But he felt scared and humiliated and helpless, and he was tired of feeling that way.

The knocking began just after midnight. *Knock knock knock* went his visitor, first at the door, then at the window. *Knock knock knock.* Door, window, window, door, until the whole house was surrounded by a fluttery, girlish knocking. Surely no one person could move that fast. Maybe all of Class Six had come to visit, here on a sadistic class trip. Again, Aaron saw Mercy with her hands around the flagpole, squinting up at him. Even when he'd been angry enough to beat her bloody, she hadn't been afraid of him, and now here he was, crouching in his house like a coward. *I came here to help you*, he thought. He stood, hooking the grass cutter over his shoulder like a baseball bat, and crept toward the door, as the knocking spread around the house like unfolding wings.

Wait.

Wait.

*Knock knock knock.*

Now.

Aaron flung open the door. Two bare brown legs floated in front of him, naked toes wiggling, and then one of them kicked out toward his face, five pearled toenails scratching down his cheek. Shrieking, Aaron swung the grass cutter wildly—but the legs slid up and away, leaving him staring at a blank doorway and the chill black night, the metal blade lodged in the crumbling wood of the frame.

Aaron buckled, gagged. He spat bile onto the place where, if blade had met flesh, a girl's severed leg would have tumbled to the floor. The shock of what he'd almost done whiplashed back to him, and curled, electric, around his spine. To think if he'd hit her. The crunch of bone. The screaming. The gushing surge of dark red blood.

But she'd escaped him. She was on the roof now, the knocking replaced by a whispery rain of *tap tap tap*s. He stumbled out into the yard, just in time to see a small, dark shadow creep across the pitched roof. She was out of sight, but trapped, because the wall on that side of the compound was far too high for any girl to climb.

"Mercy?" he begged. "Linnet? Roda? Come here and talk to me. Please."

From the other side of the house came a soft *thud* as whoever had been on the roof tumbled to the ground. Aaron loped toward the sound, cutting off the path to the exit. Impossible that she could have crept around the house without him seeing her—and yet the next noise came from behind him, a soft giggle followed by a whispered taunt. *"Meow!"*

The anger he thought he'd exorcised surged up in him again. He spun and dove to tackle her, but she slipped past him and he gave chase, out the gate and into the road, forgetting he was barefoot, forgetting he was dressed in nothing but his underwear, forgetting everything but his rage.

She ran down the night-darkened road, and he could make out nothing but the smudged outline of her shadow, first the size of a child, then as large as a man, then as small as a cat, and then the size of a girl again. He ran after her down empty streets, past shuttered houses and locked stores, into low dew-damp shrubbery and through a grove of higher trees that grabbed at him, tangling in his hair and leaving thin bloody streaks like whip marks on his chest. He ran and ran, past a church and a junkyard and into a cornfield, the young plants sharp as razors slashing at his legs, and finally up and over a wall, where he tumbled into a compound brilliantly full of firelight.

Blinking, Aaron shielded his eyes with his hand. At first, he couldn't distinguish people from shadows. What he took at first to be a tall, emaciated man wavered and resolved itself into a flagpole. He blinked again and realized that the yard was familiar, the building behind it even more so. Clustered around the firepit, which blazed now as it always did at celebrations, were the girls of Class Six. Beside them were the girls of Class Five, Class Seven, Class Eight. Many held Cokes and Fantas. Their mouths shone with the goat that had been roasting on the fire.

It was a party, celebrating the end of term. Aaron crouched before them, panting, and as the girls caught sight of him, their eyes widened, and then one of them pointed, her face contorted with horror, and let out a tiny whimper of fear. Aaron spun to look behind him, and in that instant of turning, he believed in all the creatures of Grace's stories before he saw the blank wall at his back and remembered himself to be pursuer, not pursued.

A few of the smaller girls began to cry, in keening, frightened wails, but then Roda Kudondo called out boldly, "Eh! Night runner!" and the sobs gave way to hooting jeers.

Aaron looked down and saw himself as they did: ghostly apparition, cat-eyed stranger, mushroom pale. Boxers shredded and covered in dirt; twigs and leaves clinging to the hair between his legs, his skin lit by a rising flush of shame. *Brave girls*, he thought suddenly, as their jeers rose up protectively around them. Brave girls, to transmute terror into laughter, to joke instead of cry.

"Sssst!" came a whisper from the far corner of the courtyard. "Aaron!"

He looked up to see a figure wreathed in shadows. At first, he thought she was just another schoolgirl, but then she grinned, and he recognized her long legs, and the gaps in her smile.

"Sssst!" the whisper came again. She beckoned, mouthed a Swahili phrase.

*Ukimbie nami.*

Run with me.

Grace, who did not fear him. Grace, who laughed at him and told him stories, who'd teased him and terrified him; Grace, who instead of crying or raging—ran. Tomorrow, he would begin the long trip home, but tonight, Grace sprinted naked across the yard, unseen by anyone but him.

And tonight, lithe as a cat, he ran after her.

## THE MIRROR, THE BUCKET, AND THE OLD THIGH BONE

Once there was a princess who needed to get married. No one expected this would present a problem. The princess had lively eyes and a small, sweet face. She loved to smile and to joke; she was in possession of a sharp, engaged, curious mind, and if she spent rather more time with her nose in a book than was considered ideal at that time (or any other), well, at least that meant she always had a story to tell.

Suitors came from all over the kingdom to visit the princess, and the princess received each one with equal grace. She asked them questions and answered theirs in turn; she walked arm in arm with them as they strolled around the grounds; she listened, and laughed, and exchanged one story for another, and she was so charming and so cheerful that each suitor returned home thinking that a life spent married to the princess would not be a terribly unpleasant one, even apart from the joy of someday becoming king.

After these visits, the princess would sit in the parlor with the king and the queen and the royal advisor, and they would pepper her with questions. What did she think of the most recent suitor? Did she find him handsome, chivalrous, intelligent, kind?

Oh, yes, the princess would say with a dimpled smile. Absolutely. All of those things.

And how did this suitor compare to the last one?

Indeed, that other suitor was also quite appealing.

But this one was better?

Yes, probably. Well, no. It's hard to say. They both had so many good qualities!

Shall we invite them both back, so you can compare?

Oh, no, I don't think that's necessary.

So you're saying you didn't like either of them.

I did, I did! Only—

Only?

It does seem like a bad sign, doesn't it, that I'm having such a hard time choosing between them? I was wondering, if it's not too much trouble, perhaps we could . . .

Invite another one?

Yes.

Another suitor.

Yes. Please.

If there are any left.

Yes, if there are any left. Might we? Please?

And at that, the queen would purse her narrow lips, the royal advisor would look troubled but keep his own counsel, and the king would sigh and say: I suppose.

In this way, one year passed, and then another, and then three more, and the princess worked her way through all the princes in the kingdom, and all the dukes, and all the viscounts, and all the untitled-but-obscenely-wealthy financiers, and all the untitled-and-not-very-wealthy-but-respectable craftsmen, and finally all the artists, who were neither titled nor wealthy nor respectable, and still, in the princess's eyes, not one of them distinguished himself from all the rest.

Soon, you couldn't travel ten miles without bumping into one of the princess's former suitors. And it would have been one thing, all of these suitors agreed, to have been rejected for a reason, but to be passed over simply because one was, in some vague way, not good enough—that was an unequivocal blow.

Five years in, the princess had rejected nearly every eligible man in the kingdom, and the whispers had begun to spread, and along with them, discontent: perhaps the princess was selfish. Spoiled. Arrogant. Or perhaps this was simply a game she was playing, and she did not want to get married at all.

At the close of the fifth year, the king lost patience. He informed the princess that the next day, all the rejected men would be invited back to the castle. The princess would pick one and marry him and that would be the end of it. And the princess, who was also tired of this procession, and troubled by her own inability to choose, agreed.

The suitors returned, and once again, the princess walked among them, chatting and laughing and exchanging stories, although perhaps not quite as vivaciously as before, and each of the suitors decided anew that a life spent married to the princess would not be a *terribly* unpleasant one, especially given the joy of becoming king someday.

The day passed without incident, and at sunset, the king and the queen and the royal advisor sat down in the parlor with the princess and asked for her decision. The princess did not answer right away. She bit her lip. She gnawed at her fingernail. She ran her hands through her long dark hair. Finally, she whispered:

Please, may I have one more day?

The king bellowed and overturned the table in a fury. The queen jumped up and slapped the princess's cheek. The princess buried her face in her hands and wept, and all was chaos and misery until the royal advisor intervened.

Let her have one more night to think it over, the royal advisor said. She can choose her husband in the morning.

The king and the queen were hardly pleased, but the royal advisor had never steered them wrong before, so they allowed the princess to go to bed that evening with her decision still unmade.

Alone in her room, the princess lay awake, twisting herself in the sheets and searching her heart as she'd done every night for the past five years. Why did no one satisfy her? What was she looking for that she couldn't find? Her battered heart offered her no answers. Exhausted and miserable, she had just drifted off to sleep when a knock came on her door.

The princess sat up. Was it the queen, ready to offer a kiss of apology and commiseration? The king, bearing one more threat or warning? Or perhaps it was the royal advisor, in possession of some magical task she could present to her suitors that would separate the most worthy one out from all the rest.

But when the princess opened her door, the figure standing in the hallway was not the king, or the queen, or the royal advisor. It was someone she had never seen before.

The princess's visitor wore a black cloak that fell from neck to ankle, and a black hood covering his hair. But his face, when she gazed straight into it, was lovely and captivating and warm. His cheeks were round, his lips were full and soft, and he had bright blue eyes to drown in.

Oh, the princess whispered softly. Hello.

*Hello*, her visitor whispered back.

The princess smiled, and when the visitor returned her smile, she felt as though all of her blood had been drained from her body and replaced with a mixture of soap bubbles and light and air.

The princess drew her visitor inside, and they spent the night together in the princess's canopy bed, kissing and joking and talking until dawn. When she fell asleep, just as the sun was rising, the princess was happier than she had ever been, and when she dreamed, she dreamed of a life full of more joy than she had ever dared to imagine, a life overflowing with laughter and happiness and love.

The princess awoke with a smile dancing on her lips, her lover's hand on her hip, and the king and the queen and the royal advisor standing over her.

Oh dear, the princess said, blushing. I know what this looks like. But listen—I've done it. At last, after all these years. I've made my choice.

She turned to her lover, who was still hidden under the bedsheets. I love him, she said. Nothing else matters. This is the man I choose.

The king and the queen shook their heads sadly. The royal advisor snatched the covers off the bed and threw them on the floor, and then, before the princess could object, he lifted the visitor's thick black cloak and shook it. Out of the cloak tumbled a cracked mirror, a dented tin bucket, and an old thigh bone.

The princess felt a crawling sensation on her hip where her lover's hand had been. She looked down and saw that it was only her own hand there, twitching with fear.

I don't understand, the princess whispered. What have you done with him?

We've done nothing with him, said the royal advisor. This is all he ever was.

The princess opened her mouth to speak but no words came out. Here, the royal advisor said. Let me show you.

He lifted the thigh bone from the bed and propped it against the wall. He lashed the mirror to the top of the bone with a bit of string, and he tied the bucket to the middle, and then he draped the black cloak over it all.

You see, said the royal advisor. When you looked in your lover's face, you were looking at your own face reflected in this cracked mirror. When you heard his voice, you heard only your own voice echoing back to you from this dented bucket. And when you embraced him, you felt your own hands caress your back, though you held nothing but this old thigh bone. You are selfish and arrogant and spoiled. You are capable of loving no one but yourself. None of your suitors will ever satisfy you, so put an end to this foolishness, and marry.

The princess made a choking sound. She clawed at her arms and bit her tongue until it bled and then she fell to her knees before the thing that had been her lover. When she stood up again, her face was smooth, her jaw was firm, and her eyes were dry of tears.

Yes, she said. I've learned my lesson. Call the suitors and assemble them. I am ready to choose.

The suitors gathered together in the courtyard, and the princess walked among them and apologized for having made them wait so long. Then, without hesitation or the slightest sign of doubt, she picked a husband: a young duke who was handsome and chivalrous and intelligent and kind.

One week later, the princess and the duke married. The queen was pleased. The king was satisfied. The royal advisor kept his own counsel, but he couldn't help looking a little bit smug. The mood of

discontent that had been hovering over the kingdom lifted, and everyone agreed that things had worked out for the best.

The year after the princess was married, both her parents died, which
meant she was no longer a princess, but a queen. Her husband, now
king, treated his wife with every courtesy and grace. The two of
them got along well, and the king ruled the kingdom successfully
for many years.

However, nearly a decade into the marriage, after the queen had
given birth to two of his children, the king discovered that he had
fallen in love with his wife. This complicated their relationship, as
it meant that he could no longer ignore the fact that she was very,
very sad.

The king knew that there had been some mystery surrounding
the way he had been chosen; he was not a fool, and he was well
aware that he had not made any particular impression on the princess
during their courtship. When he thought about it, which he mostly
tried not to do, he guessed something not very far from the truth:
that she had been in love with someone unsuitable, and when that
man had been forbidden to her, she had chosen him instead. The
king didn't terribly mind being a second choice, but he hated seeing
his wife pining away so miserably, and he couldn't help wondering if
their marriage was the cause of it all.

So, one night, the king asked the queen tentatively what was
wrong, and if there was anything he could do to make it better. At
first, the queen tried to deny that she was unhappy, but after so many
years together, a certain degree of trust had grown between them,
and at last, she told the king the whole strange story.

When she was finished, the king said: That is a very odd tale. And
the oddest thing of all is this: I have lived with you for a long time,

and I would say I know you very well, and I do not think you are selfish or arrogant or spoiled.

But I am, the queen said. I know I am.

How do you know?

Because, the queen whispered. I fell in love with that thing. I loved it as I have never loved anyone else: not you, not my parents, not even my own children. The only thing I have ever loved in this world is a grotesque contraption made of a cracked mirror, a dented bucket, and an old thigh bone. The night I spent with it in my bed was the only night I have ever been happy. And even knowing what it is, I ache for it, I yearn for it, I love it still. What can this mean but that I am spoiled, and selfish, and arrogant, and that I am capable of loving nothing but a distorted reflection of my own twisted heart?

With that, the queen burst into tears, and the king cradled her against his chest. I'm sorry, he said, because he could think of nothing else. What can I do?

There is nothing to be done, the queen said. I am your wife. I am the mother of my children. I am the queen of this kingdom. I am trying to be better than I am. All I ask is that you try and forgive me.

Of course I forgive you, the king said. There is nothing to forgive.

But the king went to sleep that night deeply troubled, and when he woke up in the morning, he could think of nothing but the possibility of easing the queen's misery. He loved her so much that if making her happy meant giving her up, he might have done it—but what good would it do to set her free when the person she was in love with didn't exist, except in her own mind?

The king brooded for days on this conundrum. At last, he went to visit the royal advisor, and together they came up with a plan. Even as they concocted it, the king knew it wasn't a very good plan, but the queen was growing sadder and paler every day, and the king felt he had to do something, or risk losing her altogether.

That evening, after the queen had fallen asleep, the king tiptoed out into the hallway and draped himself in a long black cloak. He knocked on the door, and when the queen opened it, he held a cracked mirror up in front of his own face.

The mirror the royal advisor had given the king was nothing but a piece of junk. The vainest, poorest woman in the kingdom would have thrown it in the trash. The front of it rippled and blurred as though it were covered in a thin layer of grease, and a deep crack ran from top to bottom, as though a long hair had been placed across the glass. And yet, as soon as the queen looked into the mirror, a look of such tenderness came over her that the king's heart nearly broke. The queen swayed, and closed her eyes, and pressed her lips to her reflection. Oh, she whispered. Oh, I missed you so much. Every day, I thought of you. Every night, I dreamed of you. I know it is impossible, and yet all I've ever wanted was for us to be together.

I missed you, too, the king whispered. But as soon as he spoke, the queen opened her eyes and jumped back.

No, she exclaimed. No! It's all wrong. You're not him. You don't sound like him. This isn't what I want! Please, you're only making everything worse.

She flung herself across the bed, and when the king came and lay beside her, she refused to look at him.

The queen did not get up again for three days. When she rose at last, her children ran to her and crawled into her lap. The queen embraced them, but she did not smile when they kissed her, and when they chattered cheerfully on about the small details of their day, she took too long to answer, as though she were speaking to them from very far away.

At first, the king tried to respect the queen's wishes and leave her to her sadness, but now, having once seen her happy, if only briefly, he found her misery even more difficult to witness than before. As the days wore on, and the queen remained sad and pale and quiet, the king convinced himself that if only he could manage to make the illusion a little more convincing, his disguise might bring the queen joy instead of sorrow.

And so, not long afterward, the king stood before the queen's bedroom door, holding a cracked mirror in one hand and a dented tin bucket in the other. The bucket was in an even worse state than the mirror—it was rusted and grimy and sour-smelling, and a patch of pale lichen had spread like spilled milk across the bottom.

The king knocked on the door, and the queen answered it, and once again, she looked in the mirror, and once again, her face softened, and the king's heart nearly broke, and she kissed the glass and whispered sweet words to her imaginary lover. But this time, the king stayed quiet, and the only sound in the room was the queen's own voice, echoing. Sobbing with joy, the queen fell against the king's broad chest—but as soon as his arms closed around her, she opened her eyes and pulled away from him.

No, she said. You can't deceive me like this. Your touch is nothing like his. Why do you insist on making me suffer?

Deaf to the king's apologies, the queen returned to her bed and she did not get out of it again—not when the king begged her, not when her daughter came and pleaded for her mother, not when the royal advisor came and demanded that she stop acting so foolishly and for once think of someone other than herself. She lay unmoving, refusing to eat or to drink, until at last the king decided that he had to take action or she would surely die.

This time, the king abandoned all hope of deception. He carried the old thigh bone into the queen's room in the middle of the day. The thigh bone was long and yellow, with bits of tendon still clinging to it, and small pocked holes along its sides where dogs had gnawed at it. The bone smelled like rotted meat and trash and bile, and the king could barely touch it without gagging. Nonetheless, he tied the mirror and the bucket to the bone with bits of string, and he draped the black cloak over it and propped it in the corner. As he finished, the queen opened her eyes and moaned.

Why, she begged. Why are you doing this to me, when I am trying so hard to be good?

You love what you love, the king said. If that means you are selfish, or arrogant, or spoiled, then so be it. I love you, and your children love you, and the people of the kingdom love you, and we don't want to see you suffer any longer.

The queen rose from her bed on unsteady legs. As the king watched, she peered into the mirror, whispered into the bucket, wrapped her arms around the old thigh bone, and smiled.

Over the next several days, the servants brought food for the queen to pick at and wine for her to sip, and soon the darkest of the shadows had vanished from around her eyes, and the hollows under her cheekbones were not quite so deep. Although he was glad she had emerged from the depths of her despair, the king found the sight of the queen cooing blissfully over her collection of trash unbearable to watch, so he left her to it, and when he returned the next day, he discovered that she had brought the filthy thing into their bed. He tried to object, but as soon as he approached, the queen hissed at him with such fury that he stumbled backward out of the room.

After a week had passed, the queen's children began asking again for their mother. The king returned to the queen's bedroom, where she lay naked among the bedclothes, nuzzling the mirror, murmuring into the bucket, and cradling the old thigh bone in her arms.

What do you want? she asked as he approached, without taking her eyes off the mirror.

Your children miss you, the king said. Could you not come out and play with them for a while?

Send them to me, the queen said. They can play in here.

Absolutely not, the king replied in disgust. Go and take care of your family. This . . . thing will be waiting for you when you get back.

The queen whispered something under her breath, and then she cocked her head, listening to her own echo. A terrible, sly expression came over her face.

Oh, she said craftily. I see.

*See*, whispered the bucket.

Yes, she answered it. I see.

What are you talking about? the king asked.

You want to lure me out of here, the queen said. You're jealous. As soon as I leave the room, you will sneak in here and steal my mirror, my bucket, and my old thigh bone, and I'll be all alone again.

*Alone*, whispered the bucket.

Yes, the queen said darkly. Alone.

Please— the king begged her. Listen to me. That's not what I—

Get out of here! the queen shouted, and then she began to scream, the words echoing from the dented tin bucket until the room resounded with a cacophony of shrieking:

*Leave us alone! Leave us alone! Leave us alone!*

———

After that, the king went mad himself. He ordered the servants' tongues cut out, so that they could tell no one of the queen's condition, and he dismissed the royal advisor, then hired an assassin to ensure he kept the secret. He lied to his children and told them their mother was an invalid, and he passed a law forbidding anyone to speak of what had befallen her. Yet despite all his efforts, the whispers spread. Rumor had it that late at night, the queen would emerge from the bedroom and stroll across the parapets, dragging her monstrous lover clacking and clanking beside her.

The king ruled the kingdom as best he could, and tried to think himself a widower. He no longer visited the queen, though on some nights, he would wander in his sleep and wake to find himself in the hallway outside her room, his knuckles poised before her door.

A year went by, then five, then ten, until at last, unable to carry the weight of his grief any longer, the king returned to his wife's bedroom, resolving to speak with her one last time and then end his own life.

The queen's bedroom was lit by a single candle that guttered in the corner. Blinded by shadows, at first the king thought the room was empty, but as his eyes adjusted to the darkness, he could make out a pale shape, writhing in the dark. From the direction of the bed came a flurry of chittering whispers, like the sound grubs make when exposed by an overturned rock. The sound was so unnerving that the king was about to flee, but then a shaft of silvery moonlight pierced the window and illuminated what lay tangled in the sheets.

The creature that lifted its face to him was a ghastly, skeletal thing, with matted hair and corpse-white skin and huge, unseeing eyes that had long ago grown used to the dark. It bared its teeth and snarled wordlessly, its naked shoulder blades flexing beneath its skin like stubby, unformed wings. In the slow motion of a dream, the monster that had once been the queen slid off the bed and began crawling toward the king, dragging the mirror, the bucket, and the old thigh bone behind her.

The king screamed and ran for the door, but just as he reached it, he was overcome by a vision of his wife as she'd been when he'd first laid eyes on her—a smiling girl with a gentle face—and his pity drowned out his fear.

Gathering his courage, he returned to the room, and kneeled down beside the woman he loved. I'm so sorry, he whispered, and in the silence, the tin bucket echoed his own words back to him.

*I'm sorry.*

Gently, ever so gently, the king began to pry the thigh bone from the queen's clenched hands. Shaking, she held on as tightly as she could, but her strength was no match for his. Without warning, she let go. The king's hand slipped. The thigh bone fell, the dented bucket landed on stone with a noise like crashing bells, and the mirror shattered into a thousand pieces.

The queen furrowed her brow in confusion, and for one brief moment she seemed herself again. Then she collapsed as though her tendons had been severed, and when the king tried to take her arm to lift her, she whipped her hand around and dragged a shard of broken mirror across his neck.

The next morning, the queen emerged from her room. She was still corpse-white and bone-thin, but when she spoke, her words were soft and clear. She told the people of the tragedy that had taken place the night before; of how the king, driven out of his mind by years of grief, had come to her bedchamber and cut his own throat. She said she had been ill for a long time, but that she was now better, and that now she was prepared to rule in her husband's stead. The story beggared belief, and the queen's eyes glittered madly as she told it, but she was still the queen, and no one, not even her own children, dared to speak against her.

The queen ascended the throne, and shortly thereafter, a figure dressed in an old black cloak appeared beside her. Although no one was permitted to come close enough to see it clearly, an unpleasant stench wafted from it, and sometimes, when the queen leaned in and listened to its counsel, those who kneeled before her thought they could see, through the folds of the hood, an image of the queen's own face, broken into a thousand jagged pieces. Thus the queen lived out the rest of her days, and when she died, she was buried according to her wishes, with the black-cloaked figure interred in the coffin beside her.

The queen's children grew up, and grew old, and died in their turn, and before long, the kingdom collapsed and was overrun by strangers. Deep beneath the earth, the tin bucket echoed with the sound of gnawing maggots, and the mirror reflected a dance of grim decay. Soon, the queen's sad story was entirely forgotten. Her gravestone toppled, the passing weather wore away her name, and by the time a century had passed, the old thigh bone was just one of many in a pile, the dented tin bucket had long gone silent, and the shattered mirror reflected nothing but a clean white skull.

# CAT PERSON

Margot met Robert on a Wednesday night toward the end of her fall semester. She was working behind the concession stand at the artsy movie theater downtown when he came in and bought a large popcorn and a box of Red Vines.

"That's an . . . unusual choice," she said. "I don't think I've ever actually sold a box of Red Vines before."

Flirting with her customers was a habit she'd picked up back when she worked as a barista, and it helped with tips. She didn't earn tips at the movie theater, but the job was boring otherwise, and she did think that Robert was cute. Not so cute that she would have, say, gone up to him at a party, but cute enough that she could have drummed up an imaginary crush on him if he'd sat across from her during a dull class—though she was pretty sure that he was out of college, in his mid-twenties at least. He was tall, which she liked, and she could see the edge of a tattoo peeking out from beneath the rolled-up sleeve of his shirt. But he was on the heavy side, his beard was a little too long, and his shoulders slumped forward slightly, as though he were protecting something.

Robert did not pick up on her flirtation. Or, if he did, he showed it only by stepping back, as though to make her lean toward him, to try a little harder.

"Well," he said. "Okay, then." He pocketed his change.

But the next week he came into the movie theater again, and bought another box of Red Vines.

"You're getting better at your job," he told her. "You managed not to insult me this time."

She shrugged.

"I'm up for a promotion, so," she said.

After the movie, he came back to her.

"Concession-stand girl, give me your phone number," he said, and, surprising herself, she did.

From that small exchange about Red Vines, over the next several weeks they built up an elaborate scaffolding of jokes via text, riffs that unfolded and shifted so quickly that she sometimes had a hard time keeping up. He was very clever, and she found that she had to work to impress him. Soon she noticed that when she texted him he usually texted her back right away, but if she took more than a few hours to respond his next message would always be short and wouldn't include a question, so it was up to her to reinitiate the conversation, which she always did. A few times, she got distracted for a day or so and wondered if the exchange would die out altogether, but then she'd think of something funny to tell him or she'd see a picture on the internet that was relevant to their conversation, and they'd start up again. She still didn't know much about him, because they never talked about anything personal, but when they landed two or three good jokes in a row there was a kind of exhilaration to it, as if they were dancing. Then, one night during reading period, she was complaining about

78

how all the dining halls were closed and there was no food in her room because her roommate had raided her care package, and he offered to buy her some Red Vines to sustain her. At first, she deflected this with another joke, because she really did have to study, but he said, *No I'm serious, stop fooling around and come now*, so she put a jacket over her pajamas and met him at the 7-Eleven.

It was about eleven o'clock. He greeted her without ceremony, as though he saw her every day, and took her inside to choose some snacks. The store didn't have Red Vines, so he bought her a Cherry Coke Slurpee and a bag of Doritos and a novelty lighter shaped like a frog with a cigarette in its mouth.

"Thank you for my presents," she said, when they were back outside.

Robert was wearing a rabbit fur hat that came down over his ears and a thick, old-fashioned down jacket. She thought it was a good look for him, if a little dorky; the hat heightened his lumberjack aura, and the heavy coat hid his belly and the slightly sad slump of his shoulders.

"You're welcome, concession-stand girl," he said, though of course he knew her name by then.

She thought he was going to go in for a kiss and prepared to duck and offer him her cheek, but instead of kissing her on the mouth he took her by the arm and kissed her gently on the forehead, as though she were something precious.

"Study hard, sweetheart," he said. "I will see you soon."

On the walk back to her dorm, she was filled with a sparkly lightness that she recognized as the sign of an incipient crush.

While she was home over break, they texted nearly nonstop, not only jokes but little updates about their days. They started saying good morning and good night, and when she asked him a question and he didn't respond right away she felt a jab of anxious yearning.

79

She learned that Robert had two cats, named Mu and Yan, and together they invented a complicated scenario in which her childhood cat, Pita, would send flirtatious texts to Yan, but whenever Pita talked to Mu she was formal and cold, because she was jealous of Mu's relationship with Yan.

"Why are you texting all the time?" Margot's stepdad asked her at dinner. "Are you having an affair with someone?"

"Yes," Margot said. "His name is Robert, and I met him at the movie theater. We're in love, and we're probably going to get married."

"Hmm," her stepdad said. "Tell him we have some questions for him."

*My parents are asking about u*, Margot texted, and Robert sent her back a smiley-face emoji whose eyes were hearts.

When Margot returned to campus, she was eager to see Robert again, but he turned out to be surprisingly hard to pin down. *Sorry, busy week at work*, he replied. *I promise I will c u soon.* Margot didn't like this; it felt as if the dynamic had shifted out of her favor, and when eventually he did ask her to go to a movie she agreed right away.

The movie he wanted to see was playing at the theater where she worked, but she suggested that they see it at the big multiplex just outside town instead; students didn't go there very often, because you needed to drive. Robert came to pick her up in a muddy white Civic with candy wrappers spilling out of the cup holders. On the drive, he was quieter than she'd expected, and he didn't look at her very much. Before five minutes had gone by, she became wildly uncomfortable, and, as they got on the highway, it occurred to her that he could take her someplace and rape and murder her; she hardly knew anything about him, after all.

Just as she thought this, he said, "Don't worry, I'm not going to murder you," and she wondered if the discomfort in the car was her fault, because she was acting jumpy and nervous, like the kind of girl who thought she was going to get murdered every time she went on a date.

"It's okay—you can murder me if you want," she said, and he laughed and patted her knee. But he was still disconcertingly quiet, and all her bubbling attempts at making conversation bounced right off him. At the theater, he made a joke to the cashier at the concession stand about Red Vines, which fell flat in a way that embarrassed everyone involved, but Margot most of all.

During the movie, he didn't hold her hand or put his arm around her, so by the time they were back in the parking lot she was pretty sure that he had changed his mind about liking her. She was wearing leggings and a sweatshirt, and that might have been the problem. When she got into the car, he'd said, "Glad to see you dressed up for me," which she'd assumed was a joke, but maybe she actually had offended him by not seeming to take the date seriously enough, or something. He was wearing khakis and a button-down shirt.

"So, do you want to go get a drink?" he asked when they got back to the car, as if being polite were an obligation that had been imposed on him. It seemed obvious to Margot that he was expecting her to say no and that, when she did, they wouldn't talk again. That made her sad, not so much because she wanted to continue spending time with him as because she'd had such high expectations for him over break, and it didn't seem fair that things had fallen apart so quickly.

"We could go get a drink, I guess?" she said.

"If you want," he said. "If you want" was such an unpleasant response that she sat silently in the car until he poked her leg and said, "What are you sulking about?"

"I'm not sulking," she said. "I'm just a little tired."

"I can take you home."

"No, I could use a drink, after that movie." Even though it had been playing at the mainstream theater, the film he'd chosen was a very depressing drama about the Holocaust, so inappropriate for a first date that when he suggested it she said, *Lol r u serious*, and he made some joke about how he was sorry that he'd misjudged her taste and he could take her to a romantic comedy instead. But now, when she said that about the movie, he winced a little, and a totally different interpretation of the night's events occurred to her. She wondered if perhaps he'd been trying to impress her by suggesting the Holocaust movie, because he didn't understand that a Holocaust movie was the wrong kind of "serious" movie with which to impress the type of person who worked at an artsy movie theater, the type of person he probably assumed she was. Maybe, she thought, her texting *Lol r u serious* had hurt him, had intimidated him and made him feel uncomfortable around her. The thought of this possible vulnerability touched her, and she felt kinder toward him than she had all night.

When he asked her where she wanted to go for a drink, she named the place where she usually hung out, but he made a face and said that it was in the student ghetto and he'd take her somewhere better. They went to a bar she'd never been to, an underground speakeasy type of place, with no sign announcing its presence. There was a line to get inside, and, as they waited, she grew fidgety trying to figure out how to tell him what she needed to tell him, but she couldn't, so when the bouncer asked to see her I.D. she just handed it to him. The bouncer hardly even looked at it; he just smirked and said, "Yeah, no," and waved her to the side, as he gestured toward the next group of people in line.

Robert had gone ahead of her, not noticing what was playing out behind him. "Robert," she said quietly. But he didn't turn around.

Finally, someone in line who'd been paying attention tapped him on the shoulder and pointed to her, marooned on the sidewalk.

She stood, abashed, as he came back over to her. "Sorry!" she said. "This is so embarrassing."

"How old are you?" he demanded.

"I'm twenty," she said.

"Oh," he said. "I thought you said you were older."

"I told you I was a sophomore!" she said. Standing outside the bar, having been rejected in front of everyone, was humiliating enough, and now Robert was looking at her as if she'd done something wrong.

"But you did that—what do you call it? That gap year," he objected, as though this were an argument he could win.

"I don't know what to tell you," she said helplessly. "I'm twenty." And then, absurdly, she started to feel tears stinging her eyes, because somehow everything had been ruined and she couldn't understand why this was all so hard.

But, when Robert saw her face crumpling, a kind of magic happened. All the tension drained out of his posture; he stood up straight and wrapped his bearlike arms around her. "Oh, sweetheart," he said. "Oh, honey, it's okay, it's all right. Please don't feel bad." She let herself be folded against him, and she was flooded with the same feeling she'd had outside the 7-Eleven—that she was a delicate, precious thing he was afraid he might break. He kissed the top of her head, and she laughed and wiped her tears away.

"I can't believe I'm crying because I didn't get into a bar," she said. "You must think I'm such an idiot." But she knew he didn't think that, from the way he was gazing at her; in his eyes, she could see how pretty she looked, smiling through her tears in the chalky glow of the streetlight, with a few flakes of snow coming down.

He kissed her then, on the lips, for real; he came for her in a kind of lunging motion and practically poured his tongue down her throat. It was a terrible kiss, shockingly bad; Margot had trouble believing that a grown man could possibly be so bad at kissing. It seemed awful, yet somehow it also gave her that tender feeling toward him again, the sense that even though he was older than her, she knew something he didn't. When he was done kissing her, he took her hand firmly and led her to a different bar, where there were pool tables and pinball machines and sawdust on the floor and no one checking I.D.s at the door. In one of the booths, she saw the grad student who'd been her English T.A. her freshman year.

"Should I get you a vodka soda?" Robert asked, which she thought was maybe supposed to be a joke about the kind of drink college girls liked, though she'd never had a vodka soda. She actually was a little anxious about what to order; at the places she went to, they only carded people at the bar, so the kids who were twenty-one or had good fake I.D.s usually brought pitchers of PBR or Bud Light back to share with the others. She wasn't sure if those brands were ones that Robert would make fun of, so, instead of specifying, she said, "I'll just have a beer."

With the drinks in front of him and the kiss behind him, and also maybe because she had cried, Robert became much more relaxed, more like the witty person she knew through his texts. As they talked, she became increasingly sure that what she'd interpreted as anger or dissatisfaction with her had, in fact, been nervousness, a fear that she wasn't having a good time. He kept coming back to her initial dismissal of the movie, making jokes that glanced off it and watching her closely to see how she responded. He teased her about her highbrow taste, and said how hard it was to impress her because of all the film classes she'd taken, even though he knew she'd taken only one summer class in film. He joked about how she and the other employees at the artsy theater probably sat around and made fun of the people who went to the mainstream theater, where they didn't even serve wine, and some of the movies were in IMAX 3-D. Margot laughed along with the jokes he was making at the expense of this imaginary film snob version of her, though nothing he said seemed quite fair, since she was the one who'd actually suggested that they see the movie at the Quality 16. Although now, she realized, maybe that had hurt Robert's feelings, too. She'd thought it was clear that she just didn't want to go on a date where she worked, but maybe he'd taken it more personally than that; maybe he'd suspected that she was ashamed to be seen with him. She was starting to think that she understood him—how sensitive he was, how easily he could be wounded—and that made her feel closer to him, and also powerful, because once she knew how to hurt him she also knew how he could be soothed. She asked him lots of questions about the movies he liked, and she spoke self-deprecatingly about the movies at the artsy theater that she found boring or incomprehensible; she told him about how much her older coworkers intimidated her, and how she sometimes worried that she wasn't smart enough to form her own opinions on anything. The effect of this on him was palpable and immediate, and she felt as if she were petting a large, skittish animal, like a horse or a bear, skillfully coaxing it to eat from her hand.

By her third beer, she was thinking about what it would be like to have sex with Robert. Probably it would be like that bad kiss, clumsy and excessive, but imagining how excited he would be, how hungry and eager to impress her, she felt a twinge of desire pluck at her belly, as distinct and painful as the snap of an elastic band against her skin.

When they'd finished that round of drinks, she said, boldly, "Should we get out of here, then?" and he seemed briefly hurt, as if he thought she was cutting the date short, but she took his hand and pulled him up, and the look on his face when he realized what she was saying, and the obedient way he trailed her out of the bar, gave her that elastic-band snap again, as did, oddly, the fact that his palm was slick beneath hers.

Outside, she presented herself to him again for kissing, but, to her surprise, he only pecked her on the mouth. "You're drunk," he said, accusingly.

"No, I'm not," she said, though she was. She pushed her body against his, feeling tiny beside him, and he let out a great shuddering sigh, as if she were something too bright and painful to look at, and that was sexy, too, being made to feel like a kind of irresistible temptation.

"I'm taking you home, lightweight," he said, shepherding her to the car. Once they were inside it, though, she leaned into him again, and after a little while, by lightly pulling back when he pushed his tongue too far down her throat, she was able to get him to kiss her in the softer way that she liked, and soon after that she was straddling him, and she could feel the small log of his erection straining against his pants. Whenever it rolled beneath her weight, he let out these fluttery, high-pitched moans that she couldn't help feeling were a little melodramatic, and then suddenly he pushed her off him and turned the key in the ignition.

"Making out in the front seat like a teenager," he said, in mock disgust. Then he added, "I'd have thought you'd be too old for that, now that you're twenty."

She stuck her tongue out at him. "Where do you want to go, then?"

"Your place?"

"Um, that won't really work. Because of my roommate?"

"Oh, right. You live in the dorms," he said, as though that were something she should apologize for.

"Where do you live?" she asked.

"I live in a house."

"Can I . . . come over?"

"You can."

The house was in a pretty, wooded neighborhood not too far from campus and had a string of cheerful white fairy lights across the doorway. Before he got out of the car, he said, darkly, like a warning, "Just so you know, I have cats."

"I know," she said. "We texted about them, remember?"

At the front door, he fumbled with his keys for what seemed a ridiculously long time and swore under his breath. She rubbed his back to try to keep the mood going, but that seemed to fluster him even more, so she stopped.

"Well. This is my house," he said flatly, pushing the door open.

The room they were in was dimly lit and full of objects, all of which, as her eyes adjusted, resolved into familiarity. He had two large, full bookcases, a shelf of vinyl records, a collection of board games, and a lot of art—or, at least, posters that had been hung in frames, instead of being tacked or taped to the wall.

"I like it," she said, truthfully, and, as she did, she identified the emotion she was feeling as relief. It occurred to her that she'd never gone to someone's house to have sex before; because she'd dated only guys her age, there had always been some element of sneaking around, to avoid roommates. It was new, and a little frightening, to be so completely on someone else's turf, and the fact that Robert's house gave evidence of his having interests that she shared, if only in their broadest categories—art, games, books, music—struck her as a reassuring endorsement of her choice.

As she thought this, she saw that Robert was watching her closely, observing the impression the room had made. And, as though fear weren't quite ready to release its hold on her, she had the brief wild idea that maybe this was not a room at all but a trap meant to lure her into the false belief that Robert was a normal person, a person like her, when in fact all the other rooms in the house were empty, or full of horrors: corpses or kidnap victims or chains. But then he was kissing her, throwing her bag and their coats on the couch and ushering her into the bedroom, groping her ass and pawing at her chest, with the avid clumsiness of that first kiss.

The bedroom wasn't empty, though it was emptier than the living room; he didn't have a bed frame, just a mattress and a box spring on the floor. There was a bottle of whiskey on his dresser, and he took a swig from it, then handed it to her and kneeled down and opened his laptop, an action that confused her, until she understood that he was putting on music.

Margot sat on the bed while Robert took off his shirt and unbuckled his pants, pulling them down to his ankles before realizing that he was still wearing his shoes and bending over to untie them. Looking at him like that, so awkwardly bent, his belly thick and soft and covered with hair, Margot thought: oh, no. But the thought of what it would take to stop what she had set in motion was overwhelming; it would require an amount of tact and gentleness that she felt was impossible to summon. It wasn't that she was scared he would try to force her to do something against her will but that insisting they stop now, after everything she'd done to push this forward, would make her seem spoiled and capricious, as if she'd ordered something at a restaurant and then, once the food arrived, had changed her mind and sent it back.

She tried to bludgeon her resistance into submission by taking a sip of the whiskey, but when he fell on top of her with those huge, sloppy kisses, his hand moving mechanically across her breasts and down to her crotch, as if he were making some perverse sign of the cross, she began to have trouble breathing and to feel that she really might not be able to go through with it after all.

Wriggling out from under the weight of him and straddling him helped, as did closing her eyes and remembering him kissing her forehead at the 7-Eleven. Encouraged by her progress, she pulled her shirt up over her head. Robert reached up and scooped a breast out of her bra, so that it jutted half in and half out of the cup, and rolled her nipple between his thumb and forefinger. This was uncomfortable, so she leaned forward, pushing herself into his hand. He got the hint and tried to undo her bra, but he couldn't work the clasp, his evident frustration reminiscent of his struggle with the keys, until at last he said, bossily, "Take that thing off," and she complied.

The way he looked at her then was like an exaggerated version of the expression she'd seen on the faces of all the guys she'd been naked with, not that there were that many—six in total, Robert made seven. He looked stunned and stupid with pleasure, like a milk-drunk baby, and she thought that maybe this was what she loved most about sex—a guy revealed like that. Robert showed her more open need than any of the others, even though he was older, and must have seen more breasts, more bodies, than they had—but maybe that was part of it for him, the fact that he was older, and she was young.

As they kissed, she found herself carried away by a fantasy of such pure ego that she could hardly admit even to herself that she was having it. Look at this beautiful girl, she imagined him thinking. She's so perfect, her body is perfect, everything about her is perfect, she's only twenty years old, her skin is flawless, I want her so badly, I want her more than I've ever wanted anyone else, I want her so bad I might die.

The more she imagined his arousal, the more turned-on she got, and soon they were rocking against each other, getting into a rhythm, and she reached into his underwear and took his penis in her hand and felt the pearled droplet of moisture on its tip. He made that sound again, that high-pitched feminine whine, and she wished there were a way she could ask him not to do that, but she couldn't think of any. Then his hand was inside her underwear, and when he felt that she was wet he visibly relaxed. He fingered her a little, very softly, and she bit her lip and put on a show for him, but then he poked her too hard and she flinched, and he jerked his hand away. "Sorry!" he said.

And then he asked, urgently, "Wait. Have you ever done this before?"

The night did, indeed, feel so odd and unprecedented that her first impulse was to say no, but then she realized what he meant and she laughed out loud.

She didn't mean to laugh; she knew well enough already that, while Robert might enjoy being the subject of gentle, flirtatious teasing, he was not a person who would enjoy being laughed at, not at all. But she couldn't help it. Losing her virginity had been a long, drawn-out affair preceded by several months' worth of intense discussion with her boyfriend of two years, plus a visit to the gynecologist and a horrifically embarrassing but ultimately incredibly meaningful conversation with her mom, who, in the end, had not only reserved her a room at a bed-and-breakfast but, after the event, written her a card. The idea that, instead of that whole involved, emotional process, she might have watched a pretentious Holocaust movie, drunk three beers, and then gone to some random house to lose her virginity to a guy she'd met at a movie theater was so funny that suddenly she couldn't stop laughing, though the laughter had a slightly hysterical edge.

"I'm sorry," Robert said coldly. "I didn't know."

Abruptly, she stopped giggling. "No, it was . . . nice of you to check," she said. "I've had sex before, though. I'm sorry I laughed."

"You don't need to apologize," he said, but she could tell by his face, as well as by the fact that he was going soft beneath her, that she did.

"I'm sorry," she said again, reflexively, and then, in a burst of inspiration, "I guess I'm just nervous, or something?" He narrowed his eyes at her, as though suspicious of this claim, but it seemed to placate him.

"You don't have to be nervous," he said. "We'll take it slow."

Yeah, right, she thought, and then he was on top of her again, kissing her and weighing her down, and she knew that her last chance of enjoying this encounter had disappeared, but that she would carry through with it until it was over. When Robert was naked, rolling a condom onto a dick that was only half-visible beneath the hairy shelf of his belly, she felt a wave of revulsion that she thought might actually break through her sense of pinned stasis, but then he shoved his finger in her again, not at all gently this time, and she imagined herself from above, naked and spread-eagled with this fat old man's finger inside her, and her revulsion turned to self-disgust and a humiliation that was a kind of perverse cousin to arousal.

During sex, he moved her through a series of positions with brusque efficiency, flipping her over, pushing her around, and she felt like a doll again, as she had outside the 7-Eleven, though not a precious one now—a doll made of rubber, flexible and resilient, a prop for the movie that was playing in his head. When she was on top, he slapped her thigh and said, "Yeah, yeah, you like that," with an intonation that made it impossible to tell whether he meant it as a question, an observation, or an order, and when he turned her over he growled in her ear, "I always wanted to fuck a girl with nice tits," and she had to smother her face in the pillow to keep from laughing again. At the end, when he was on top of her in missionary, he kept losing his erection, and every time he did he would say, aggressively,

"You make my dick so hard," as though lying about it could make it true. At last, after a frantic rabbity burst, he shuddered, came, and collapsed on her like a tree falling, and, crushed beneath him, she thought, brightly, *This is the worst life decision I have ever made!* And she marveled at herself for a while, at the mystery of this person who'd just done this bizarre, inexplicable thing.

After a short while, Robert got up and hurried to the bathroom in a bow-legged waddle, clutching the condom to keep it from falling off. Margot lay on the bed and stared at the ceiling, noticing for the first time that there were stickers on it, those little stars and moons that were supposed to glow in the dark. Robert returned from the bathroom and stood silhouetted in the doorway. "What do you want to do now?" he asked her.

"We should probably just kill ourselves," she imagined saying, and then she imagined that somewhere, out there in the universe, there was a boy who would think that this moment was just as awful yet hilarious as she did, and that sometime, far in the future, she would tell the boy this story. She'd say, "And then he said, 'You make my dick so hard,' " and the boy would shriek in agony and grab her leg, saying, "Oh, my God, stop, please, no, I can't take it anymore," and the two of them would collapse into each other's arms and laugh and laugh—but of course there was no such future, because no such boy existed, and he never would.

So instead she shrugged, and Robert said, "We could watch a movie," and he went to the computer and downloaded something; she didn't pay attention to what. For some reason, he'd chosen a movie with subtitles, and she kept closing her eyes, so she had no idea what was going on. The whole time, he was stroking her hair and trailing light kisses down her shoulder, as if he'd forgotten that ten minutes ago he'd thrown her around as if they were in a porno and growled, "I always wanted to fuck a girl with nice tits" in her ear.

Then, out of nowhere, he started talking about his feelings for her. He talked about how hard it had been for him when she went away for break, not knowing if she had an old high-school boyfriend she might reconnect with back home. During those two weeks, it turned out, an entire secret drama had played out in his head, one in which she'd left campus committed to him, to Robert, but at home had been drawn back to the high-school guy, who, in Robert's mind, was some kind of brutish, handsome jock, not worthy of her but nonetheless seductive by virtue of his position at the top of the hierarchy back home in Saline. "I was so worried you might, like, make a bad decision and things would be different between us when you got back," he said. "But I should have trusted you." My high-school boyfriend is gay, Margot imagined telling him. We were pretty sure of it in high school, but after a year of sleeping around at college he's definitely figured it out. In fact, he's not even a hundred percent positive that he identifies as a man anymore; we spent a lot of time over break talking about what it would mean for him to come out as non-binary, so sex with him wasn't going to happen, and you could have asked me about that if you were worried; you could have asked me about a lot of things.

But she didn't say any of that; she just lay silently, emanating a black, hateful aura, until finally Robert trailed off. "Are you still awake?" he asked, and she said yes, and he said, "Is everything okay?"

"How old are you, exactly?" she asked him.

"I'm thirty-four," he said. "Is that a problem?"

She could sense him in the dark beside her vibrating with fear. "No," she said. "It's fine."

"Good," he said. "It was something I wanted to bring up with you, but I didn't know how you'd take it." He rolled over and kissed her forehead, and she felt like a slug he'd poured salt on, disintegrating under that kiss.

She looked at the clock; it was nearly three in the morning. "I should go home, probably," she said.

"Really?" he said. "But I thought you'd stay over. I make great scrambled eggs!"

"Thanks," she said, sliding into her leggings. "But I can't. My roommate would be worried. So."

"Gotta get back to the dorm room," he said, voice dripping with sarcasm.

"Yep," she said. "Since that's where I live."

The drive was endless. The snow had turned to rain. They didn't talk. Eventually, Robert switched the radio to late-night NPR. Margot recalled how, when they first got on the highway to go to the movie, she'd imagined that Robert might murder her, and she thought, *Maybe he'll murder me now.*

He didn't murder her. He drove her to her dorm. "I had a really nice time tonight," he said, unbuckling his seat belt.

"Thanks," she said. She clutched her bag in her hands. "Me too."

"I'm so glad we finally got to go on a date," he said.

"A date," she said to her imaginary boyfriend. "He called that a date." And they both laughed and laughed.

"You're welcome," she said. She reached for the door handle. "Thanks for the movie and stuff."

"Wait," he said, and grabbed her arm. "Come here." He dragged her back, wrapped his arms around her, and pushed his tongue down her throat one last time. "Oh, my God, when will it end?" she asked the imaginary boyfriend, but the imaginary boyfriend didn't answer her.

"Good night," she said, and then she opened the door and escaped. By the time she got to her room, she already had a text from him: no words, just hearts and faces with heart eyes and, for some reason, a dolphin.

She slept for twelve hours, and when she woke she ate waffles in the dining hall and binge-watched detective shows on Netflix and tried to envision the hopeful possibility that he would disappear without her having to do anything, that somehow she could just wish him away. When the next message from him did arrive, just after dinner, it was a harmless joke about Red Vines, but she deleted it immediately, overwhelmed with a skin-crawling loathing that felt vastly disproportionate to anything he had actually done. She told herself that she owed him at least some kind of breakup message, that to ghost him would be inappropriate, childish, and cruel. And, if she did try to ghost, who knew how long it would take him to get the hint? Maybe the messages would keep coming and coming; maybe they would never end.

She began drafting a message—*Thank you for the nice time but I'm not interested in a relationship right now*—but she kept hedging and apologizing, attempting to close loopholes that she imagined him trying to slip through ("It's okay, I'm not interested in a relationship either, something casual is fine!"), so that the message got longer and longer and even more impossible to send. Meanwhile, his texts kept arriving, none of them saying anything of consequence, each one more earnest than the last. She imagined him lying on his bed that was just a mattress, carefully crafting each one. She remembered that he'd talked a lot about his cats and yet she hadn't seen any cats in the house, and she wondered if he'd made them up.

Every so often, over the next day or so, she would find herself in a gray, daydreamy mood, missing something, and she'd realize that it was Robert she missed, not the real Robert but the Robert she'd imagined on the other end of all those text messages during break.

*Hey, so it seems like you're really busy, huh?* Robert finally wrote, three days after they'd fucked, and she knew that this was the perfect opportunity to send her half-completed breakup text, but instead she wrote back, *Haha sorry yeah* and *I'll text you soon*, and then she thought, Why did I do that? And she truly didn't know.

"Just tell him you're not interested!" Margot's roommate, Tamara, screamed in frustration after Margot had spent an hour on her bed, dithering about what to say to Robert.

"I have to say more than that. We had sex," Margot said.

"Do you?" Tamara said. "I mean, really?"

"He's a nice guy, sort of," Margot said, and she wondered how true that was. Then, abruptly, Tamara lunged, snatching the phone out of Margot's hand and holding it far away from her as her thumbs flew across the screen. Tamara flung the phone onto the bed and Margot scrambled for it, and there it was, what Tamara had written: *Hi im not interested in you stop textng me.*

"Oh, my God," Margot said, finding it suddenly hard to breathe.

"What?" Tamara said boldly. "What's the big deal? It's true."

But they both knew that it was a big deal, and Margot had a knot of fear in her stomach so solid that she thought she might retch. She imagined Robert picking up his phone, reading that message, turning to glass, and shattering to pieces.

"Calm down. Let's go get a drink," Tamara said, and they went to a bar and shared a pitcher, and all the while Margot's phone sat between them on the table, and though they tried to ignore it, when it chimed with an incoming message they screamed and clutched each other's arms.

"I can't do it—you read it," Margot said. She pushed the phone toward Tamara. "You did this. It's your fault." But all the message said was *Okay, Margot, I am sorry to hear that. I hope I did not do anything to upset you. You are a sweet girl and I really enjoyed the time we spent together. Please let me know if you change your mind.*

Margot collapsed on the table, laying her head in her hands. She felt as though a leech, grown heavy and swollen with her blood, had at last popped off her skin, leaving a tender, bruised spot behind. But why should she feel that way? Perhaps she was being unfair to Robert, who really had done nothing wrong, except like her, and be bad in bed, and maybe lie about having cats, although probably they had just been in another room. But then, a month later, she saw him in the bar—her bar, the one in the student ghetto, where, on their date, she'd suggested they go. He was alone, at a table in the back, and he wasn't reading or looking at his phone; he was just sitting there silently, hunched over a beer.

She grabbed the friend she was with, a guy named Albert. "Oh, my God, that's him," she whispered. "The guy from the movie theater!" By then, Albert had heard a version of the story, though not quite the true one; nearly all her friends had. Albert stepped in front of her, shielding her from Robert's view, as they rushed back to the table where their friends were. When Margot announced that Robert was there, everyone erupted in astonishment, and then they surrounded her and hustled her out of the bar as if she were the president and they were the Secret Service. It was all so over-the-top that she wondered if she was acting like a mean girl, but, at the same time, she truly did feel sick and scared. Curled up on her bed with Tamara that night, the glow of the phone like a campfire illuminating their faces, Margot read the messages as they arrived: *Hi Margot, I saw you out at the bar tonight. I know you said not to text you but I just wanted to say you looked really pretty. I hope you're doing well!*

*I know I shouldnt say this but I really miss you*

*Hey maybe I don't have the right to ask but I just wish youd tell me what it is I did wrog*

*\*wrong*

*I felt like we had a real connection did you not feel that way or . . .*

*Maybe I was too old for u or maybe you liked someone else*

*Is that guy you were with tonight your boyfriend*

*???*

*Or is he just some guy you are fucking*

*Sorry*

*When u laguehd when I asked if you were a virgin was it because youd fucked so many guys*

*Are you fucking that guy right now*

*Are you*

*Are you*

*Are you*

*Answer me*

*Whore.*

# THE GOOD GUY

By the time he was thirty-five, the only way Ted could get hard and remain so for the duration of sexual intercourse was to pretend that his dick was a knife, and the woman he was fucking was stabbing herself with it.

It's not like he was some kind of serial killer. Blood held no erotic charge for him, either in fantasy or in real life. Key to the scenario, moreover, was the fact that the woman was *choosing* to stab herself: the idea was that she wanted him so badly, had been driven so wild with obsessive physical desire for his dick, that she was driven to impale herself on it despite the torment it caused. She was the one taking the active role; he just lay there as she thrashed around on top, doing his best to interpret her groans and facial twitches as signs that she was being crushed in an agonizing vise between pleasure and pain.

He knew it wasn't great, this fantasy. Yes, the scene he was imagining was ostensibly consensual, but you couldn't ignore its underlying aggressive themes. Nor was it reassuring that his reliance on the fantasy had increased as the quality of his relationships had declined. Throughout his twenties, Ted's breakups had been reasonably painless. None of his affairs had lasted longer than a few months, and the women he'd dated had seemed to believe him when he told them he wasn't looking for anything serious—or at least to believe that the fact he'd said this meant they could not accuse him of wrongdoing when it ultimately proved to be true. Once he reached his thirties, though, this strategy no longer worked. More often than not, he'd have what he thought was a final breakup conversation with a woman, only to have her text him shortly afterward, telling him she missed him, that she still didn't understand what had happened between them, and that she wanted to talk.

Thus, one night in November, two weeks before his thirty-sixth birthday, Ted found himself sitting across a table from a crying woman named Angela. Angela was a real-estate agent, pretty and polished, with sparkly chandelier earrings and expensively highlighted hair. Like all the women he'd dated over the past several years, Angela was, by any objective measure, way out of his league. She was two inches taller than he was; she owned her own home; she made an amazing fettuccine with clam sauce; and she knew how to give a back rub with essential oils that she'd sworn would change his life, which it had. He'd broken up with her more than two months earlier, but the subsequent texts and phone calls had become so relentless that he'd agreed to another face-to-face meeting in the hopes of gaining some peace.

Angela had begun the evening chattering brightly about her vacation plans, her work drama, and her adventures with "the girls," performing a happiness so clearly calculated to make him see what he was missing that he writhed with vicarious embarrassment, and then, at the twenty-minute mark, she dissolved into tears.

"I just *don't understand*," she cried.

What followed was a hopeless, absurd conversation in which she insisted that he had feelings for her that he was hiding, while he insisted, as kindly as he could, that he did not. Through sobs, she marshaled her evidence of his affection: the time he'd brought her breakfast in bed, the time he'd said, "I think you'd really like my sister," the gentleness with which he'd taken care of her dog, Marshmallow, when Marshmallow was sick. The problem, it seemed, was that while he'd told Angela from the beginning that he wasn't looking for anything serious, at the same time, confusingly, he'd also been nice. When what he ought to have done, apparently, was to tell her that she could get her own damn breakfast, inform her it was unlikely that she'd ever meet his sister, and been a jerk to Marshmallow when Marshmallow was puking, so that both Marshmallow and Angela would have known where they stood.

"I'm sorry," he said, over and over and over again. Not that it mattered. When he failed to admit that he was secretly in love with her, Angela was going to get angry. She was going to accuse him of being a narcissistic, emotionally stunted man-child. She was going to say, "You really hurt me," and "The truth is, I feel sorry for you." She'd announce, "I was falling in *love* with you," and he would sit there, abashed, as though the claim damned him, even though it was obvious Angela didn't love him—she thought he was an emotionally stunted man-child and she didn't even like him all that much. Of course, it was hard to feel entirely self-righteous about all this when the reason he knew what was coming was that this was not the first such conversation he'd had with a woman. It was not even the third. Or the fifth. Or the tenth.

Angela sobbed on, a figure of perfect, abject misery: her reddened eyes, her heaving chest, her mascara-stained face. As he watched her, Ted realized that he couldn't do it any longer. He couldn't apologize one more time, could not continue with this ritual of self-abasement. He was going to tell her the truth.

The next time Angela stopped for breath, Ted said, "You know none of this is my fault."

There was a pause.

"*Excuse* me?" Angela said.

"I was always honest with you," Ted said. "Always. I told you what I wanted from this relationship from the very beginning. You could have trusted me, but instead you decided you knew better than I did what I felt. When I said I wanted something casual, you lied and said you wanted the same thing, and then immediately you started doing everything you could to make it something else. When you didn't manage to make what we had into a serious relationship—the thing you wanted, and I didn't—you got hurt. I see that. But I am not the one who hurt you. You did this, not me. I'm just—just—the tool you're using to hurt yourself!"

Angela let out a little cough, like she'd been punched. "Fuck you, Ted," she said. She pushed back her chair, preparing to storm out of the restaurant, and, as she left, she picked up a glass of ice water and threw it at him—not just the water, but the whole, full glass. The glass—it was more of a tumbler, really—cracked against Ted's forehead and landed in his lap.

Ted looked down at the broken tumbler. Well. Maybe he should have expected that. Because who was he kidding? This many crying women couldn't be wrong about him, no matter how unfair their accusations felt. He reached up and touched his forehead. His fingers came away red. He was bleeding. Awesome. Also, his crotch was really, really cold. In fact, as the ice water soaked through his pants, his dick started to hurt even more than his head did. Maybe there should be a legal limit on how cold restaurant water could be, the way there was a limit on how hot coffee could be at McDonald's. Maybe his dick would get frostbite and shrivel up and fall off, and then everyone he'd ever dated would come together to throw a party in honor of Angela, the fearless heroine who'd ended his reign of terror over the single women of New York.

Wow, he was bleeding more than he'd originally thought. In fact, so much blood was streaming from his forehead that the water in his crotch was turning pink. People were running over, but sound was coming to him kind of scrambled and he couldn't make out what they were saying. Probably something along the lines of: you deserved this, asshole. He remembered what he'd said right before Angela had flung the glass at him—*I'm just the tool you're using to hurt yourself*—and he wondered if this was related somehow to the dick-stabbing fantasy, but he was bleeding and freezing and possibly concussed, and he didn't have it in him right then to figure it out.

He hadn't always been this way.

Growing up, Ted was the kind of small, bookish boy female teachers described as "sweet." And he was sweet, at least where women were concerned. He spent his childhood and early adolescence floating through a series of crushes on older, unattainable girls: a cousin, a babysitter, his big sister's best friend. These crushes were always sparked by some small gift of attention—a minor compliment, genuine laughter at one of his jokes, remembering his name—and they contained no overt or sublimated aggression at all. Just the opposite: in retrospect, they were remarkably chaste. In a recurring daydream he had about his cousin, for example, he envisioned himself as her husband, puttering around the kitchen as he prepared breakfast. Dressed in an apron, he hummed to himself as he squeezed fresh orange juice into a pitcher, whisked the pancake batter, fried the eggs, and placed a single daisy in a small white vase. He carried the tray upstairs to the bedroom and sat down on the side of the bed, where his cousin was snoozing beneath a hand-stitched quilt. "Rise and shine!" he said. His cousin's eyes fluttered open. She smiled sleepily at him, and as she sat up, the quilt slid down, revealing her bare breasts.

That was it! That was the entire fantasy. And yet he nursed it so long, and with such devoted attention (Should the pancakes have chocolate chips in them? What color should the quilt be? Where should he put the tray so that it would not fall off the bed?), that it imbued his aunt and uncle's house with a sexual aura that remained palpable to him even as an adult, even though his cousin had long ago become a lesbian and immigrated to the Netherlands and he hadn't seen her in years.

Never, not even in his wildest imaginings, had young Ted allowed himself to believe that his crushes might be reciprocated. He wasn't stupid. Whatever else he might be, he'd never been that. All he'd ever wanted was for his love to be tolerated, maybe even appreciated: he yearned to be permitted to linger worshipfully around his crushes, lightly bumping up against them every so often, the way a bee might brush against a flower.

Instead, what transpired was that as soon as Ted fixated on a new crush, he would start to moon over her, gazing at her and smiling like a dope, concocting reasons to touch her hair, her hand. And then, inevitably, the girl would recoil—because for some impenetrable reason, Ted's affections provoked in their targets a reaction of intense and visceral disgust.

They were not cruel to him, these crushes. Ted was drawn to the kind of dreamy girls to whom open cruelty was anathema. Instead, perhaps understanding that their earlier small attentions had been the doorway through which Ted had entered uninvited, the girls set about locking themselves down. Instituting some universally understood emergency girl protocol, they refused to make eye contact, spoke to him only when necessary, and stood as far across the room as it was possible to get. They barricaded themselves inside fortresses of chill politeness, where they hunkered down and waited for as long as it took for him to go away.

God, it was awful. Decades later, remembering those crushes made Ted want to die of shame. Because the worst part was, even after it became obvious that the girls he adored found his attentions excruciating, he still desperately desired to be around them and to make them happy. He struggled in the grip of this conundrum, trying to exert self-control in the form of brutal self-punishment (standing naked in front of the mirror, forcing himself to look at his skinny legs, concave chest, small penis: *She hates you, Ted, face it, all girls hate you, you're ugly, you're disgusting, you're gross*) and then losing control and finding himself awake at three in the morning, crying with frustration and typing *states where its legal to marry your cousin* into the internet search bar, playing an endless game of whack-a-mole with his hopes.

The summer before high school, after a particularly humiliating episode with a camp counselor, Ted went for a long solitary walk and considered his future. Fact: He was short and ugly and greasy-haired and no girls would ever like him. Fact: Just knowing that someone as gross as Ted liked them creeped girls out. Conclusion: If he didn't want to spend his whole life making women miserable, he needed to figure out a way to keep his crushes to himself.

So that was what he did.

His freshman year of high school, Ted crafted a new persona: cheerfully asexual, utterly unthreatening, scrubbed clean of any whiffs of need. This Ted was a sixty-year-old comic in a fourteen-year-old's body: hilarious, self-deprecating, and much too neurotic to ever have actual sex. When pressed, this Ted claimed to have a crush on Cynthia Krazewski, a cheerleader who was so unattainable that he might as well have claimed to have been in love with God Himself.

Thus disguised, Ted was free to befriend the girls he really did like, and to channel all his energy into being nice to them without ever hinting that he wanted any more than that. The truth was, he *didn't* want more, not really. He had no faith in love's capacity to cause him anything but pain. Far easier, and more pleasant, to be friends with girls: to chat with them, to hear their stories, to drive them places, to tell them jokes that made them giggle, and then to go home and masturbate himself into a frenzy, banishing his desires to the realm of the imagination, where they couldn't do any harm.

By his junior year, all of Ted's romantic energy had coalesced around a single target: Anna Travis, who not only tolerated him, but considered him a friend. This was the magic of his new persona: As long as Ted kept his feelings hidden from them, girls—some of them, at least—liked him quite a lot.

Though she was considerably more popular than he was, when it came to love, Anna was as hopeless as Ted. For three weeks in ninth grade, Anna had dated Marco, a soccer player who'd dumped her when he'd gotten promoted from the freshman team to junior varsity, and she'd never gotten over it. Years later, Anna still had an insatiable desire to talk about Marco with anyone who would listen, and since everyone else was sick of the topic (and, perhaps, a bit unnerved by how crazy her eyes got when it came up) her sole partner for these conversations was Ted.

Obviously, Ted didn't exactly *want* to help Anna spend hours analyzing what it meant that Marco had said, "Miss you, kid," and punched her in the shoulder when he'd seen her in the hallway the week before . . . but at the same time, he also did. Because telling Anna how stupid Marco was for dumping her, and how infinitely superior she was to Marco's new girlfriend-of-the-week, was the closest he'd ever come to confessing how he felt. Plus, watching Anna yearn for Marco provided fuel for Ted's fantasies in which Anna yearned for him.

Fantasy: It's late at night, Ted's phone rings. Anna.

"Anna," he says. "What is it? Is everything okay?"

"I'm outside," she says. "Can you come down?"

Ted puts on his bathrobe and opens the door. Anna is on his stoop, looking miserable: hair messy, shirt askew. "Anna?" Ted says.

Anna flings herself against Ted and starts sobbing. He wraps his arms around her, patting her back as her chest shakes against his. "It's okay, Anna," he says. "Whatever it is, it's okay, I promise. Shhhh, shhhh."

"No!" she cries. "You don't understand. I—" and then she tries to kiss him. Her lips brush warmly against his, but then he pulls away. She's shocked, heartbroken. "Please," she says. "Please, just . . ." He stands there stiffly, allowing her to slide her tongue into his mouth, and after a moment of hesitation, kisses her back, tenderly, but then, once again, he pulls away.

"I'm sorry, Anna," he says. "I don't understand. I thought we were just friends."

She says, "I know—I mean, I tried to keep it that way. But I can't hide anymore. It's always been you, this whole time. I know you don't feel that way about me. I know you love Cynthia. But I just . . . if you would just give me a chance. Please. Please."

And then she's kissing him again, and pushing him toward the bedroom, and he's trying to resist, saying things like, "I just don't want to ruin our friendship," but she's so insistent, she won't stop begging him, she's unbuttoning his pants, and sliding on top of him, and putting his hand on her breast. Once they're both naked, Anna is gazing at him in a way that is both worshipful and anxious, and she says, "Tell me what you're thinking," and he sighs heavily and says, "Nothing," and stares off into the distance, and she says, "You're thinking about

Cynthia, aren't you?" and he says, "No," but they both know that he is. Anna says, "I promise, Ted, if you just give me a chance, I will make you forget about Cynthia," and then she slides her head down between his legs.

Every so often, Ted wondered if there was a chance Anna might like him as more than a friend. She didn't like him as much as he liked her, that was obvious, and she was never going to show up at his doorstep sobbing from frustrated passion, but . . . maaaaaaaaaaybe? She sat close to him on the couch sometimes, and she was always trying to talk him into asking girls out, which in and of itself was probably not a good sign, but when she did it, she'd say things like, "You're a lot cuter than you think you are, Ted," and "Any girl would be lucky to go out with a guy like you." So even though she didn't *like* like him, maybe there was some latent potential that he could activate if he only told her how he felt. But there was also a kind of Heisenberg's uncertainty principle thing going on, whereby any serious attempt to determine the state of the relationship would invariably alter it—and because change was scary, and he was 99 percent sure Anna didn't like him like that and never would, he let things stay the way they were: good-old friendly, utterly dishonest Ted.

Anna was a year ahead of him in school, college-bound for Tulane, and the week before she left for New Orleans, she coaxed her parents into throwing her a huge good-bye bash. The party was a performance with an intended audience of one, Marco; an elaborate setting designed to show off Anna at maximum sparkle—and sparkle, dazzlingly, she did. She wore a short lace dress with a plunging neckline, and high heels, and lots of eye makeup, and she piled her tawny hair on top of her head. She surrounded herself with a coterie of other beautiful girls, all of them crying and laughing and shouting and posing for pictures and emoting so brightly that the rest of the world went dim.

Ted lurked around the edge of the party, hating himself. He and Anna had mostly hung out one-on-one, when she was feeling down about Marco and didn't have the energy to go out. On these occasions, they sat around on the couch and ate pizza and talked. Anna was usually wearing sweatpants. Ted had rarely seen her like this, broadcasting her charisma at full force. He was painfully aware of his natural role at the party—fawning courtier—and he didn't want to play it. Maybe he'd been deluding himself that he'd kept his feelings hidden all this time, when really he'd been walking around with his dick dangling out of his fly, unknowingly exposed. Maybe everyone in the room was thinking, oh, there's Ted, he's in love with Anna, isn't it embarrassing, isn't it cute. Maybe Anna knew, too.

Of course, Anna knew.

Ted's pride bristled inside him, cutting into the soft parts. For the first time, he was angry at Anna, at the way she'd allowed a random distribution of physical resources—height, facial symmetry, soccer-playing ability—to determine the outcomes of both their lives. He was smarter than Marco, and kinder than Marco, and had more in common with Anna than Marco, and he knew how to make Anna laugh harder than Marco ever would—but none of that mattered, because who he *was* didn't matter, to her or to anyone else.

The evening dragged on, and as the party started to break up, the remaining guests decided to wander down to the beach. Ted could have gone home, but instead he stayed and sulked. Someone lit a campfire, and Ted sat in the literal shadows as he watched the glow from the flames play across Anna's face. He felt like something deep inside had broken. He'd asked for nothing; he'd tried to content himself with as little as it was possible to want. Yet here he was, feeling humiliated and small once again.

Anna was roasting a marshmallow, twirling it contemplatively over the coals. She was wearing a boy's sweatshirt over her short dress, and her bare legs were crusted with sand. The wind shifted, sending a plume of smoke billowing over her. She coughed, and stood, and then she circled the fire and plunked herself down next to Ted.

"Getting hard to breathe over there," she said.

"Did you have fun at your party?" Ted asked.

"It was all right," said Anna. She sighed, probably because Marco was long gone. He'd only stayed an hour. Looking at Anna, her forlorn expression mirroring his own, Ted felt bad about how angry he'd been only a few minutes before. He unrequitedly loved Anna; Anna unrequitedly loved Marco; Marco probably unrequitedly loved some rando none of them had ever met. The world was pitiless. Nobody had any power over anyone else.

He said, "You look beautiful. Marco's an idiot jerk."

"Thanks," Anna said. She looked like she might be about to say something more, but instead, she put her head on his shoulder, and he put his arm around her. She closed her eyes and settled against him, and when he was pretty sure she was asleep, he let himself kiss her forehead. Her skin tasted like salt and smoke. Maybe I was wrong, Ted thought. Maybe I could be content with this.

Unfortunately, he could not.

Ted had hoped that when Anna left for college, his feelings for her might torment him less, but they didn't. Indeed, with Anna's physical presence in his life so diminished, Ted could see with greater clarity the astonishing amount of space she took up in his head. In the morning, as he waited for his alarm to go off, he imagined holding her in his arms and nuzzling her neck; the first thing he did when he got up was check his email to see if she'd sent him a message overnight; all day, he filtered his experience for amusing bits and pieces that he could turn into stories to write to her about. Whenever he was bored or anxious, his brain distracted itself by worrying at the question of whether he could ever make Anna like him, like a dog working the last bits of marrow from a bone. And for hours at night, his bedroom turned into the set of an imaginary porn film starring the two of them, with the occasional movie star or classmate as a walk-on guest. Given how little contact Ted had now with actual Anna, it was like he was in a relationship with an imaginary friend.

Ted would have preferred not to live like this, but he wasn't quite sure what to do about it. He supposed the answer was to develop a crush on someone else, someone who might like him back. As it happened, that wasn't as wild a prospect as it might have been a year earlier—while Ted was still short and nerdy, his braces had come off, he'd gotten a decent haircut, and there was this girl he tutored in biology, a sophomore named Rachel, whose crush on him even he wasn't oblivious enough to overlook.

Ted wasn't remotely attracted to Rachel, who was thin and frizzy-haired and abrasive, but he was seventeen years old and had never even held hands with a girl, so who was he to keep his standards high? Maybe if he and Rachel hooked up, he'd start to develop feelings for her. Stranger things had happened. Besides, he had to admit that dating Rachel couldn't *hurt* his chances with Anna—after all, how many stories had he heard about girls who didn't realize the love of their lives was standing right in front of them until the moment he fell for someone else?

So, one afternoon after tutoring, Ted, mumbling, asked Rachel what she was doing that weekend and if she wanted to hang out. As soon as the words escaped his lips, he regretted them, but it was too late. Rachel took charge immediately, acquiring his phone number and giving him her own. She told him what time, precisely, she'd be expecting him to call her, and when he dutifully phoned, she let him know what movie she wanted to see that weekend, what time it was showing, and where they should eat dinner beforehand, and then she gave him directions to her house so he could pick her up.

As they walked out of the theater, she was already making plans for future hangouts, chattering about how much she wanted to try the new Thai place on Seventh, and how they shouldn't forget to go see that romantic comedy they'd watched the trailer for, and did Ted have any plans for Halloween, because she and her friends were putting together a group costume and he'd be welcome to join.

Ted was wildly uncomfortable. He wasn't quite sure who Rachel was on a date with, but it didn't seem to be him. He'd contributed nothing to the outing; as far as he could tell, she could have brought an inflatable doll with her to the movie and had an equally good time. As he drove her home, he resolved to politely make it clear there would not be a second date. Rachel would hate him for dumping her, obviously, which meant he might need to drop out of the tutoring program, but he figured it'd be worth it to avoid the awkwardness that would otherwise follow. They didn't have any other activities in common, so if he played his cards right, he might never have to see her again.

When they reached Rachel's house, he put the car in park but left it running.

Rachel unbuckled her seat belt. "Good night," she said, but she didn't move.

"Good night," he said, going in for a hug. What, precisely, were his responsibilities here? Did he even *have* to explicitly break up with her, since they'd only been on the one date? Could he just quit tutoring and hope she got the hint? He was patting Rachel's back in a way that he hoped signaled: *Please don't hate me, I'm sorry about what*

*I'm about to do to you*, when she took his cheeks between her palms, held his face steady, and kissed him on the mouth.

Ted's first kiss! The shock of it briefly drove all other thoughts from his head. He froze, jaw slack, and Rachel plunged her tongue into his mouth and wriggled it around. Just as his brain caught up with his body, and he remembered he was supposed to be kissing her back, she broke away and started covering his lips with light little pecks. "Like this," she said breathily, and he realized she was taking it on herself to *teach* him how to kiss her, because he obviously didn't know how. A hammer of shame swung down and flattened him. Dorky, know-it-all Rachel, condescending to teach him how to kiss!

Well, since it was too late not to humiliate himself, he might as well take the opportunity to learn. After a few minutes, he decided that kissing wasn't that hard, really, although it certainly wasn't everything it was cracked up to be. Overall, it wasn't an unpleasant sensation, but there was nothing particularly erotic about it. Rachel's glasses kept bumping up against the bridge of his nose, and it was weird to see her this close up. She looked like a different person, paler, more . . . vague, somehow, like a painting. He tried closing his eyes but it made him uncomfortable, like someone was going to sneak up behind him and plunge a knife into his back.

So this was kissing. He had to admit Rachel seemed into it. She kept kind of rolling around and sighing. Would he be enjoying himself more if he were kissing Anna? Frankly, it was hard to ever imagine being turned on by this activity. Two boneless slabs of flesh, flopping around, like a pair of slugs mating in the cavern of your mouth. *Gross*, Ted. What was wrong with him? Rachel's breath smelled like popcorn butter: slightly metallic, with a hint of the burnt grease that stuck to the bottom of the machine. Or was that his breath? He could think of no way to tell.

Rachel was basically on top of him now, moving her hand in an exploratory way, like maybe she was trying to figure out if he had a boner. Needless to say, he did not have a boner; he actually felt like his dick might have snuck up inside his body to hide. Was the fact that he didn't have a boner going to hurt Rachel's feelings? Should he try to fantasize about Anna so that he could get a boner so that Rachel wouldn't feel bad about the fact that he hadn't gotten a boner for her? No, that could not be the right course of action. But what did Rachel *want*? She was full-on straddling him now, grinding her hips against his knee and groaning. Did she want to have sex? Surely not. They were parked outside her parents' house, and she was only a sophomore, and besides, he was *Ted*. It was one thing to accept that Rachel might have developed a minor crush on him during biology tutoring, another to think that he'd made her so wildly hot for the D that she was ready to bone him in the front seat of his car.

Still, she really did seem to be absurdly into this. It was almost existentially unsettling, that two people in such close physical proximity could be experiencing the same moment so differently.

Unless . . . she was faking her enthusiasm? Or if not faking, entirely, then exaggerating. A lot. But why would she do that? Pretend he was turning her on with his clumsy tongue fumblings when he wasn't?

Oh.

As soon as it occurred to him, he realized the answer was obvious. She knew he was nervous, and she was trying to coax him through it. His ineptitude and discomfort were probably visible from space. She was pretending to enjoy herself so that he'd relax and stop being such a bad kisser. She was faking sexual excitement out of *pity*.

If before he'd felt like his dick had crawled up inside his body, now he felt like a two-ton lead slab had dropped on his crotch from the heavens, paralyzing him for life.

*Kill yourself, Ted*, a voice in his head said. Seriously.

He might have done it, too—just leaped out of the car and pitched himself in front of the nearest oncoming vehicle—but then Rachel picked up his hand and pressed it to her breast. He felt the no-thoughts shock again. Rachel's breasts were small but her shirt was low-cut, so he was touching a lot of very soft skin. Tentatively, he squeezed, and then he rubbed the spot where he was pretty sure her nipple would be. Holy shit, it *was* there, and after a second of rubbing, it popped up under his thumb.

Whoa.

Closing his eyes like he was jumping off a diving board, he plunged his hand under her shirt and bra, and then he didn't have to worry about the no-boner problem, because the bare nipple he was pinching was the dirtiest, sexiest thing in the world, and it was somehow only dirtier and sexier for being attached to a person he barely knew, whose breath smelled like popcorn and whose transparent parody of arousal was an insult to them both.

He pinched it again, a little harder. She yelped, but then quickly recovered. "Oh, my *God*, Ted," she moaned, fakely.

They dated for the next four months.

Looking back, Ted thought Rachel was the first woman he could truly be said to have treated badly. Yeah, he'd inadvertently creeped out some of his crushes, but he'd been a kid, and he'd wrestled mightily to keep himself under control. And there was probably an argument to be made about the way he'd acted around Anna when they'd been in school together—that he should have been honest with her about his feelings instead of skulking around in the friend zone—but while he might have been cowardly with Anna, he'd also done his best to be kind. Rachel, though . . . if there was a hell, and he ended up in it, he was pretty sure the devil would hold up a picture of Rachel, shake it in his face, and say, "Hey, buddy, what was the deal with this one?"

But he didn't know! He really, truly didn't.

In the four months they were together, he never started liking Rachel any more than he did on their first date. Everything about her bugged him: her stupid hair, her nasal voice, her habit of bossing him around. The thought of people saying, "There goes Rachel, Ted's girlfriend!" made him cringe. He saw, in her, all the parts of himself he tried so hard to repress: her sycophantic overtures to people who treated her like shit, her faux-patrician condescension toward the handful of people below her on the popularity ladder, the sarcastic jabs she used to distance herself from all the other losers on her social plane.

Like him, she was prone to embarrassing bodily mishaps—period stains, bad breath, sitting in ways that inadvertently exposed her underwear—but, unlike him, these episodes didn't seem to cause her inordinate shame. *He* was the one who felt ashamed: when he caught sight of her in the hallway ahead of him, sauntering on with a rusty patch on the back of her jean skirt, or when Jennifer Roberts fanned the air in disgust after Rachel, who'd been standing much too close, finally turned away. In these moments, Ted didn't just dislike Rachel: he *hated* her, more than he'd ever hated anyone else in his life.

So why didn't he break up with her?

At home, alone, Ted knew he did not like Rachel and that he did not want to date her, and so breaking up with her seemed straight-forward, the right thing to do. But then they would meet up, and as soon as Rachel saw him, if he hesitated, or pulled away, or signaled with even the tiniest of expressions that something was wrong, then her face would darken. At the first hint of her anger, he would feel an onrush of guilt and cold fear. He'd get swept up in a current of conviction that he was a total garbage asshole jerk, his sins stretching in an unbroken chain back to his original decision to agree to go on even one date with her when he'd been in love with Anna the whole time. Skewered by guilt, he would decide that rather than confront Rachel directly, and add to the immeasurable wrongs he'd already done her, it'd be *so much better* to wait for a more opportune moment, like maybe one where she'd do the breaking up herself. After all, it wasn't like he was such a prize; surely if he just sat it out, sooner rather than later she'd free herself of this delusion that he was remotely datable and dump him of her own accord. With that in mind, he'd agree to whatever she was suggesting with a sense of profound relief—and then it'd be ten minutes later, or fifteen, or an hour, and he'd surface and think, wait a second, I was going to break up with her, why are we sitting here in this Olive Garden, eating lunch?

With Rachel prattling on, that dark cloud of incipient anger nowhere to be seen, the idea that just seconds ago it had felt impossible to end the relationship seemed absurd—but it also seemed absurd to break up with her out of nowhere, when he'd just been sitting there acting like everything was fine and saying things like, "Sure, I'll go with you to visit your cousin on Sunday." Because if he tried to break up with Rachel right now, while she was halfway through a breadstick, surely the first thing she'd say would be, "If you knew you were going to break up with me, why did you literally *just* agree to go with me to visit my cousin on Sunday?" and he would have no answer.

Well, what if she did, Ted? What. If. She. Did. Couldn't he have just shrugged his shoulders and said, "Whelp, sucks for your cousin, I changed my mind?" No. He could not do that, because that was something that only an asshole would do, and he, Ted, was not an asshole. He was . . . a nice guy.

Yes, okay, everyone agreed that nice guys were the worst, but this was different. To feel incapable of interrupting Rachel in the middle of a meal and dumping her without warning—that wasn't Nice Guy Syndrome, that was just being humane. He'd never empathized with Rachel more than he did in those moments, imagining what it would be like to be innocently eating lunch with a person who had been acting for all the world as though he liked you, who had given you no hint that anything was bothering him at all, when suddenly, out of nowhere, *wham*, it turned out you were completely wrong about him, and that everything he'd been telling you was a lie.

His whole life, Ted had clung to the idea that he was misunderstood—that the girls who'd rejected him were wrong to treat him as though there was something inherently creepy about him. He might not have been the handsomest guy around, but he wasn't *bad*. And yet sometimes he'd lie awake at night imagining Rachel telling her story to a tribunal of all the girls who'd ever rejected him, regaling them about his deceptions, the way he'd pretended to like her when he didn't, the mask of "niceness" he wore when the truth was he was a selfish, lying piece of shit—and he saw all those girls, Anna at their center, shocked but not shocked, nodding and agreeing that yes, of course, they'd known something was wrong with him all along.

And so Anna took on another role in his head: forewoman of a jury that stood ready to convict. The longer the relationship with Rachel went on, the more he needed her to return to his imaginary tribunal with a story that vindicated him. He needed his first-ever girlfriend not simply to say, but to believe, that while things might not have worked out between them, he wasn't creepy or scary or bad; he was, fundamentally, a good guy.

To placate this imagined version of Anna, he stayed with Rachel, and he lied. He finished his lunch at the Olive Garden, he went to visit the cousin, and he tried to lay the groundwork for his escape. He did his best to keep his distance from Rachel, not enough to make her angry, just enough to keep the relationship from getting any more serious than it already was. He didn't call her very often, and he was busy a lot, but always apologetic about it. He did exactly what was required of him, but no more. He felt a bit as though he were playing dead, remaining limp and pliable in the hopes that she would eventually lose interest and wander away. All right, the tribunal would say at the end of it. He's not the *best* person. He's not a saint. But he's no Marco, manipulating girls just for the hell of it. It could have been worse. He deserves another chance. We find the defendant . . . reasonably okay.

But wait, a voice pipes up, just before the gavel comes down.

Yes?

Just one thing, though. I have a question.

Go ahead.

What about the sex?

Uh . . . what about it? Ted and Rachel did not have sex. He wanted to be very clear with the tribunal about that. Ted did *not* take Rachel's virginity. (And Rachel did not take Ted's.)

Did they hook up?

Yeah, obviously. They dated for four months.

*When* they were hooking up, did Ted "do exactly what was required of him, but no more"? Did he "play dead" with Rachel, so to speak? Was he the polite, slightly distant, withdrawn person that he was with her otherwise?

Um. Well. No.

What was he like?

. . .

What were you like, Ted?

I was . . .

You were . . . ?

119

I was . . . kind of . . .

Yes?

. . . mean.

Mean?

Mean.

Before Ted got old and sexually experienced, before he mastered a range of fetish keywords on Pornhub and started paying for a yearly subscription to Kink.com, "mean" was the word he used in his head for the things he did to (with?) Rachel, that squirmy, compelling dynamic. The word predated her. He'd used it when he was a kid to describe certain kinds of comics and cartoons and movies and books where people were "mean" to girls. Wonder Woman was chained to the railroad tracks. On the cover of one of his sister's Nancy Drew mysteries, Nancy was gagged and tied to a chair.

Young Ted liked stories where people were "mean" to girls, but that didn't imply he wanted to *do* mean things to them. When he imagined himself into these stories, which he only rarely did—being mostly content to watch them play out—he, Ted, was never the one tying girls up. No, he was the one who was *rescuing* them. He untied the ropes and rubbed their wrists to get the circulation flowing, gently undid the gags, stroked their hair as they cried against his chest. To be the villain, the tie-er up-er, the inflictor of pain? No, no, no, no, no. Meanness had nothing to do with Ted's love life, or his fantasy life, either. Until Rachel came along.

As far as possible, Ted avoided hooking up with Rachel. He rarely touched her affectionately, and he kept his mouth closed when they kissed. Though he recognized that it bothered her, he felt like he was being a good person when he did this: since he didn't like her, he had no right to pressure her into doing sex stuff. After all, if he made an effort to hook up, and then later he broke up with her, she'd be justified in returning to the tribunal and accusing him of using her for sex. By this logic, therefore, the only way he could exculpate himself from guilt was to require Rachel to prod and nag him and push him to be alone with her, to ask him two or three or five times, so that, in the end, no one could claim that it was his fault.

Once they were in her bedroom, with her door closed, she'd start kissing him in that way that never ceased to feel fake: those light pecks, those melodramatic sighs. *Ugh, Rachel*, he would think, as the annoyance he'd been fighting all day pushed to the surface. *Why are you so bossy and pushy and oblivious? Why do you like me? Why can't you tell I'm not that into you?* But she would keep throwing herself at him . . . and eventually, surrendering to temptation, he would channel his irritation into a pinch or a bite, or even, later, a light slap.

She claimed to be into it when he was "mean" to her, and he guessed she must be, if how wet and flushed and wriggly she got meant anything at all. Yet he still felt, gut-deep, that there was a patina of falseness over everything she did, and that in claiming to enjoy what he did to her, she was telling him what she thought he wanted to hear. Part of what it meant to be "mean" to Rachel, therefore, was to scrape away that falseness, to dig under it, to force her to show a true reaction: he wanted to catch that real part of Rachel, but it kept slipping away from him, like an eel dipping under the water, and chasing it drove him up the wall with lust. *I hate you, I hate you*, he'd think, pinning her bony wrists above her head and biting the meat of her shoulder and dry-humping her leg until he came.

"That was *amazing*," she'd sigh afterward, cuddling up to him, but he did not, could not, believe her.

Sometimes, he wondered if, more than the hookups themselves, she liked their aftermath, because in those brief periods he was different with her. He needed her to salve his guilt over what he'd just done so badly that he was vulnerable, open and raw. He'd kiss her and bring her water, and afterward he'd lie beside her and hide his face in her hair. In those moments, he could look at Rachel's face and see her not as ugly or pretty or good or bad or loved or hated but just as a person lying next to him, stripped of all the judgment he was continually imposing on her, his obsessive critical analysis of everything she did. What if he *could* like Rachel? If he liked her, then he wouldn't be a bad person for dating her. He'd have nothing to atone for. They could be happy. He'd be free. The thought made him feel fantastically light, like some sponge inside him, heavy with poison, had finally been wrung dry.

It never lasted. As the postcoital bliss began to fade, Anna would manifest beside him like a ghost. *Think about me, think about me*, she'd whisper in his ear, and he would. His brain would rev up again, thinking, churning, judging. He'd fucked up by hooking up with Rachel, letting Rachel see him like this, exposed. Now she'd be even more sure that he liked her; now she'd be even more hurt when he dumped her; now he had even more sins against her to expiate; now it would be even harder to get away.

He'd sit up, pull on his underwear.

"What's wrong?"

"Nothing. I just have to get going."

"Why don't you just lie here with me for a little while?"

"I've got homework."

"It's *Friday*."

"I told you before, I have a lot to do."

"Why do you always get like this?"

"Like what?"

"Like *this*. All cranky. After."

"I'm not cranky."

"Yes, you are. Mr. Cranky. Cranky-pants."

"I've got a calculus midterm, a project due for history I haven't even started, I told a friend I'd help her study for the SAT, and the final draft of my college essay is due to the guidance counselor on Monday. I'm sorry if I seem stressed but it doesn't exactly help for you to pester me and call me Mr. Cranky-pants when I've already wasted like an hour here."

"Just come lie down for a minute. Let me rub your back."

"Rachel, I don't want you to rub my back. I want to go get my work done. This is why I said we shouldn't do this."

"Oh, come on, cranky. My mom won't be home for another hour. Here, just let me . . ."

"Hey, cut it out!"

"What, you don't *liiike* it? Because it seems like you *liiike* it. Oooh, yes it does."

"Stop, I said!"

"Make me, baby."

"Goddamnit, Rachel—"

"Oh, *Ted*!"

And above them, like a heavenly chorus, the girls of the tribunal would resume their chattering: *Look at them, those two uggos, doing their weird ugly-person shit, oh my God, he's so nasty, did you see that, did he? I think he just . . . yes, he did, he did, oh no, I think I might vomit, oh, gross, that's the most disgusting thing I've ever seen, I don't know who's grosser, her or him, how could she, how can she bear it, I would never, ever, ever let him do anything like that to me . . .*

While Imaginary Anna remained Ted's constant companion, helpfully sharing her detailed opinions on the evolution of his relationship and the state of his soul, Actual Anna continued obliviously on at Tulane, receiving a friendly email from her good friend Ted every couple of weeks—none of which, notably, mentioned the existence of an Actual Rachel.

Ted's self-presentation to Anna was as carefully curated as a museum exhibit, and he wrestled unsuccessfully with the question of how to incorporate Rachel into the display. The problem was that while an abstract "sophomore" could conceivably be a sexy rival to Anna, raising Ted's status in her eyes, Rachel *herself* could be nothing but a liability. If Anna asked him follow-up questions he couldn't avoid, he feared that the discovery that he'd been romantically linked with Rachel Derwin-Finkel might be enough to taint him forever with her loser's stench.

Rachel, on the other hand, knew *all about* Anna. Boy, did she. Sometimes, Ted suspected that Rachel was a very low-level clairvoyant, her psychic powers limited to a tiny and useless handful of realms. The slightest flicker of discomfort on his face would be immediately met with "Ted? Ted? What's wrong? What are you thinking about? Ted?" Since he was usually thinking about how annoying Rachel was and/or daydreaming about Anna, he had no choice but to lie when this happened; he lied more to Rachel, on a day-to-day basis, than he'd ever lied to anyone in his life. And yet every once in a while, she would interrogate him in a way that sent him spasming, unable to keep himself from revealing a piece of the truth.

For example, he once—*once*—mentioned Anna to Rachel, but he might as well have tattooed ASK ME ABOUT MY FEELINGS FOR ANNA TRAVIS.

"Gilda Radner was basically an underrated genius," he said that night in the Blockbuster, as they browsed past a rack featuring *The Best of SNL*. "My friend Anna is a huge fan of hers."

"Your friend, Anna?" Rachel echoed.

Ted froze. "Yep." He felt as though he were walking across a lake in winter, and the ice had begun to crackle all around him. No sudden movements, he told himself. You can still get yourself to safe ground.

"I don't think I know Anna," Rachel said. Her voice was studiedly casual.

"Probably not," he said. "She graduated last year."

"How do you know her?"

"I don't remember. I think we had class together one time."

There was a silence. Side by side, they gazed at the movies under the bright fluorescent lights. Rachel picked up the case for Steve Martin's *The Jerk* and studied the back of the box. Was it over? Had he escaped?

"You mean Anna Zhang?" Rachel asked.

The ice gave way, plunging him into the water.

"No."

"Anna Hogan?"

"No." Dammit, he knew Anna Hogan! Why hadn't he just said Anna Hogan? YOU ARE SUCH A FUCKING IDIOT, TED, his brain screamed at itself.

"Well, which Anna is it?"

Ted felt his throat starting to close up. "Anna Travis," he managed.

"Anna Travis!" Rachel was ostensibly still reading the box, but she raised her eyebrows in such a way as to evince dramatic skepticism at the idea of Ted moving in the same exalted social circles as Anna Travis. "I didn't know you knew Anna Travis."

"Yup."

"Huh."

A pause.

"How come you never mentioned her before?"

"I don't know. It just never came up."

It occurred to Ted that if Rachel flew off the handle and gave him an ultimatum about Anna, he would have to break up with her, because obviously if he had to choose between Rachel and Anna, he'd choose Anna, and since nothing had ever happened between him and Anna, Rachel would be the unreasonable one, and the breakup wouldn't even end up being his fault.

But Rachel was savvier than that. She put *The Jerk* back on the shelf, and they wandered through the Blockbuster in silence.

"She's pretty," Rachel said after a minute.

"Who?"

Rachel's face twisted briefly into a sneer. "*Who?* Gilda Radner. No, Anna Travis, dummy. She's hot."

"I guess so," he said.

"You guess?"

"We're just friends, Rachel," Ted said, with exaggerated patience.

"I mean . . . obviously," Rachel said. "Anna *Travis*."

Rachel, Ted thought, you are a fucking cunt and I hope you die in a fire.

"Did you go to her good-bye party? Over the summer?" Rachel asked.

"Yeah. Why?"

"No reason." Rachel took another movie off the shelf and thoughtfully read the description on the back. Without looking up, she said, "I just heard this rumor that at that party she banged Marco Hernandez in her parents' bedroom while her mom was getting the cake ready downstairs."

Image: Ted is strapped to a gurney with Rachel standing over him, perusing a selection of knives, as she decides which one to jab into his tenderest parts.

126

"That's ridiculous," Ted scoffed. "Who told you that? Shelly?" Shelly was Rachel's flighty, obnoxious best friend. Ted thought maybe he could start a fight about Shelly that could serve as a distraction. Or maybe he should just knock over the nearest video display and flee the state.

Rachel did not take the bait. "It wasn't Shelly, actually. But everybody knows Anna Travis is obsessed with Marco. Like genuinely, crazy obsessed." For the first time, Rachel looked directly at him, her eyes blank behind her glasses. "*I* heard that she's been writing him all these messages from college, and calling him all the time at his dorm, and it got so bad that he had to have her number and email address *blocked*."

Ted felt sick. How long had she been carrying this piece of information around, and how had she known she should use it?

"Oh my God, Rachel," Ted said. "It's like honestly embarrassing the way you do this, gossiping about people you don't even know. You treat people you think are cool like they're celebrities or something. Anna's just a regular person and you don't even know her, so maybe you and Shelly should stop obsessing about her love life like a couple of dorks."

"Well," Rachel said, pursing her lips. "I actually do know her. So."

"You do not."

"I do," she said, coldly triumphant. "We went to nursery school together and our moms are friends. It was her mom who told my mom the thing about Marco blocking her number. She said Anna's been so messed up about it that she might need to take a semester off. I guess *your friend Anna* just didn't tell you."

Ted's stomach contracted around the knife Rachel had just shoved into his gut.

Rachel wrapped her cold hand around Ted's limp one. "I don't think I'm in the mood for a movie, actually," she said. "My parents won't be back home until midnight and my brother is at a sleepover. Let's go."

A few nights later, Ted sat in front of the computer, trying to compose an email to Anna. He'd written and deleted twenty variations on the question *Are you sure everything's okay?* but nothing had come out right. He'd already sent her two emails that had gone unanswered, and he knew he should just chill. The problem was that he didn't just want to find out if Rachel's story was true; he *needed* to find out—his itch to know felt like bugs crawling under his skin.

Driven by anxiety to unforeseen heights of bravery, Ted found himself picking up the phone. He had Anna's number at school memorized, even though he'd only ever called her once before— on her birthday, when he'd sung the entire "Happy Birthday" song into her voice mail. She'd never called him back, but he did get an email eventually (subject line: *Thank you SO much!!*) that she'd signed with a bunch of *x*'s and *o*'s, which had felt significant at the time.

Anna picked up on the first ring.

"Hello, Anna, it's Ted calling," Ted said, as though he were speaking directly into her answering machine.

"Ted!" she said. "What's up?"

"Uh . . . I was just thinking about you," he said. "Are you doing okay?"

"I guess," she said. "Why?"

Because my girlfriend, whose existence I'm keeping a secret from you, told me a secret you're keeping from me, because she was jealous of the crush I have on you, which I'm also keeping secret from you, though I was unable to keep it a secret from her?

"Um, I'm not sure exactly. It's weird, but I just had the . . . feeling . . . that something was wrong."

Using covertly acquired information to feign a mysterious psychic bond was a new realm of deception for Ted, and he didn't fully understand the potency of what he'd done until Anna started to cry.

"I'm not okay," she said. "I'm not okay at *all*." Between sobs, she began gasping out a tangled story that involved not only Marco, but a guy in a frat who'd treated her badly, a nasty fight with her father's new wife, an ongoing war with her roommate, and the fact—which she mentioned as almost an afterthought—that she was failing most of her classes and would be on academic probation next year.

"I'm sorry," Ted said, stunned. "I'm so sorry. That sounds really hard."

"I can't believe you called me," Anna said. "Nobody else from home has called me in forever. It's like they forgot about me. You think you're so close to people but when it comes down to it, they just *forget*."

"I didn't forget about you," Ted said.

"I *know*," Anna said. "I know you didn't forget. You were always there for me, always, but I never appreciated it, I took you for granted. I was so selfish. I hate who I was in high school, God, I wish I could change everything about myself but it's just—it's too late to *do* anything, that's the problem. It's all so fucked up, and I just don't know who I am anymore, you know? Like, who is this person who made all these choices that I just have to live with? I look back at that person and I hate her, I hate her so much for what she did to me, that person is like my nemesis, my worst enemy, but the problem is, that person is *me*."

As Anna poured her heart out over the phone, Ted's own heart lit up like a solar flare. He wanted nothing more than to show Anna how he saw her: how beautiful and perfect she was in his eyes. He needed to let her know that he was going to carry that memory—that *knowledge*—of her inside him, so that no matter what happened between them, no matter how down she got on herself, he could do this for her: he could love her, selflessly and unceasingly, with total commitment and purity, for the rest of his life.

An hour later, Anna sniffled. "Thank you for listening, Ted," she said. "It really means a lot to me."

*I would die for you*, Ted thought.

"No problemo," Ted said.

After that, Ted and Anna began talking on the phone almost every night. Never in his life had Ted experienced anything that matched the thrill of those late-night conversations, and he found himself constructing an elaborate set of rituals around them, the way that a primitive tribe might need to perform rituals around the lighting of a fire, to keep its power contained.

Part of the ritual involved keeping the conversations a secret—from Rachel, of course, but also from his parents and everyone else. He moved the phone in the den away from his computer and up by his bed. He ran the fan outside of his door to create a mask of white noise. He took a shower, brushed his teeth, and got under the sheets. Before Anna even answered the phone, his skin would have grown warm, almost feverish.

"Hey."

"Hey."

Their voices were husky and low; they murmured to each other, Ted thought, as though they were lying beside each other in bed, whispering across the pillow. He closed his eyes and pictured this.

"How was your day?" he asked.

"Oh. You know."

"Still. Tell me. I want to hear."

As Anna began telling him the story of her day ("Well, so, I woke up at four A.M. because fucking Charise had fucking crew . . .") Ted stroked his hand slowly down his chest and around his rib cage, imagining it was Anna's hand, his skin goose-pimpling beneath Anna's fingers.

As she talked, he said very little, mostly just sympathetic "uh-uh"s and "oh-no"s. Once, when she sounded particularly upset, he said, "I'm sorry," and then mouthed silently, ". . . sweetheart."

Meanwhile, his hand progressed in slow sensuous circles down his torso, along the waistband of his boxers, and under the elastic band, hesitantly stroking the edge of his pubic hair.

"Tell me more about Kathleen," he said, when Anna seemed to be running out of story. Kathleen was Anna's stepmother. He began playing with his dick—tapping it with his fingertips, flicking it on the shaft. "Do you think your dad will stand up to her, or will he take her side?"

"Oh my God, are you *kidding*?" Anna practically shrieked.

"Shhhh, shhhh," Ted hushed her. "Charise has practice in four hours."

"Fuck Charise," Anna whispered. Ted laughed. Anna laughed, too. He could practically feel her breath on his face. He squeezed his dick, arcing his back with pleasure, and gritted his teeth to force himself to keep quiet.

"Are you getting sleepy?" he asked at last.

"Yes," Anna said.

"Do you want to fall asleep together?"

"I do . . . but you have to get up so early . . ."

"It's okay," he said. "I'll sleep in study hall."

"You're sweet, Ted. I like falling asleep with you."

"I like falling asleep with you, too. Good night, Anna."

"Good night, Ted."

"Sweet dreams, Anna."

"Sweet dreams, Ted."

In the ensuing quiet, he imagined Anna watching him with fascinated disgust; he imagined her touching him; he imagined that on the other end of the line, in the humid New Orleans night, Anna, racked with desire, was touching herself and thinking of him. He listened to her breathe in and out as his hand worked steadily beneath the sheets. He felt ashamed of himself, of course, but the warmth of that shame pooled in his crotch, amplifying his pleasure. He came in a torrent, making no sounds other than those that could be explained away as sleepy breathing. Only when he'd calmed himself completely, his pulse and his breath both fully slowed, did he dare to whisper: "Anna, are you asleep?"

He imagined Anna lying awake, eyes wide, staring at the ceiling, her heart full of yearning, but there was only silence.

"I love you, Anna," he whispered, and he hung up the phone.

And then it was winter break, and Anna was coming home to visit. Would Ted see her? Of course he would see her. They were practically best friends! They talked every night. She'd said, "You were always there for me, always." He would see her, obviously. The only question was when.

And where.

And how.

In high school, making plans with Anna had been a process as delicate as surgery, and occasionally as brutal. If he asked her directly to hang out, she'd always smile and say, "Sure! Sounds great! Call me tomorrow and we'll figure it out." Only a slight tightness around her mouth, and the heaviness of her exhale, would suggest that he'd imposed. But inevitably, a conflict would appear at the last minute, or else, when he tried to pin down the details, she'd simply fail to answer the phone. If he called her out on her flakiness, or even made reference to the broken plans, as opposed to pretending they'd never existed in the first place, she'd pull away even further, in a way that made him feel ashamed of himself, and needy for pressing her.

On the other hand, she happily kept him informed about plans she had with other people, providing a steady flow of information about excursions that were about to happen, details of dates or parties that were always *this close* to coming together. As long as he listened, without complaint, to an endless description of activities that were supposed to happen without him, there was a 30 percent chance, at least, that Anna would change her mind at the last minute, claim to be unable to handle the unbearable burden of whatever her social plans were supposed to be, and decide to hang out with him instead. She'd arrive at his house and collapse in exaggerated relief: "I am *so glad* we're doing this, I was *so* not in the mood for another house party at Maria's." As though they were both equally at the mercy of circumstance, similarly oblivious to the power dynamic that governed their "friendship."

But surely something had changed between them! Surely she wouldn't treat him, now, the way she had then, not after she'd spoken the words aloud: *You were always there for me, always, but I never appreciated it, I always took you for granted.* What could those words be but a confession? And what was a confession if not a promise, or at least a willingness, to change? He loved the way her voice had caught and hitched a little before that second "always." *You were always there for me, always.* When they got married, she could include them in her wedding vows: *You were always there for me, always. You were always there for me, always. You were always there for me, always.*

They were the most beautiful words he'd ever heard.

---

The night before she got on the plane to New Jersey, Ted tried to nudge Anna, as gently as he could, into saying what he wanted to hear. "I'm excited to see you," he said.

"Me too! For sure."

"Have you talked to anybody else from here lately? Like, friends, or anybody? I remember you saying that your friends from home were bad at being in touch."

Was he imagining the slight hesitation before her answer? She still hadn't confided in him about Marco; the other day, Rachel's obnoxious friend Shelly had announced, out of the blue, that she'd heard that Marco Hernandez had an actual *restraining order* out against Anna that required her to stay five hundred feet away from him at all times. This was obviously an idiotic rumor of the type that was Shelly's specialty, but he still wished Anna would do something to reassure him—ideally burst into tears and say, *You were always there for me, always*, and plead with him to forgive her for all her years of neglect—but he'd have settled for even a hint that she intended to make an active effort to meet up.

Instead, the conversation took a sharp and unsettling turn.

"Actually," Anna said. "I was talking to Missy Johansson, you know her? And *she* told *me* you were dating somebody! Rachel Derwin-Finkel? And I was like, no way, that's not possible. But she insisted that it was!"

"Hahahahahahahaha!" Ted said.

And then, when Anna's silence indicated that cackling like a madman was an insufficient response, he added, "Um. Yeah. We've been hanging out."

"Hanging out as in *dating*?"

"I mean, I don't know. We haven't really put a label on it." (They had.) "It's complicated." (It wasn't.) "You know how I am." (She did not.) "But . . . yeah."

Ted, who had been leisurely erect at the beginning of this conversation, now felt like he might puke. There was something deeply wrong, almost violating, about having Anna talk to him about Rachel; it was like having his parents walk in on him having sex.

"Maybe all three of us can hang out when I'm there! I'd like to see Rachel again. It's been way too long."

"Um, sure. If you want."

"Did you know our moms were friends? We used to have play-dates, like, constantly. We don't know each other that well anymore, 'cause we went in different directions, socially, in school, but Rachel's a really good kid. Mostly what I remember about Rachel is that she was super into horses when we were little. And My Little Ponies and stuff. Remember?"

Clever, Anna. Very clever. What had *actually* happened was that a rumor had spread around school that Rachel Derwin-Finkel masturbated with My Little Ponies. It was one of those rumors that no one really believed, not really, but that they passed along enthusiastically nonetheless. Ted himself had argued passionately with the other boys at his lunch table about whether that was even possible (Did she just stick it in there, or . . . ?), and then, when the controversy had threatened to die down, he'd willfully revived it, because the Rachel scandal had taken the focus off the previous scandal roiling the third grade, which was the question of whether or not he, Ted, had been caught by the music teacher pooping in the instrument closet during the spring recital, WHICH OF COURSE HE HAD NOT.

What did Anna know about what it was like to have a rumor like that spread about you, that overpowering and helpless shame? He wished he could believe Anna was jealous, but he didn't; she was just marking her territory, like a dog peeing on a patch of grass. Did he even exist in her mind, as a living, breathing, thinking person? He spent so much time trying to figure out what she was thinking, but what kind of a consciousness did she imagine lived behind the mask of his face?

For the first time, Ted imagined fucking Anna the way he (almost) fucked Rachel: cruelly, without concern for her comfort, fully acknowledging that as much as he loved her, he hated her, too. In his fantasy, Anna was underneath him, his hand was around her throat, and, oh shit, there was Rachel: they were in a three-way. Rachel was naked, on her hands and knees, and Ted was grabbing Anna by the hair and forcing her—

Making her—

They were both—

"Did you hear what I said, Ted?" Anna asked.

"No—sorry—listen, I, uh, I've got to go!"

On Anna's fourth day in New Jersey, Ted was in Rachel's bedroom, dressing himself after another round of not-quite-copulation, when Rachel asked him what he wanted to do for New Year's Eve.

"I don't know," Ted said as he pulled on a sock. "I think I might just stay home."

"You can't do that," Rachel said. "Ellen is having a thing and I told her we'd go."

"What? Why would you do that?"

"Do what?"

"Make plans without asking me first. Don't you think that you should have checked in with me to see if maybe there was something I'd want to do other than being dragged to some party with a bunch of sophomores I don't even know? I have a life outside of you, you know."

"Um. You literally just said you had no plans on New Year's and were going to stay home."

"I said I *might* stay home."

"Okay. What else *might* you do?"

"I don't know. There's this party at Cynthia Krazewski's I was thinking of checking out."

"At *Cynthia Krazewski's.*"

"Yeah. What?"

"Cynthia Krazewski invited *you* to a party."

"So?"

"Ted. You're telling me Cynthia Krazewski invited you to her New Year's party, and you're *thinking* of *checking it out.*"

"Are you, like, having a stroke?"

"I'm just trying to get my facts straight. Cynthia Krazewski called you up on the phone and was like, 'Hi, Ted, it's me, Cynthia, and I would like you to come to my party'?"

"No. Obviously."

"So who invited you?"

"What? What are you talking about? Anna invited me. Who cares? I didn't even say I was definitely going, I said I was *thinking* about it."

"Oh, *now* I see. Now I get it. Now everything is very clear."

"You don't see anything! I was on the phone with Anna and she mentioned the party at Cynthia's and we talked about going. We don't even have concrete plans."

That was not what had happened. What had happened was that Anna had complained to him at length the previous night about the painful obligation she was under to go to Cynthia Krazewski's party, despite the fact that it was the absolute last thing she'd ever want to do, and thus Ted had inferred there was a strong likelihood that if he should happen to be home alone on New Year's, he would get a last-minute phone call from Anna, and the two of them would wind up spending New Year's together, most of which they would pass watching *SNL* in Ted's basement, but then at midnight, they'd switch to network television to watch the ball drop, and he'd "discover" a bottle of chilled champagne in his fridge, and after they'd toasted each other, he'd turn to her with a wry, amused smile on his face and say, "I know this is silly, but we might as well!" and she'd giggle and say, "I guess so!" and so he'd kiss her in an almost-friendly way, on the lips but closed-mouthed, and then he'd pause as he was pulling away and wait, and she would wait, and then *she'd* go in for the kiss, and then they'd be making out for real, grappling on the couch and then on the floor, and when he took her shirt off, he'd pull it up but then kind of twist it around her arms so they were pinned above her head, which was a trick he'd recently discovered with Rachel, and Anna would make this kind of sexy, surprised Oh face with her mouth, and she'd be panting underneath him and they'd fuck and he'd make her come so hard that afterward they would be together for the rest of their lives.

It was a *foolproof plan*.

Oh, wait. No, it wasn't. It was a sexual fantasy, and he was an idiot.

Then, just as he was acknowledging this to himself, Rachel—his girlfriend, his mirror—began to dance. Clad in only her underwear, her tiny tits shaking, she did a hideous little dance, a mocking-Ted dance. A dance that, in a moment, fused everything he loathed about her with everything he loathed about himself.

"*Hi, I'm Ted!*" Rachel sneered, shimmying. "Look at me! I'm Anna Travis's dorky sidekick. I follow her around hoping that if I do every-thing she tells me all the time, I can somehow make her like me. *Look at me, look at me, look at meeeeeeeeeeeeee!*"

Was there a point at which your ego was crushed so completely that it died, and you no longer had to lug around the burden of yourself?

There must be a German word for this feeling, when the elaborate contortions of your own thinking rose to the surface and became suddenly and unpleasantly visible. Like walking past a mirror in a crowded mall and thinking: Who is that dude with the terrible posture, and why is he cringing like he expects someone to punch him, *I'd* like to punch him—oh wait, that's me.

"Did she invite me?" Rachel practically spat. "Am I invited with you to the cool kids' party?"

Ted didn't answer her.

"So she *didn't* invite you? Did she just say she was going, and you were just going to lurk creepily around her like, oh *Anna*, I've missed you so much since you've been at *college*, I wish we could just run away together and watch like twenty hours of *SNL* while I make you popcorn and breathe heavily into your ear?"

"Yep," said Ted. "That's pretty much what happened."

"I have an idea," Rachel said. "We'll go to Cynthia Krazewski's party together. Sure! Why not? I'll call Anna. I told you our moms are friends, right? I'll ask her if we can come to Cynthia's. I'm sure she'll say yes. It'd be fun to see her. You'd like that, wouldn't you, Ted?"

"No," he said. "I would not."

But that was precisely what they did.

In New York City in the year 2018, Ted lay on his back on a hospital gurney, shoved into a hallway of a crowded ER. Unable to turn his head either left or right, he stared directly up into a blinding fluorescent light and wondered if he was dying. That's ridiculous, he told himself. I am absolutely not dying. A lady threw a glass of water at me; it's a minor injury; it's absurd to think a person could die because of that. Immediately, he imagined Rachel saying scornfully: "People die of head injuries *all the time*, Ted."

Ted thought: I am probably not dying but I am scared and alone and I don't like this.

"Excuse me," he shouted, through a dry, cracked throat. "Could someone please tell me what's going on?"

No one responded to his plea, but eventually some blurry shadow-creatures came swimming toward him. They asked him questions in a nonsense language, and he answered in an equally unintelligible garble, and he was rewarded by a prickle in his arm, followed by a flooding ease of bliss.

As the drugs took hold, Ted's memories began to entwine with a strange yet perversely lovely hallucination. In this hallucination, the tumbler Angela flung at his head had not bounced off his skull but had shattered instead. One piece of glass had become lodged in his forehead, and he could see that piece of glass in the center of his vision, rising like a tower, impaling him, pinning him down, refracting a shimmering circle of rainbows in the light. Through the glass, he could see himself reflected in all his miserable glory.

There he was.

There he *is*.

Trenton, New Jersey, on the last day of 1998.

Ted and Rachel are standing on Cynthia Krazewski's front porch. Rachel has prepared herself as though for battle. She is clad in a skin-tight black dress and shiny high heels, her hair sprayed and bound in a tight French twist. Ted rings the doorbell, and after what feels like a pointedly long time, Cynthia Krazewski opens the door.

"Hi," says Ted. "I'm Ted."

Rachel nudges herself between them. "Anna invited us," she says.

Cynthia says: "Who?"

"Anna Travis," says Rachel.

Cynthia shrugs her shoulders like she's never heard of Anna Travis. Maybe she hasn't. "Whatever," she says. "Beer's in the fridge."

Inside the party, Ted locates Anna immediately. She is in the corner, talking to Ryan Creighton. She's wearing a dowdy smock dress over leggings, and she's dyed her hair an unbecoming shade of red. In contrast to Rachel, Anna looks a little . . . bland? She looks what Ted knows her to be: tired, overwhelmed, and sad. Ted thinks: Is it possible that Rachel is hotter than Anna? Or that they're both equally hot? His world trembles on its foundations, but then Ted sees Anna put her hand on Ryan Creighton's bicep and laugh flirtatiously, and once again she body-slams his heart.

Rachel sees Ted looking at Anna looking at Ryan Creighton. She stiffens, and she grips Ted's hand until it hurts.

Realizing she's being watched, Anna takes Ryan Creighton's arm and leads him over to Rachel and Ted. There is a bunch of superficial hugging and some *Oh my God it's been so long*s. Anna and Rachel giggle over some small embarrassing habit of Ted's—*Have you ever noticed how he*—while Ryan Creighton looks seriously bored.

Ted thinks: Everyone at this party could die tonight, including me, and I wouldn't even care. He gets very drunk.

At some point in the night's festivities, the doorbell rings, followed by a slight commotion. Anna disappears from sight. Ted tries to go after her, but Rachel holds his wrist in a firm and brutal grip. Rumor filters back to them that Marco Hernandez was at the party briefly, but left when he found out that Anna was there. There is more talk about the restraining order, and whether it's real or not, and how that would even work.

Midnight comes.

Ted kisses Rachel with tongue and squeezes her ass. In doing so, he discovers that it is possible to enjoy something and yet not care about it in the slightest. He finds this sensation—feeling pleasure, and simultaneously feeling detached from the pleasure—to be, itself, quite pleasurable. He wonders if he has miraculously become a Buddhist, or suffered a psychotic break.

When Ted finally withdraws his tongue from Rachel's throat, he sees that Anna is watching them. Anna looks upset. Rachel sees Anna watching them, and kisses Ted again, in triumph. Ted once more feels like a patch of peed-on grass.

Anna disappears, but when Rachel leaves to go to the bathroom, she returns.

"Ted, can I talk to you?" she asks.

"Sure," he says. "What's up?"

"In *private*."

She leads him outside, onto the porch. It's freezing, sleeting a little, but he's wrapped in enough drunken warmth that he doesn't really mind it. Anna lights a cigarette. She exhales a gray wave of smoke and scratches at her thighs. It's news to Ted she smokes.

"I can't believe you," she says at last. "I can't believe you did that."

"Did what?"

"Made out with your girlfriend like that. Groping her and everything. Right in front of me."

"Huh?" Ted says. "What?"

Anna slumps forward. "I don't know . . ." she says. "I guess I just thought . . ." She starts again. "I guess, we've been talking for weeks about how hard this was going to be for me, and about how worried I was about how it'd be, seeing everyone. You knew I didn't even want to come here, but then you decided you were going to come with your new girlfriend, so I had to. And then Marco showed up, and it was like, super traumatic, and when I come to you and try to get support, you're in the corner making out with Rachel Derwin-Finkel. It just . . . I feel like our relationship isn't the same anymore, that I've lost you somehow. I miss you, Ted."

There are tears in her eyes. Ted has never seen her look so despondent, and Anna often looks very, very sad.

"Why aren't you saying anything?" Anna asks, sniffling.

"I guess . . ." Ted says. "I'm not sure what to say." Awkwardly, he puts his arms around her. "I'm here for you, Anna. You know that."

"I know," she says. She puts her head on his shoulder, and for a second, it's like that other good night, the night of the bonfire, the brief lifting of the yoke, freedom from the circle: Marco hurting Anna, Anna hurting Ted, Ted hurting Rachel, these endless rounds of jealousy and harm.

Anna says, weeping, "I'm so tired of chasing after all these shitty guys. I want to be with someone I can trust. I want to be with someone *good*."

And then Anna, luminous Anna, beautiful Anna; Anna, with her dimples and smooth skin and the freckles on her nose and her pretty, pretty hair; Anna, whose smell enchants him; Anna, who has ruined him for all other women; Anna, the one he'd die for. Anna, the most perfect girl in the world—

Anna kisses him.

*I will be good for you, Anna*, Ted thinks, embracing her. *I will be good for you for the rest of my entire life.*

Just give me one quick minute to break up with Rachel first.

Anna waits on the porch while Ted goes back inside to tell Rachel he is leaving. "It's Anna," he says. "She . . . We . . ."

He doesn't finish his sentence. He doesn't have to. The look that

Rachel gives him penetrates deep, deep, deep into whatever tattered mess he has of a soul.

Of course, there is screaming.

There is crying.

There is beer-throwing. (Just the liquid, not the glass.)

But then, at the end of it, Ted leaves the party with Anna. He walks out of a party with Anna Travis that he walked into with Rachel Derwin-Finkel, and if there is a heaven, this is the feeling he will be allowed to live inside of for eternity; the greatest, most triumphant moment of his entire life.

Twenty years later, from the perspective of his hospital gurney, he has to admit that everything pretty much went downhill from there.

Ted loses his virginity to Anna Travis on March 13, 1999, in the top bunk of her dorm room, after they've been dating long-distance for three and a half months. To the surprise of both parties involved, Ted has difficulty maintaining an erection. The reason for this, though he would never, ever confess it, is the look on Anna's face. She just seems so dutiful. She looks like she is taking medicine, or eating vegetables. She looks like she is thinking, *Whelp, my life sucks so bad I guess I might as well have sex with Ted.*

No, that's not fair. Anna is having sex with him because she loves him. Since they started dating, she's told him that she loves him, dozens and dozens of times. She's having sex with him *because* she loves him, and because he loves her, and sex is a normal part of this equitable exchange. She loves him because he is "good." But by "good," she means "safe." And by "safe," she means "You love me so much that you'll never, ever hurt me, right?"

Anna loves Ted, but she does not want him in a way that causes her to suffer; she does not want him desperately, despite herself. And it turns out that is how Ted has always wanted to be wanted: the way he has always wanted women. The way Anna wanted Marco, and he wanted Anna, and Rachel (or so it seems, in retrospect) wanted him.

In the absence of this painful wanting, Ted has trouble getting hard. At first, he tries to address the problem of his vanishing erection, by shouting at himself, TED YOU ARE HAVING SEX WITH ANNA TRAVIS! But that doesn't work. What lifts his dick, finally, is thinking about Rachel. About how, if she knew he was having sex with Anna Travis, she would be so jealous and so pissed. Look at me now, Rachel, he thinks triumphantly as he comes.

You fucking slut, you stupid fucking bitch.

Ted dates Anna, long-distance, for the next year and a half. For the first year, he struggles valiantly to make it work, but for the last six months, he cheats on her: first with a girl on the floor of his dorm at college, and later, with the girl who will eventually become the next in his series of girlfriends, and in between these women, he also cheats on her with Rachel Derwin-Finkel, while they're both home over Thanksgiving break. The whole time Ted is having sex with Rachel, Imaginary Anna flutters around him, waving her angel's wings in his face: *I'm so beautiful and perfect*, she sighs. *How could you possibly prefer having this creepy weirdo sex with Rachel Derwin-Finkel? Is that really the kind of person you are?*

The thing is, it's such a relief, having sex with Rachel Derwin-Finkel. He doesn't have to pretend around her. She knows exactly who he is.

As he gets older, he finds himself refining the technique he first used, however inadvertently, on Anna; his secret seduction trick. This is what you do: drag your heart like bait in front of them. Pretend to be an easy catch, while always staying slightly out of reach. Oh look, it's me, here I am, I'm just nerdy old Ted. You're so much better-looking than me, you're so much cooler than me, you're the greatest you're the smartest you're the best. With you, for you, I'd be the greatest boyfriend who ever, ever lived.

Pathetic Ted, short nerdy Ted, ladykiller Ted, using a thousand tiny hooks to catch onto a woman's ego, like a burr clinging to the cuff of her pants. All he has to do is smile, and make a few self-deprecating comments, and women start telling themselves he's so "nice" and "smart" and "funny." They argue themselves into settling for him, talk themselves into just one date. They feel proud of themselves for giving him a chance.

The older he gets, the higher his stock rises. More and more women want out of that endless chase after Marcos; they yearn to collapse into the arms of their Teds.

Ted hears other men congratulate themselves on this new reversal of power, the fact that now, in their thirties, it's so much easier for them to get dates. Maybe there are men who can enter into this bargain wholeheartedly, who can look into the eyes of their Annas and not mind the truth of what they see there . . . but not Ted. What Ted saw in Anna's eyes, he also sees in Sarena's and Melissa's and Danielle's and Beth's and Ayelet's and Margaret's and Flora's and Jennifer's and Jacquelyn's and Maria's and Tana's and Liana's and Angela's: that tiredness, that willful giving up. He sees how smug they feel about settling for a "good guy," which means: a guy they secretly think they're too good for. He sees them think they're safe.

He gets pleasure out of it, a kind of pleasure, fucking these women, but it's entwined with loathing, both for them and for himself. He gets his revenge in his fantasies, which grow more and more elaborate, until at last they involve sharp knives and utter desperation. It's like the game kids play: *Why are you slapping yourself? Stop slapping yourself!* Only in this case, it's: *Stop impaling yourself on my dick!*

The women he dates all turn on him eventually, of course. The more they feel like they've compromised themselves by being with him, the more passionately they pursue him when he launches his retreat. He becomes an instrument of pure self-punishment: What is wrong with me, that even *this fucking loser* won't give me what I want? They identify all sorts of problems in him that he needs them to fix: he isn't "in touch with his emotions," or he's "afraid of commitment," but they never question the basic premise, that somewhere deep down, underneath it all, he wants to be with them. Of course you have feelings for me, Angela might as well have been saying, right before she threw the glass at him. Admit it, dammit!

I'm *me*.

And you're *Ted*.

In 2018, Ted is Facebook friends with both Anna and Rachel, though he hasn't seen either of them in years. Rachel is married, a pediatrician, and the mother of four kids; Anna lives in Seattle as a single mom. She seems to be doing okay, now, but for a while she was going through a rough time; Ted suspects she may be in some kind of recovery program. She posts inspirational quotations that strike him as beneath her: *I can't change the direction of the wind, but I can adjust my sails to always reach my destination* and *It is in the darkest moments that we must try to see the light.*

He thinks of Anna, now, as he's lying on the gurney. In fact, he sees her. She's coming at him through the rainbows, accompanied by a chorus of voices, a fluttering of wings.

What time is it? What day is it? What year? Here is Anna, but she's not alone. She's with all the women of the tribunal. They're here, at his bedside, whispering about him, observing him closely, judging him the way they always have. They're fighting, disagreeing about something, and he senses there is a misunderstanding at the center of all of it, some base confusion. He could clear it up, if only there weren't a giant shard of glass embedded in his forehead, if only this blood would stop pooling in his mouth.

I didn't mean to hurt anyone, he tries to tell them. I just wanted to be seen, and loved for who I am. The problem was, it was all a misunderstanding. I pretended to be a good person, and then I couldn't stop.

No, wait. Let me start over. That's not right.

All I've ever wanted is to be loved. Well, to be worshipped. To be desired, madly and painfully, to the exclusion of all else. Is that so wrong?

No, *wait*. That's definitely not what I meant.

Listen, listen. I can explain. There's a bad Ted underneath the good Ted, yes, but then, under *that*, there's a Ted who's good for real. But no one ever sees him; his whole life, no one ever has. Underneath it all, I'm just that kid who wanted nothing more than to be loved and didn't know how to make it happen, even though I tried and tried and tried.

Hey, stop. Put me down. I'm trying to tell you something. Would you stop talking and listen to me, please? The light up there is hurting my eyes. But also, maybe turn on the air-conditioning? It'd be a little easier to explain myself if it wasn't so damn warm. Are those flames licking at my feet?

I'm trying to say something important. Where are you taking me?

Listen to me, will you—

I'm a nice guy, I swear to fucking God.

# THE BOY IN THE POOL

"Let's watch it again," says Taylor. She's sitting so close to the television that Kath can see its cool pastel glow reflecting off her cheekbones as the credits roll.

"I thought we were going to play Light as a Feather, Stiff as a Board," complains Lizzie, but Taylor is already crawling toward the VCR. Kath suspects that Lizzie likes the movie as much as Taylor does, but that she's embarrassed to show it. Meanwhile, nothing embarrasses Taylor: "What was you guys' favorite part?"

"Um, all of it?" Lizzie says.

Kath swirls a handful of popcorn seeds from the emptied bowl and sucks the salt off them, buying time. "I liked . . ." she begins. There was a point during the movie when Taylor had squeezed her knees together, rocking a little, as a flush spread up the hollow of her neck. Kath had been riveted. "I liked the part where the lady dunks the boy underwater, and then he comes up for air . . ."

There's a dizzying pause as Lizzie stares at her, blankly, but then Taylor giggles and Kath knows she's guessed right. "Oh my God, yes. The way he looked at her? Imagine somebody looking at you like that. Like Eric Harrington. Or . . ." Taylor's eyes dart toward Lizzie. "Or Mr. Curtis. Lizzie, imagine Mr. Curtis looking at you that way."

"Shut up," Lizzie says, throwing a pillow at Taylor. Taylor bats the pillow away, laughing, and then slumps against Kath, unexpectedly dropping her head onto Kath's lap. "Hey, it's the good part," she says, waving at the TV, where a teenage boy is doing the butterfly stroke in reverse across the screen. "Let's just watch from here."

Kath is closest to the TV, but if she shifts position, Taylor will have to move, too, so she waits to see if Lizzie will start the movie, and she does.

On-screen, a boy swims in only his underwear, watched by a woman whose lips are the same shade of red as her long, sharp nails. Taylor sighs contentedly and settles herself against Kath. The woman emerges from the shadows and dangles her toe in the deep end of the pool, like bait. Kath is unsure what to do with her hands. The boy swims up to the woman and says something Kath can't quite hear, since they're keeping the sound low because of Taylor's mom. The woman begins toying with the boy, teasing him, letting him come close before pushing him away. Kath decides to put one hand on the floor and the other on her leg. The boy grabs the woman's foot, cradles it, then plants a kiss on each of her painted toes. Lizzie snorts. "That's ridiculous," she says. "Who wants to kiss someone's disgusting feet?" The woman rests her foot on the boy's bare shoulder and pushes him under the water. Very, very lightly, Kath begins stroking Taylor's hair. The boy surfaces, gasping, and the woman dunks him under again. He kicks and thrashes, gripping her calves with his hands. The boy looks a little like River Phoenix, and a little like Leonardo DiCaprio: those soft, bruised eyes. Kath trails her fingers along the hairs on Taylor's temple, and they prickle up beneath her touch. The woman releases the boy, and he rises, droplets of water clinging to his eyelashes, to his

150

dark feathered hair. Opening his eyes, he gives the woman the look Kath knows that Taylor loves: the one that says, *I'd let you do anything to me.* Taylor tenses and shivers with pleasure, sending a sparkler of sensation fizzing along Kath's spine. The woman laughs and kisses the boy, then slides onto his shoulders. The boy buries his head between the woman's thighs.

That night, during Light as a Feather, Stiff as a Board, Kath and Lizzie raise Taylor all the way above their heads and she floats there, weightless, for a miraculous half-second before she comes tumbling down. They play MASH and learn the names of their future husbands, and when Lizzie falls asleep, Kath and Taylor try to get her to wet herself by putting her hand in a cup full of warm water, but it doesn't work.

The movie remains a staple at their sleepovers for the next several weeks, but then Taylor's mom finds the tape and confiscates it, so they switch to *Candyman.* Taylor stays obsessed with the movie for a month or so, but then out of nowhere she starts hanging out with Greta Jorgensen, whom neither Kath nor Lizzie can stand, and so they're in a fight for a few weeks, and by the time they're friends again, the sleepovers feel like a long time ago.

Still, in tenth grade, when Taylor tries to explain to Kath why she's dating Jason McAuliffe, she says, "I like the way he looks at me," and Kath remembers the boy in the pool. The boy in the pool, Kath decides, is a boy who will kiss your feet and be grateful for it, a boy who suffers, a boy who will suffer for *you.* She uses this concept as a way to explain to herself why Taylor spends most of high school dating a series of burnouts and depressive alcoholics; why it becomes a common experience at parties for total strangers to ask her what her pretty, popular, high-achieving best friend could possibly see in him—"him" being any one of a dozen sad and useless boys.

Kath comes out uneventfully during her senior year of high school, and soon she's so consumed by being in love with her first real-life girl-friend that it's easy for her to forget all the time she spent mooning over Taylor. Or not to forget, exactly, but to remember it slightly falsely, as just a very intense adolescent friendship, which, in some ways, is exactly what it was. What remains in the wake of her crush is the habit of observing Taylor very, very closely, straining toward interpretation, reading all her signs.

One night, when they are both very drunk, Taylor gets morbid and weepy about yet another breakup, and Kath says, "You are such a disaster. I can't believe I spent so much time in love with you."

This shocks Taylor out of her crying fit. "You *loved* me?" she says.

"Never mind. Forget I said anything," snaps Kath, and after they sober up, neither of them mentions it again.


The three friends scatter across the country for college. Taylor meets a new boy, Gabriel, during welcome weekend, and over the course of the next four years, she and Kath drift apart. The relationship with Gabriel, which Kath hears about mostly through Lizzie, is apparently all-consuming, an endless series of fights and tearful resolutions: they scratch and claw at each other, then tend each other's wounds. For the first time in their lives, Taylor's passions threaten to derail her. Senior year, she and Gabriel break up, and he flees to California. She follows him and puts college on hold when he agrees to reconcile. Lizzie goes to visit her and reports that she's not doing great: she's lost twenty pounds, which is maybe standard in L.A., but she's also downing vodka tonics pretty much nonstop, and she's got shadows under her eyes, and a ring of bruises around her upper arm.

"Do you think we should, like, stage an intervention?" she asks Kath, but Kath refuses to get involved.

"She wants what she wants," Kath says.

Don't we all?

A decade later, Kath and Lizzie live in Brooklyn. Lizzie works at an education nonprofit; Kath's an attorney, specializing in contract law. Kath dates men and women, while Lizzie is hapless about romance in an ironic, self-deprecating way. Taylor's still out in California. The relationship with Gabriel is finally over, but before it ended, there were infidelities, suicide attempts, police involvement. Lizzie knows more of the details than Kath does. Every once in a while, the three of them will Skype, and during these calls, Kath and Taylor do most of the talking, in brief intense bursts, as though nothing has changed—but the calls are always instigated and organized by Lizzie, and when Lizzie's too busy to facilitate, months will pass where Kath and Taylor do not talk at all.

Free of Gabriel, Taylor seems to be doing a lot better. She's switched jobs, found a new therapist, finished her degree. And, Lizzie reports, she's started dating someone, this producer or something, a guy named Ryan, who seems really good for her. "That's amazing!" Lizzie screams, over Skype one night, when Taylor announces that she and Ryan are engaged. "That's the best news I've ever heard!"

On the couch beside her, Kath experiences a moment of confused dislocation, as though her soul has suddenly relocated into her body from very far away. *Ryan?* she thinks, *Who the fuck is* Ryan?—before coming to herself and offering her own congratulations, doing her best to echo Lizzie's ecstatic tone.

"Of course, I want you both to be in the wedding," Taylor says.

Kath nods, and Lizzie says, "We wouldn't miss it for the world." But as the conversation moves toward venues and shoes and dresses, Kath registers a faint discomfort, as though Taylor wants to tell them something she can't quite bring herself to say. The reason for this becomes clear the next morning, when Kath and Lizzie are at brunch and a text message arrives to Kath's phone.

Kath's face contorts so dramatically that Lizzie freezes, a forkful of eggs Benedict halfway to her mouth. "What?" Lizzie demands, and when Kath doesn't answer right away, she repeats, "What's wrong?"

Kath turns her phone around to show Lizzie the message.

Lizzie's eyebrows knit together. "Oh."

"Is she serious?" demands Kath. "I've never even *met* this guy. Doesn't she have any friends in L.A.?"

"Wow, where did that come from? What a rotten thing to say."

Kath says, "You're the one who's been there for her this whole time. If she was going to ask one of us to be her maid of honor, she should've asked you."

"Well, she didn't. So."

"So, I don't want to do it."

"You have to," says Lizzie, but she's wrong. That night, Kath drinks three beers in quick succession and calls Taylor on the phone. "Listen . . ." she begins, and then launches into a long, rambling monologue, sentimental and self-serving. "I've always had really complicated feelings about weddings . . . They're just not really my thing . . . Money's kind of tight right now . . . June is my busiest time at work . . . I know that she won't show it, but I'm afraid that Lizzie will be really hurt . . ."

Taylor listens bravely, interjecting only the occasional "yeah," and "sure," and at the end of twenty minutes, they've agreed that Lizzie will be the maid of honor and that Kath will be an "honorary bridesmaid," with exact responsibilities TBD.

"The wedding-industrial complex is inherently capitalist and anti-feminist, and I don't support it," Kath tells Lizzie the next time they meet for drinks.

"Alternative explanation: you're a heartless bitch."

"I'll read a poem or something," Kath says. But she doesn't get off so easily. A few days later, Lizzie informs her that she is in charge of planning the bachelorette.

"So, like, tiaras and penis straws?"

"No," says Lizzie. "*Not* tiaras and penis straws. Do me a favor: pull your head out of your own ass for two seconds, and try to figure out something she'll like."

So Kath tries. She tries so hard she surprises herself. She emails the other women in the wedding party to ask if any of them are vegetarian or religious or pregnant, then makes a spreadsheet to coordinate every-one's preferences and availability. She narrows the possibilities down to three solid options and sends out a poll. When the results are in, she calls Lizzie and announces they'll be spending the bachelorette week-end at a cabin in the Sierras. "You did good!" Lizzie exclaims, when she sees the cabin website: huge fireplace, lux hot tub, gorgeous views.

Kath is proud of what she's accomplished. She and Taylor have a couple of good conversations, just the two of them. She learns more about Ryan: where he comes from (Colorado), how he and Taylor met (eHarmony), and what Taylor loves most about him (his steadiness, his honesty, his concern for the environment, his close-but-not-*too*-close relationship with his mom). Maybe this will be the start of a flourishing second act of their friendship, the distance bridged, the old wounds finally healed.

But then: disaster. Lizzie, knees curled up on Kath's couch, drink-ing wine: "So, here's the thing. Taylor's embarrassed to tell you, but she wants to change the plan for the bachelorette."

"What? She doesn't like the cabin?"

"No, I mean, she did. She does. But I guess what happened is, Ryan decided he's going to Vegas with his friends, and it's going to be all gambling and blackout drinking and strippers, and Taylor feels like a girls' weekend in the mountains can't compete."

"Strippers? I thought Ryan was, like, Mr. Responsible."

"He is. It's out of character. Which I think is why she's so upset."

Kath shivers. "So, what now?"

"She just wants something a little . . . wilder. Like what bachelor parties are supposed to be for guys. A last chance for a little excitement, before she settles down."

"If she thinks of marrying this guy as the end to all excitement, maybe she shouldn't be getting married," Kath says.

"Don't be melodramatic. Can you plan something else, or not?"

"I can't think of anything she'll like."

"Just try, okay? She needs this. Be her friend."

Kath, trying, runs through a hundred ideas, but is dissatisfied with all of them. What's the female equivalent of a guy taking all his friends to Vegas? A pack of shrieking, tipsy ladies shoving dollar bills into some greased-up hunk's banana hammock? That's not wild or sexy or transgressive, it's a joke. A dude dressed up as a police officer knocking on the door, then ripping off his pants? Thinking about it too hard makes her angry: ardent Taylor, who *wants* more passionately than anyone Kath has ever met, deserves more than these insulting parodies of lust. But what does Taylor want?

*Hey Liz, is there any flexibility in the budget for Taylor's thing?*

*Idk, maybe? Why?*

*If I threw in some extra $ for a surprise for Taylor, could you too?*

*Sure, I guess. Whatcha planning?*

*Ahhhhh, I don't wanna tell you yet. It's a crazy long shot. If I make it happen, you'll find out.*

Here's the first difficulty: she doesn't even remember the name of the movie. Taylor had taped it off cable by accident, trying to record something else. But she'd set the timer wrong, and so she'd ended up with this sleazy softcore horror film none of them had ever heard of; a movie that, even at age twelve, they'd known was terrible, and that they'd have been embarrassed to watch were it not for the fact that the boy who starred in it drove Taylor wild.

The boy. Did she know his name? It feels like she did, at some point. First name, one syllable, she thinks. Chad or Nick or Brad. And maybe he had three names, the way a lot of actors back then did—Chad Michael Nickerson. Nick Bradley Chaderson. Brad Chad Daderson.

No. It's gone.

Okay. So what actually happened in the movie? Well, there was a sex scene. In a pool. Between the teenage boy, Chad-Brad-Whoever, and an older woman, who later turned out to be some kind of vampire; she can remember that scene nearly frame by frame. But, unsurprisingly, googling *Movie sex scene pool vampire woman* doesn't get her anywhere. Neither does adding *90s* or *Cinemax*. Or *oral sex*. What else? She strains to remember. Wasn't there something about . . . a gravedigger? A resurrection? She has an image of the boy and the woman lying together in a coffin, the boy nestled against the woman's chest. There was something about a knife, right, that had to be hidden. Or was that a different movie? This feels impossible, but she knows it's not. Nothing is lost any longer. She just needs a detail. Something searchable. Just one thing.

It's 3 A.M. when it comes to her, another scene. The woman, and another man, and the boy. They were all three of them vampires by then, lying in bed together, drinking each other's blood. What the fuck *was* this movie, twelve years old and they were sitting around giggling and eating popcorn and watching horror porn. But the man, who was maybe the woman's husband or vampire master or maker—

he gave the boy a . . . scar, or a tattoo? She can remember the boy on his back, and the man and the woman looming over him, and they wrote something on his body and it said, it said . . . she can't remember.

But she can *almost* remember, because Taylor wrote it in her notebook the next week in class. There was a heart, and a knife dripping blood, and a quote, and the quote was something about love. Kath remembers because later Taylor had forgotten the notebook at her house and Kath never gave it back; she'd read that quote a dozen times, tracing Taylor's daydream with her finger:

*Love is—*

*Love is—*

Her memory like a skipping record, bumping continually up against the scratch.

*Love is, love is.*

She backs up, relaunches—

*Love—*

*Love—*

*Love bears—*

*Love breeds—*

And hurls herself over the chasm.

*Love breeds monsters.*

That's it.

That's enough.


From IMDb:

*Jared Nicholas Thompson is an actor, writer, and producer who is best known for his debut performance as the unnamed Boy in the Pool in the movie* Blood Sins *(1991), a straight-to-video horror release which became a staple of late-night cable television in the early 1990s. He also appeared in the films* Save Me *(1994),* Pushing the Limit *(1995), and* Fatal Exposure *(2000), as well as the Lifetime Original Movie* A Sister's Promise *(1993). After a decade-long hiatus from acting, during which he worked as a carpenter, a professional dancer, and a mother's helper, Jared returned to the industry to work behind the camera as a screenwriter and producer. His most recent project is the web series* DadZone *(currently in development), which he created in partnership with his longtime friend and collaborator Doug McIntyre. Thompson currently lives in Los Angeles with his wife and six-year-old son.*

The boy in the pool is now a man, pushing forty, with a soft webbing of lines around his eyes. He has a Twitter account and a YouTube channel, as well as a tiny, passionate coterie of female fans who maintain his Facebook page and call him, presumptuously, by his first name. Most of these women seem to be fans of his performance as The Boy in the Pool, though they feign an interest in his more recent projects in transparent bids for his attention: *So excited for @jnthompsn's new series #dadzone—been a fan ever since #boyinthepool.* Jared faithfully retweets all of the #dadzone mentions, while ignoring the more lascivious references to his earlier work (*tracked down old #skinemax crush @jnthompsn—omg still super hotttttt*), and Kath crafts her first message with that in mind.

The opportunities available to actors who achieved the peak of their fame as nameless characters in 1990s softcore horror porn films must be limited: Kath writes to him at 7 P.M.; he answers her a little after midnight, and two days later, they set up an appointment to Skype. His face appears on her computer screen, sharper than memory, a vivid emissary from a time before.

Jared's voice is soft, a little raspy, and he has an unexpectedly high, fluting laugh. He's older, but almost eerily unchanged: the same pale skin, dark hair, and wide uncertain eyes. Kath spends the first few minutes of their conversation dancing around the specifics of why she's calling him, feeling him out. His expressive face might be his greatest asset as an actor, but as a negotiator, it betrays him utterly. When she hints that he might not be quite what she's looking for, he wilts; when she praises him, he fills and straightens like a freshly watered plant.

She explains the opportunity to him, skirting around the details, and emphasizing how much she'll pay him: five hundred dollars for showing up for two hours, another five hundred as a bonus if it all goes well. He hesitates before agreeing, and she wonders if he knows what's really going on. She's certain that if she'd mentioned the words *bachelorette party*, he'd have refused her offer—he visibly aches to be taken seriously, burdened by what she imagines as an aging ingenue's misplaced pride. But what's the definition of *bachelorette party*, anyway? They're just a group of women who are interested in meeting him, that's all. Chatting politely. Flirting a little. Seeing if they can convince him to take his shirt off. Maybe trying to coax him into the pool.

Having secured the surprise guest of honor, Kath relocates the party from a cabin in the Sierras to a hotel in downtown L.A. Instead of girls-only hikes and campfires and sleeping bags in the basement, there will be a group spa day, aromatherapy massages, karaoke, dancing, and lots of free-flowing wine. She organizes, reserves, orders, corrals—then flies into LAX, where Taylor picks her up. It's their first time seeing each other in person in . . . *how long?* they demand of each other as they hug. *Time goes by so fast. Can it really have been so many years?*

Taylor's rose-gold engagement ring, capped by a blocky, prismatic diamond, sprays rainbows onto the roof of her car. She, too, has changed little in the intervening years—the only real difference Kath can detect is a certain thickness around the knuckles of her hands. Her Echo Park bungalow, which she shares with Ryan, is beautifully appointed, with bright geometric art glowing on its smooth white walls. There's a dry-erase board hanging from the refrigerator, and on it is a list of wedding-related tasks in Taylor's careful, rounded handwriting; the list is labeled: *Honey-do.*

Lizzie arrives that night, and unlike Kath, she remembers to bring a hostess gift. Even though it's the first night all three of them have been under the same roof since high school, they go to bed early, and the bachelorette kicks off the next morning with a heavily Instagrammed brunch.

As the day goes by, they move from brunch to the spa to the sangria bar for happy-hour drinks, and the whole time, Kath compulsively searches Taylor's face for any signs of what the future holds. In ten years, will she be surrounded by abundance: healthy children, an overgrown garden, a joyfully messy house? Will she have a couple extra pounds around the middle, a few wild, untamable gray hairs? Or will she be one of those women who subsist on salad and stress, their bodies Botoxed and bleached and starved into submission, locked in an endless war against the flesh?

Jesus Christ, Kath. Get a grip. A more reasonable voice in her head, one that sounds a lot like that of a therapist she had in college, gently inquires if all this angst is truly about Taylor and her choices. As many, many exes have informed her, Kath's an expert in making things about her that aren't. So maybe something else is going on? But she refuses the most obvious explanation, that she's still carrying a torch for Taylor. She doesn't know what to call it—this free-falling sensation she feels every time she looks at Taylor, like her hands are closing again and again on emptiness—but she thinks she knows better than to call it love.

And then it's evening, and they're sitting on a hotel patio strung with fairy lights. Beside them, an infinity pool spills into the horizon, creating the illusion that you could tumble right over a waterfall into the glittering Los Angeles night. The women of the wedding party have now spent eight hours together, which, it turns out—nice job, party planner!—is way too goddamned long. Everyone's faces are stretched taut and sore from too much smiling, and because they started too early, even though they feel increasingly like garbage, they have to continue downing drinks in order to keep their encroaching hangovers at bay. The ones who don't know each other have run out of small talk; the ones who see each other all the time have nothing left to say. At some point in the afternoon, Taylor began texting with Ryan, and Kath can tell, from the way she keeps snatching her phone and thrusting it away from her, that they have gotten into a fight.

Jared was due to arrive at 8 P.M., but he's more than an hour late; he's stuck in traffic, sending an apologetic stream of incomprehensibly L.A.-specific updates about what exit he just passed on the freeway. The guests are mostly finished eating, and a few have begun making tentative noise about going home (*God, I can't believe how wiped I am, ever since I started doing this early morning boot camp, my bedtime is like, nine o'clock*). Kath keeps them around by dropping clues about what's coming next, but all her hints make it sound like the surprise is a stripper. When Jared texts her that he's finally found parking and is heading in, Kath shields her eyes with her hands, and scans the crowd, but he enters from an unexpected doorway, and so it's Lizzie who sees him first.

Breaking off her conversation midsentence, she squints. "That guy . . ." she says. "He seems familiar." She elbows Taylor, who's busy texting. "Do we know him? Is he famous?" But Taylor doesn't look up right away, and so it's another woman entirely, someone whose name Kath doesn't even know, who cries, loudly enough to catch Jared's attention: "Oh, my God, you guys! It's that guy! From that TV movie! What's it called—you remember what I'm talking about? The Boy in the Pool!"

Chaos erupts at the table: a full third of the women recognize Jared; know exactly who he is.

*I used to be obsessed with that movie!*

*I didn't know anyone else remembered it!*

*He's still so cute!*

*I used to have such a crush on him!*

Jared jerks his head like a spooked horse and looks about to flee. Kath stands up, waves her arms above her head, and signals to him. "Jared," she says. "*So* thrilled you could make it. Over here." A burbling of excitement erupts from the women. Jared, like a lamb to the slaughter, comes as called.

Lizzie asks, "You did this? He's here for us?"

"He's here for Taylor," Kath says. What a fantastical place adulthood has turned out to be: with the power of social media and a thousand dollars, she's summoned Taylor's dream crush out of an ancient VHS tape and brought him here, to life.

Kath takes a skittish Jared by the arm, turns to Taylor, and presents her gift: "Jared, I'd like you to meet Taylor. She's a longtime fan."

Taylor doesn't look *quite* as impressed as Kath thinks she should be, given that Kath's just made all her teenage dreams come true. She offers her hand for Jared to shake, but Jared, catching Kath's pointed glance, opens his arms for a hug. As they embrace, Kath watches closely for the smallest tremble, a crack in Taylor's pristine reserve. Does she linger a little, resting her hands on his back? Did she turn her head into his neck on purpose, to inhale his smell? Maybe. Maybe not.

Taylor steps back. "It's so good of you to come," she says, an adult hostess, not a breathless girl. "I'm so sorry—I know exactly who you are, of course, but remind me of your name?"

Jared introduces himself with a little bow, prompting a wave of giggles from the table. "So," he says, "you're getting married?"

In a practiced gesture, she displays her ring. "I am." Taylor says, "I'm sure Kath's told you this, but you were quite the star of our sleepover parties, back when we were kids."

"No," Jared says. He bares his teeth at Kath. "She didn't mention that, funnily enough," he says, and they all smile tightly at each other until at last Lizzie leaps in.

"Jared! What have you been up to this whole time? Are you still acting, or . . . ?"

Jared launches into a meandering explanation of *DadZone*. Taylor raises her eyebrows at Kath. *I can't believe you*, Taylor mouths, and Kath ostentatiously shrugs.

"Jared," Kath says, hoping to liven things up. "Can I order you a cocktail?"

"No thanks!" Jared says cheerfully. "I don't drink."

"Jared!" one of the women interrupts. "Tell us what it was like to make *Blood Sins*. How did you end up taking that role?"

"It's a funny story, actually . . ." Jared says, and all the women at the table bend toward him, flowers in the sun. For all his desire to be taken seriously, it's clear to Kath that this is not his first evening dining out on twenty-year-old lust. He's a skillful courtesan: attentive, charming, and with an astonishing ability to deflect overt sexual advances with jujitsu speed. Over and over again, the women try to flirt with him, and over and over again, he parries and returns the subject to *DadZone*, until Kath starts to feel like they're at war: her goal is to push the night toward sex, riskiness, excitement . . . while he, very politely, is trying to schmooze them all to death.

Thirty minutes tick by, then an hour, then an hour twenty-five. The women appear to be mildly enjoying themselves, peppering their guest with questions, but Kath wants to chomp a bite out of her wineglass, feel the shards splinter and crunch between her teeth. She's paying *a thousand fucking dollars* for this meet-and-greet?

"Jared," she says, the sudden thickness in her voice informing her she's drunk. "I have an idea. Do you want to go swimming?"

"Ha, ha!" he says. "It's a bit chilly for that, don't you think?"

"I don't think so," Kath says. "Lizzie and Taylor and I grew up in Massachusetts. We've gone swimming in weather way colder than this."

She looks at the other two for confirmation. Taylor ignores her, but Lizzie rises to the occasion with a wicked smile. "Swimming could be fun," she says. She takes Taylor by the wrist. "Remember that time we cut French class senior year and went to the kettle pond?"

Taylor looks up, mid-text. "And snuck back into school soaking wet."

"And Mr. Swan was all, 'Why are you two drenched?' And we were like, 'We needed to take showers after gym!'"

Kath knows this story only from Lizzie's insistence on continually retelling it—it's one of a few just she and Taylor share—but she'll take any chance to break the night out of its stagnation, so she smiles encouragingly at Lizzie.

"Come on. Let's do it. Let's go swimming," Lizzie says, and the other women pick up and carry her excitement. When Taylor says, "I don't know . . ." they chant her into acquiescence, pounding their fists lightly on the table: "Taylor! Taylor!" until she finally agrees.

The women swirl tipsily toward the pool, shedding shoes and purses as they go, but Jared remains seated, his arms folded across his chest.

Kath stands over him. "Aren't you coming?"

"Nah," he says. "I think I'll sit this one out."

He loathes her for getting him into this, it's obvious, but so what? She loathes him, too. He's a lightning rod, that's all, for a kind of wild reckless energy; the target of desire, not its source.

"Come on, get in the pool," she says.

"No, thank you. I didn't bring my suit."

"Hey," she says and leans in close. "I paid you a lot of money to be here, so how about you get the fuck over yourself and go swimming with my friend?"

Jared frowns, stares straight ahead, and does not look at her, and she wonders if underneath the stiffness and the dullness and the pride is shame. "Please," she says. "It would mean so much to Taylor . . ." but when he doesn't answer, she adds: "I'll throw in an extra hundred bucks."

"Two hundred," he says grimly.

"Fine. But this next half hour better be good."

And in a movement so fluid that she can't help but wonder if some part of him knew exactly how the night would go, he kicks off his shoes and walks to the pool, pulling his shirt off as he goes. "*Ladies*," he says, his voice oily and self-mocking. The guests are all still clustered at the edge, not yet having gathered the courage to jump in. Jared tosses his shirt in a crumpled ball off to the side, and stands, wide-legged, in front of Taylor. "As much as I'd like to believe you all were intrigued by the premise of my web series, as your friend was kind enough to remind me, I was invited here for a reason," Jared says. "Who would like to join me for a swim?" Gyrating his hips, he unbuckles his belt, unsheathes it from its loops, and twirls it around his head.

The guests ooh and ahh, but Kath cringes, furious. He's doing exactly the thing she dreaded, that she sought him out in order to avoid: he's turning himself into a joke and taking Taylor with him. He wriggles out of his jeans, dancing to imaginary music, smoothing his hands down his thighs, while Taylor looks on, vicariously humiliated, like the unwilling object of a rendition of "Happy Birthday" performed by the waitstaff at a themed restaurant. Fuck you, Jared Nicholas Thompson, Kath thinks. Fuck you straight to hell.

Now Jared's pants are pooled around his ankles, and he's in just his underwear, still dancing like a fool. But at least he looks the way he ought to: lithe and hairless, tender-skinned. Despite all his efforts to make himself ridiculous, he's beautiful, and as she sees this, Kath sees Taylor register it, too—not through any obvious change in her expression, but just a kind of softening around the edges of her face.

Jared cracks his back and stretches, displaying the twin dark bursts of hair beneath his arms, and Taylor reaches up and tugs her ponytail loose from its band. Then, without warning, Jared crouches and dives into the pool, inexpertly, drenching the women closest to the edge. One woman takes out her cell phone and begins snapping photos. "What's the wedding hashtag again?" she whispers, but no one answers her.

The boy in the pool is doing the butterfly stroke, just like he did in the movie twenty years before. His arms crash operatically down into the water in perfect synchrony, while the rest of his body pulses in a tight wave that ripples down his stomach, hips, and thighs. Each time he finishes a lap, he flips direction with a dramatic kick, leaving a champagne trail of bubbles in his wake. They might as well be in a seedy motel, past midnight, because the noise he makes churning through the water is the only sound any of them can hear. He finishes three laps, swimming the final distance underwater, his body a shining ribbon of motion trembling in the stillness of the pool. He comes to Taylor, who's sitting at the edge, her legs tucked beneath her, and treads water, waiting patiently, until she stands. Her eyes half-closed, as though she's dreaming, she slides her sandal off and offers him her foot. He takes hold of it, and cradles it, and then, with only a flicker of a glance toward Kath, he sucks Taylor's toe deep into his mouth. All the women watching take one collective breath. Forgotten on the table, a silenced cell phone glows three times and then goes black. Taylor pulls her foot free, rests it lightly on top of his bare shoulder, and pushes him violently under. He slips down, his hands splayed against her calves, and as the seconds go by, though she knows it's just a game, a paid performance, Kath can't help but imagine him underwater, trapped and thrashing, waiting for Taylor's permission to breathe. At last, with a ragged gasp, he surfaces, water droplets jeweling like diamonds in his hair. He gazes up at Taylor, and she looks down at him.

*Oh*, Kath thinks, *I did it. I gave her what she wanted. What will happen now?*

Taylor laughs. "I think that's enough for tonight," she says. She lifts her foot out of the water, and that's when Kath comes up behind her, puts her hands on her shoulders, and shoves her in.

# SCARRED

I found the book shoved behind a shelf in the library. Hardly a book at all, really. No covers, just a bunch of Xeroxed pages stapled together. No space for a card in the back, or one of those little scanner strips, either. I rolled it up, put it in my pocket, and walked straight past the librarian. Rebel rebel.

When I got home, I opened it to the first page and did exactly as instructed. I drew a chalk circle on the floor of my basement, crushed together basil and blackberry from my cupboard like I was mixing up a fancy summer cocktail, then added a burnt lock of my hair and a fresh drop of my blood, gouged with a pin from the ball of my thumb. Not because I believed it would bring me my heart's desire—I wasn't even sure I had one of those—but because I've read enough books in my life to know that when you find a collection of spells hidden behind the shelf at your local library, you have to try at least one.

To my disappointment, but not my surprise, nothing happened. I flipped through the rest of the book, curious about what else I could have conjured: wealth, beauty, power, love. They all seemed a bit redundant: at least some of those must have been covered under the category *heart's desire*. Frankly, the whole concept was a little too New Age–y for me. I got up to go. If I hurried, I could still make it to the bar in time for happy hour. The thought of summer cocktails had made me thirsty, and the basement reeked of burnt hair.

He wasn't there, and then he was. His knees were scraped bloody on the concrete, his palms splayed out as though he'd fallen. His head was bowed. Shaking like a dog just come from the bath.

Naked.

I almost laughed. That was the part of my brain that started working again first, the part that thought, *A naked man, what a literal definition of desire.* Then the rest of me caught up and I scrambled up the basement steps shrieking, tripped, and fell against the door.

As I blubbered and pawed at the door handle, he stood up. Swayed. His ankle turned in a way that made me wince. He stumbled, righted himself again.

He lifted his head and looked at me.

"Don't be scared," he said.

Only, he had an accent, Scottish, maybe, or Irish, so he swallowed the *a* and the *r* came out long and burred: "Don't be sca*rr*ed."

Finally, I forced the door open, then slammed it and locked it shut behind me. Fleeing into the kitchen, I snatched the two biggest knives from the knife block and crouched down into a defensive position. I'd expected him to chase me, to try to kick the door down—it was flimsy—but thirty seconds passed, and the basement stayed quiet.

Keeping my knives at the ready, I edged over to my purse and knocked it over with my elbow, so that my phone skittered out across the table.

I could call 911 and I wouldn't even have to explain.

"There is a naked man in my house."

"How did he get there?"

"I don't know."

That would bring them, sirens wailing. If, when they arrived, he had vanished—if I were hallucinating all of this—I could tell them he had escaped through the window. Calling the police was a low-risk solution.

But.

If my sense of the absurd was the first chunk of my brain to recover from shock, and fear the second, curiosity was coming in a slow third.

I had done *magic*.

Sometimes, when people in stories encounter the paranormal, they react with horror as the fabric of reality shreds and they are faced with the dawning recognition that everything they once believed was a lie. As I stared down at my phone, I had that exact feeling, except the opposite: not horror but a giddy, mounting joy. This was what all those books had promised. *I knew it*, I thought. *I knew the world was more interesting than it was pretending to be.*

I put my phone in my back pocket, double-checked that I knew exactly which button to push to make an emergency call, and put on my black leather jacket, partly for warmth but mostly for psychological reinforcement. Knives at the ready, I descended the stairs.

He was still in the middle of the circle, where I'd left him.

If I describe him to you in terms of hair, eye color, shape of face, the effect will be all wrong, because he was the living, breathing incarnation of my deepest desires, not yours. You must imagine your own naked man, and I will tell you only this: he was larger than I would have expected, more fully embodied, and that is only half a dirty joke. There was no prettiness about him, and nothing effeminate. Nothing angelic, either, so if that's what you had started to picture, start again.

I sat down on the top step of the stairs and jabbed my knife at him. "Don't move."

"I can't," he said. "Look." He took a half step forward and then fell back, as though he'd walked into a glass door.

It looked real enough, but for all I knew, the universe had sent me a naked, duplicitous mime. I poked the knife in the air again in warning.

The spell book was lying half-open a step below me, and I swiped for it.

I scanned the page of the spell again, looking for clues, but I saw only the title at the very top, in a blurred, old-fashioned typeface: Heart's Desires.

"Who are you?" I asked.

He opened his mouth, closed it, and wrapped his arms around himself. "I don't know," he said. "I don't remember."

"You don't remember your name? Or you don't remember anything?"

He shook his head. "Anything," he said sadly. "Nothing at all."

"Do you grant wishes?"

"No," he said, and then his mouth curved up into a small, rueful smile. "Not that I know of, at least. I guess we could try."

"I wish for a cat," I said. It just slipped out. I was trying to think of something small and not dangerous, something I'd know immediately had arrived. "No. Stop. I take that back. I don't want a cat, that doesn't count. I want a hundred million dollars. In dollars, not coins. In hundred-dollar bills, I mean. Right here in front of me. Make it appear."

The man looked at me with a slightly amused expression, and when no cat or money appeared, he turned his palms up and grinned. "I'm sorry," he said. "I didn't think it would work."

His smile sent a rush of blood to my face, but I forced myself not to smile back. That was how I responded to beauty, in both women and men: drawn to it at first, and then recoiling. Ruled by my own shallow impulses, then angry at the trick.

"It's a bit cold in here," he said gently. "I wonder if I might have a blanket?"

"I'll think about it," I said.

Upstairs in the kitchen, I paced around, flipping the knife back and forth in my hand. Part of me thought, okay, just give the naked guy a blanket! But another part resisted. This spell was not straightforward. If it wasn't black magic, then it was slippery magic at least. Because if he'd said, "I'm a pediatric oncologist, but I write poetry on the side," all right, maybe, heart's desire. But what good was a handsome amnesiac to me? Also, historically, chalk circles contain devils and demons, not potential boyfriends. Giving him anything might mean bridging the circle and setting him free. If I screwed this up, I might not get another chance to make it right. Before I did anything else, I needed to give the spell book another look.

He'd be fine. After all, the basement wasn't *that* cold.

When I made my way downstairs several hours later, my guest— sitting on the ground, his arms wrapped tightly around his legs—was looking rather pale. There was a damp spot on the far side of the circle, and the basement smelled now not only of burnt hair, but of piss.

Oops.

"I'm sorry I kept you waiting so long," I said. "I've got that blanket for you now. And I'll run upstairs and grab you an empty Gatorade bottle or something in just a bit."

The man looked up at me. "Listen," he said. "I know this must seem strange to you, but I swear, it's even stranger to me. I'll do whatever you ask me to do, and I won't hurt you, I promise, but please, at least try: If you were to smudge this circle up a bit, or wash it off entirely, maybe I could get out, and we could go upstairs and talk this over?"

"Yeah . . ." I said. "I'm not going to do that. I'm sorry, it's just, you could be a demon or something, and I can't take that chance. But I think I've come up with a way to figure it out. Listen, I'm going to hand you the blanket, assuming I can reach through the circle. I want you to take it, but then I want you to leave your hand right there, at the edge, where I can reach it. Don't try anything. Got it?"

"I've got it," he sighed.

I thrust the blanket at him. He took it, keeping his hand outstretched, as I'd told him to do, and I slashed the blade of my knife across the back of his arm.

"What the fuck?" he shouted. As he jumped back, he collided with the other side of the chalk circle, bashing his head against it, and it was dizzying to watch, the way the empty air seemed to catch him as he slid down the invisible barrier. I'd cut him more deeply than I'd meant to, and a thick line of red was welling from his forearm. He stared at me in horror, jamming his back against the far edge of the circle as though if he pushed hard enough he might be able to break through.

"Give me your arm again," I said.

"Hell no," he answered, cradling it with his other hand.

I took a wad of gauze out of my back pocket. "I need your blood," I said. "I'm sorry. I just need to test something. Once I do, I'll let you out right away, I promise."

He actually *snarled* at me. "Get the fuck away from me, you crazy bitch," he said.

The next morning, I came downstairs with a tray laden with every delicious thing the coffee shop next door had on offer: a steaming mug of French roast coffee, thick with cream and sugar; a buttery, flaky croissant; a yogurt parfait jammed full of red berries; a sliced onion bagel slathered with cream cheese and draped with slabs of bright pink lox. The basement itself stank worse than before, but the aroma of the food cut through it, even so.

I set the tray on the floor, averting my eyes from the worst of the mess in the circle as my guest eyed me with loathing. If I was wrong about how the spell book worked, and the universe *had* been trying to send me my soul mate, I'd blown my chance for sure.

With gritted teeth, he shoved his arm at me. The wound had closed up, black and crusty.

"Give me your other arm," I said, taking the knife out again. He glared at me, his lip curled up, and didn't move.

I know, I know, but listen: I'd read it wrong. Heart's Desires, printed at the top of the page; not the name of the spell, but the name of the book. That first spell was nameless, like the man I'd summoned. But the next spell, Wealth, contained, in its long list of ingredients, along with silver and juniper, green candles and rosemary, not blood, but heart's blood, written in that same blurry font. I'd tested the spell myself the night before, pricking another small hole in my thumb, and nothing had happened. It was his blood I needed. I had to take it from him.

I pointed at the food, still well outside his reach. "I'll wait as long as it takes," I said.

I did the spell in the basement, while the man in the circle gobbled his breakfast. No wads of bills miraculously appeared. I was about to call the police and ask them to come arrest the crazy squatter who'd broken into my house when my phone rang with a call from an unknown number.

A *laughing heir* is what you're called when the relative who dies and leaves you everything is so distant you don't know them well enough to mourn.

I gave him a pillow to go with the blanket, a pair of shorts, one of those little camping latrines, as much water and good food as he wanted, as long as he cooperated. "Please, don't," he said when I came back, but what would you have done?

After a week, he tried to wrestle the knife away from me, drag me back to the circle with him, but he was a day too late: I'd already done the spell for *strength*.

I swear, I treated him as well as I could. I stopped cutting up his arms; I drew the knife as lightly as possible across his back and bandaged him up afterward. They healed reasonably well, especially given the dampness of the basement: no more ugly, crusty wounds, just a web of thin pink lines, fading prettily to silver.

It wasn't easy, even after weeks had gone by. No one had ever been afraid of me before, and every time he flinched at the sight of me, I felt as though my heart had gotten caught on a nail.

Only when I'd finished the third spell, *intelligence*, could I articulate my defense. Nameless, history-less, a body tailored precisely to my lust . . . even his lilting accent had come from somewhere deep in my dreams. I hadn't just called him but *created* him. Therefore, since I'd gathered him together out of herbs and blood and magic and desire, he wasn't quite real. He was another part of the book, like the spells themselves, or the lists of ingredients that prefaced them. Not a person, not really, but an idea, brought into being by the play of my mind and the words on the page.

Intelligence was a good gift. I should have conjured it first, because I slept a whole lot better after that.

"You look different," he said to me one morning, and it was true. Sometimes, it took a few hours or days for a spell to unravel its thin skein of logic, winding its way toward my inheritance, or my astonishingly rapid promotion to CEO. But other times, I just woke up different: that's how it had been with *strength* and *intelligence* and now *beauty*.

"Yes," I said. Given that I had myself fairly well convinced of his fundamental unreality, it came as a surprise, how much I enjoyed the look he gave me then—desired it, desired him. Now that I had my own beauty, my own set of tricks, I could let down my guard a bit.

I started to spend more and more time in the basement. He didn't say much back, but at least he listened. We were both lonely. I couldn't talk to anyone else about all the astonishing things that had begun to happen to me, and after long days alone in that cramped, dark little circle, he couldn't help but crave my company. Or he did a good job pretending he did.

One night, late, more than a little drunk, I promised him that when I was finished, when the book was done and there were no more spells to cast, I'd let him out of the circle and share it all with him. *After all*, I slurred, *it's as much yours as mine.* I wasn't naive—I knew I could never trust him. But he was so lovely I couldn't help but want him, and I was now in the habit of getting what I wanted. Of course, I knew he wouldn't be able to forgive me. Not without my help. I'd tried to avoid looking too closely at the upcoming spells—it felt strangely disrespectful, like skipping ahead to the last page of a book—but I knew the title of the last one was *love*.

And then a new ingredient appeared on the list.

By then, we'd established a kind of equilibrium, so when I came down-stairs carrying the knife, he offered his back to me. I looked at him and felt sick. His once-perfect muscles had softened into loose, unhealthy flesh; his skin was pasty white from days spent crouching in the dark. I saw how, despite the care I'd taken, the newest cuts were still raw, weeping through the bandages, and the way each of the knobby bones of his spine cast its own distinct shadow. I felt the stinging guilt of it, and I thought about stopping, scuffing over the circle, and setting him free. I had never desired him more than I did then, broken and ugly and need-ing me. Besides: Given everything I already possessed—wealth, success, luck, intelligence, strength, beauty—what more could *power* offer me?

I spun the knifepoint in my palm, torn. We were only halfway through the book.

"I'm sorry," I said, still spinning the knife, spinning until my hand burned and bled. "We have to do something different today."

One spell, then another, then another. Every night, the tears became harder and harder to wring out of him. I screamed, I begged and pleaded, I cried myself. I even said, in a moment of weakness: *Don't you realize I'm doing this for us?* But I also became creative, and not only with the knife. He cried from pain, he cried from fear, he cried from loneliness, he cried from exhaustion and confusion. And he cried for me. Some nights, I crept into the circle with him and held him as he wept, and I whispered to him about how it would be when we were together at last, when all of this was done.

A year went by. He cried, I collected every salty drop, and the world cracked open like an egg at my feet. I didn't just have everything I wanted, or thought I wanted, or had imagined wanting; I had every-thing that could be wanted. I invented new needs just to satisfy them.

On the day I reached the last page of the book, I gathered up all the other ingredients and carried them down to the basement: herbs from the farmer's market, trinkets from the dollar store.

He was curled on the ground, unmoving, pale and still, and when I saw him, I let out a little cry. His eyes fluttered open.

"Shhhhhhh," I said, and smiled. I reached into the circle and stroked his arm. No place on his body was unmarked by a crisscrossing of silver shining scars. I wondered if they'd all be erased by this last spell, if he'd come to me fresh-skinned, as good as new.

"My love, my love," I crooned.

He hadn't formed coherent words in months, but he groaned and twitched, and I gently squeezed his shoulder, stroked what was left of his hair.

I flipped open the book to the last page, folding it backward. We'd burn the book together, he and I, once the spells were done. My love brought back to me, reborn and whole.

Except—wait.

No. Oh, no.

Before my eyes, the spell blurred, and changed. Demanded something else from me. From him. I could have cried, but instead, I laughed. I laughed and laughed and laughed. It always turns out this way, doesn't it? You can't have everything your heart desires, because what would be the moral in that?

I stared back at the spell, willing it to rearrange itself, but it did not.

So I entered the circle and dragged him out. I remembered, a year ago, screaming and scrambling away from him. How tall and intimidating he'd been. Now I had *strength*, and he weighed next to nothing. I unfolded his limbs, peeled off his tattered shirt. I took my knife, straddled his chest. I bent down to kiss his dried, cracked lips and placed the tip of my blade at his breastbone. I would find some other love, my own heart's true desire. The promise was right there in the book.

"Don't be scared," I whispered.

heart's blood
heart's tears
heart

# THE MATCHBOX SIGN

This, before anything—

Laura, studying in a bar in Red Hook in the middle of the day. A stack of library books at her elbow, a pencil stabbed through the tangled black bun of her hair. Dusty jeans, a ragged sweater, and a dark red lipstick that seems to David, who is watching her from across the room, both seductive and completely out of place. She yanks the pencil out to underline a page and, in doing so, knocks her beer over with her elbow; in saving the books, she allows herself to be drenched from knee to thigh. That night, as David rubs traces of it off his chin, Laura will tell him that the lipstick is a strategy: put on red lipstick as soon as you get up in the morning, she'll say, and no matter how unkempt you are otherwise—stained clothes, leftover eyeliner, greasy hair—people will think you're glamorous instead of slovenly. But the truth is that Laura is both glamorous and slovenly; her slovenliness is glamour; there is no contradiction there. And, David thinks, the decision to combat grime with lipstick is surely a fashion philosophy safely adopted only by the young and very beautiful; the kind of effortlessly luminous girl on whom even dirt and ugly clothes can serve as a kind of boast: *see, not even this can diminish me.*

Six months in, even though they say I love you, do ordinary couple things like complain about their friends and squabble about what time to go to brunch, there remains a part of David that expects Laura to look up at him one day, startled, and say: *Wait, this is a joke, right? Who the fuck are you?*

Then, one evening, she arrives an hour late to dinner. Instead of announcing the breakup he always suspects is imminent, she declares that she has quit her grad program; she wants him to take that job offer he's been wavering on, so that they can move across the country, "try out California," start afresh.

Does David want to quit his job and move to California? Laura's sudden passion for this new life she has imagined for them is so dazzling that he genuinely cannot tell. But that night, Laura is brushing her teeth with the same reckless energy she brings to everything she does, and when she spits into the sink, the white foam is shot through with stringy gobs of red. She bends toward the mirror and grimaces at her reflection, fascinated, her teeth bared in a bloodstained snarl. In the wake of what comes after, David will return to this memory, as a kind of omen: Laura, rapt before a mirror, marveling at the sight of her own blood.

A year later, Laura accosts David as soon as he walks in the door.

"Look at this," she demands, before he even has a chance to put his briefcase down. "Look at my arm. I have a bite."

David takes her wrist gingerly in one hand, and she presents the soft, speckled underside of her arm for his inspection. "Oh, shit," he says. "What is this? Bedbugs?" Rumors of bedbug infestations have run rampant throughout their San Francisco neighborhood, though it seems impossible that any such shy, night-loving creatures could survive for long in their gleaming apartment of steel and glass.

"No," Laura says. "Bedbugs are small and red and come in clusters. This isn't bedbugs."

Making a claim about the bite requires him to look closer at her arm than he is fully comfortable with—just thinking about itching makes him want to scratch—but he can see a fat, white welt, two inches across, nestled inside her elbow. It's crisscrossed with pink lines from where she's been working at it. Too big for a mosquito bite. "A spider bite, maybe?" he asks.

"Maybe . . ."

"Anyway, don't touch it." This advice is as much for his benefit as hers: he hates that sound, nail on skin. It reminds him of the nauseating squish of gum chewing, or a nasal hack in the back of the throat.

Laura flops back on the couch, stretching her arm as far away from her as she can, as though to distance herself from temptation. David knows her resolve will last all of five minutes unless he helps her out.

As he scoops calamine lotion onto her arm, massaging it into her skin, he asks, "How was your day off?"

She says, "Itchy. Otherwise uneventful."

"Did you get a chance to . . ."

They've been dancing around this subject for what feels like forever. Laura, who struggled to find work when they first came to California, is now furiously dissatisfied with her job as an assistant to a despotic local gallery owner—but she also (or so it seems to David) cannot resist the gallery's swirl of drama and complaint. She hates it when David hints she might be happier elsewhere, and accuses him of nagging whenever he suggests she look for other work.

True to form, she does not even allow him to finish his sentence.

She snatches her arm away from him, spattering an arc of pink lotion across the couch.

"You really can't stop picking on me, can you?" she says. "You just can't leave me alone."

Three days. Three more bites. Laura grows even more irritable, sensitive to even the slightest provocation. When the third bite appears on her face, popping from the hard curve of her cheekbone, she scratches at it so much that her eye swells shut.

"You should see a doctor," David tells her over breakfast on Friday morning, unable to look directly at her. Her swollen eye makes it seem like she's winking at him.

"Can't," she says. "Deductible."

"Laur. Come on."

"There's a free clinic on Langford Street. I've got an appointment on Monday. So."

A free clinic, when the last time they went out to dinner, they spent two hundred dollars on the wine alone. The force of Laura's self-punishment can be a visceral shock to witness; it's like watching her willfully slam her fingers in a door. But he refuses to rise to her provocation and counters instead: "If I can get the afternoon off, want me to come with?"

She offers him a brilliant smile. "David. That's so sweet of you. Sure."

Only after spending a full forty-eight hours at home with Laura over the weekend does David realize how completely she has given herself over to the war against her skin. The number of bites has tripled overnight; her entire day is built around her attempts to soothe the relentless itching and trying not to scratch. A soak in a baking soda

bath in the morning is followed by a basil and aloe rub. She obses-
sively trims her fingernails, washes and rewashes the sheets, carefully
applies bandages that she immediately removes. The rest of her time
is spent on internet searches, the frantic rephrasing of keywords: *skin
lump bite itch*; *itchy bite skin help*; *bites arms stomach face*, along with the
close analysis of a succession of awful, cringe-inducing images and
the deep excavation of message boards filled with fellow sufferers:
thousands of endless, plaintive, fruitless threads.

David crawls through the apartment on his hands and knees, looking for culprits—flies or larvae, fleas or mites—but he comes up empty-
handed. Ten minutes of his own internet research offers up so many
possibilities that he concludes such searches are worse than useless; itching is a symptom so common that it stymies diagnosis. "I really think
you should consult someone more qualified than WebMD," he tells her.

Laura digs her fingernail under the welt on her arm, which is now
a glistening, cratered circle, ringed with yellow like a cigarette burn.
"Do me a favor," she says as she scratches. "Stop trying to help, okay?
You're only making things worse."

On Sunday night, he wakes to an empty space in the bed beside
him. He walks out to the living room and finds her on the couch,
surrounded by crumpled tissues, each one stained with a little red
blossom of blood. "I can't sleep," she whimpers. "It's like something
is *crawling* in there, under my skin."

David has never seen her so undone. He presses his lips to the part
in her hair, tucks a blanket around her shoulders, and makes her a pot
of tea, and they stay awake together until the sun rises, and then he
helps her wash and dress.

The clinic waiting room is crowded with sick people, and the air itself
feels oily, laden with disease. They wait more than an hour past the

scheduled time of Laura's appointment, and when the nurse finally calls her name, Laura lifts her chin and insists on going in alone.

She emerges less than fifteen minutes later, carrying a thin sheet of yellow paper, a disbelieving look on her face. "She recommended non-prescription *antihistamines*," she says, not even slowing down as she passes him on the way to the exit. "She told me not to *scratch*."

"She didn't have any idea what might be causing it?"

"She didn't have any fucking clue."

Briefly, they are joined in their shared indignation, but soon enough that temporary alliance falls apart. Another itchy spot has appeared on the top of Laura's head, and she has scratched away a tiny bald patch the size of a quarter. The skin beneath it is thick and scaly, lined with dandruff. "Are you sure you don't have any bites?" she asks him. "Even small ones? It doesn't make any sense. We share everything. Why would they go after me and not you?"

A thousand times over the past week, he felt a phantom itch start to crawl across his skin, but he always rubbed it with a flat finger instead of scratching, and it vanished back into the ghostly realm from which it came.

"I don't know," he said. "I'm sorry, hon."

"Why would you be sorry?" she snaps. "How is this your fault?"

"It's just—I want you to know that we're in this together."

"Oh, sure," she says, blowing her nose into a bloodstained tissue. "I know."

David goes to work as usual on Tuesday, losing hours to the same Google searches that he'd decided two days earlier were a waste of time. He returns home to find Laura examining her arm with a magnifying glass, using a Q-tip to dig deep into the little wound. She barely glances up at him, so intent is she on her hunt. "There's something *there*. I can see it. It's like this . . . little . . . white . . . smudge."

He stands over her, horrified. "What are you doing?"

She pushes the Q-tip into the welt, and the blood foams up around it. She lifts the cotton tip in triumph. "There!" she cries. "You see?"

On the very tip of the blood-soaked cotton puff, he thinks he can maybe make out a very tiny, pale, and glistening dot. Squinting, he tries to make out the shape: A bug? An egg? A bit of fuzz?

Laura peers at the Q-tip. "Oh, my God. It's still *moving*. You know what? I read about these. They're called botflies. They lay eggs in you, if you have like a small cut or a burn I think, and then the eggs turn into larvae that burrow up under your skin. Or, actually, it could be these worms, that you can pick up from swimming in contaminated water . . . anyway, it's some kind of parasite. That's why you're fine, why we couldn't find anything. It wasn't hiding in the apartment. It was hiding in me, all along."

"That's disgusting."

"I know!" she says, but she doesn't sound disgusted, she sounds relieved. David can understand why—at last, she's found some kind of answer—but he cannot share in her relief, because even through the magnifying glass, he can see nothing but a little white dot.

Laura digs out four more of the mysterious specimens, saving them in a small Ziploc baggie that she keeps in the refrigerator beside the orange juice. Still adamant that she cannot afford a visit to the doctor, she returns from the grocery store carrying a smelly assortment of pseudomedicinal ingredients: coconut oil, garlic, apple cider vinegar. She measures out dosages of this home remedy in careful teaspoons, refusing to eat or drink anything else. Parasites feed on sugar, she tells David. This regimen is meant to starve them out.

David believes in none of this, neither the diagnosis nor the cure—but at least her eyes are brighter, she's a little more cheerful, and the rawest of the scratch marks have begun to fade. They even manage to have a handful of short, calm conversations about something other than her skin. Perhaps, he thinks, the episode will pass without him ever understanding it, a little eddy of unhappiness in an already difficult time.

But then, he wakes up to the sound of scratching. He reaches over to bat her hand away from her face, and his fingers come back slippery and dripping. He turns on the light and recoils; in her sleep, Laura has torn open the scab beneath her eye, and the left side of her face is covered by a slick red mask of blood.

The fight that follows lasts hours; when the sun rises in the middle of it, David calls in sick to work. Laura screams for so long she loses her voice. David punches a wall.

The fight begins, of all things, with a spreadsheet. David made it when they first moved to San Francisco. It's titled *David and Laura Live Together*, and contains all their shared expenses: rent, and car, and food, and travel. They divide those costs each month, in proportion to their income. David, an engineer, makes more money than Laura, who's still technically a temp. Therefore, Laura pays 18 percent of their shared expenses while he contributes the remaining 82 percent.

As he mops the mess off her face, David says, "You need to go to the doctor."

"I can't afford one."

"Well, we can put it on the spreadsheet," David says.

Laura rolls her eyes.

"What?"

"Nothing, I just get so sick of this sometimes."

"I'm sorry, I was trying to help. Can you explain what I did wrong?"

"Let me ask you something," says Laura. "When I die, are you going to put eighty-two percent of my funeral expenses on your spreadsheet and send a bill for the rest to my heirs?"

David says: "You're literally covered in blood and still you'd rather attack me than ask for help!"

And then Laura says, "You know what, David?" and off they go.

"People who love each other take care of each other," Laura shrieks as the fight rises to its peak. "They don't keep track of every single dollar they spend on each other on a fucking *spreadsheet*. That's not how it's supposed to work!"

"So what?" David shouts back. "You want me to pay for everything so you can keep on working at your shitty job, which you hate?"

"Is that what our life looks like to you? No wonder you resent me so much, if that's how you feel!"

"I don't feel any way! I just think it's not too much to ask you to contribute something to—"

"Oh sure. You don't feel any way. That is very evenhanded of you, David, thanks."

"Of course I feel, I just—"

"The problem with you," Laura says, "is that you're not invested in this relationship, not really. You're always holding back, you—"

"Oh. Come *on*. I'm invested—"

"Yeah, you're invested! You've invested exactly eighty-two percent. How could I forget? You pay, and keep track of every cent."

"I'm not supposed to keep track of my money?"

She shakes her head furiously, as though it might help fling the words out of her mouth. "That's not what it's about. It's about—about knowing how to love a person!"

The words hang in the air, until David echoes her: "You're telling me I don't know how to *love a person*?"

"No," Laura says, setting her chin stubbornly, like a child. "You don't."

That's when it happens, the little moment of grace that can descend, all of a sudden, to signal the end of a fight. Her frown wobbles a little. She sees she's being ridiculous. And he sees her see.

"That's funny," he says, in a quieter voice. "Because I was definitely under the impression that I'd been loving you all this time."

"Well," she says, sliding almost imperceptibly into performance. "You've been doing a bad job of it."

"Really?"

"Mostly. Yeah."

"Even on your birthday?"

"On my birthday, I guess you did okay."

"So what am I supposed to do? Tell me. I'm genuinely asking."

"You're not supposed to *do* anything. You're supposed to say: 'Laura. I love you. It's going to be okay.'"

"Laura," he says, taking her hands in his. "I love you. It's going to be okay."

As Laura naps fitfully on the couch, David makes an appointment with his PCP. He tells the secretary it's an emergency, and she manages to fit them in that afternoon. When Laura wakes up, he tells her he's made an appointment. Before she can object, he says, "Please, just let me do this, all right?"

The doctor is an elderly man with smoky puffs of hair protruding from each ear, and when David wraps one arm around Laura and asks if he can accompany them to the exam room, the doctor does not object.

Dr. Lansing clucks with concern over Laura's torn-up cheek, and asks her to show him each of her welts in turn. She displays them one by one, and he asks gentle, prodding questions that she answers as best she can. When she finishes, she reaches into her purse for her little plastic baggie, and tells him her theory about the botflies, and about the evidence she's found.

Something strange happens then: the doctor's face goes empty; it's as if his curiosity has drained right out. He accepts the baggie, giving it only a cursory inspection, and then sets it on the table, crumpling it up.

"Aside from the itching, how have you been feeling?" Dr. Lansing asks.

Laura shrugs, and says, "All right."

David stays quiet in the face of this obvious untruth. Dr. Lansing pushes: "How have the past few months been for you, emotionally?"

Laura shrugs again. "Fine, I guess."

"How have you been sleeping?"

"I can't really sleep, because I'm scratching all the time," Laura says, at the same time that David says, "Laur! Come on!"

Laura and Dr. Lansing turn toward him, startled, and despite the warning glance that Laura gives him, David pushes on. "I mean, I'm not trying to—the itching has been bad, I know. But don't you remember, honey, you were having trouble sleeping even before that, because of the stress at work, you said—and I mean, am I wrong in saying that, since the move, things have been pretty hard?"

He keeps waiting for Laura to pick up the thread of the story from him, but when she doesn't, he tells Dr. Lansing everything, recounting it with as much messy desperation as if it is his own story, and part of him feels as though it is. As he finishes, he sees Laura looking utterly betrayed.

Only then does he realize the full impact of what he's done: in trying to help, he's exposed all her weaknesses without asking her permission; used her secrets to prove to an outsider that her pain is all in her head.

The doctor says, "Laura, what I'd like to do, if you'll allow me, is to write a prescription that might help treat the underlying cause of some of your distress. It sounds like you've been under a great deal of pressure these past few months, and I think you may be surprised, once your mood improves, how quickly the issues with your skin will follow suit."

Scrambling to make up for his error, David says: "But what about the actual itching? Do you have anything for that? Because if not, a referral to a dermatologist might be in order." He turns to Laura: "Don't you think?"

But Laura looks exhausted, all the fight gone out of her. Her wounded face is dull and blank with pain. She says, "If you think mood medication will help, I'm willing to try it. I'll try anything you say."

The doctor writes the prescription, and David, stunned, follows Laura out of the office. Guilt floods him. He says, "Honey. Wait right here?" and rushes back into the exam room, where Dr. Lansing is finishing up his notes.

"David?"

"I'm sorry—I just. Listen. I feel like I gave you the wrong impression. Laura isn't crazy. She's been stressed out lately, yeah, but she's had good reasons—the job, the move. I maybe haven't been the most supportive. And I think—I think if she says the itching is real, we should trust her. That's all I'm saying. That's all."

Dr. Lansing rubs his hand across his deeply wrinkled forehead. "I understand your concerns," he says. "I do. But let me ask you something." He picks Laura's plastic baggie off the exam table, and passes it to David. "What do you think this is?"

David stares down at the crumpled bag. "It's the . . . stuff . . . she found. Where she was scratching."

"But what exactly do you think is in there?"

"Eggs, I guess? Or larvae? It's too small for me to see. But that's why she came in for tests!"

"Too small for you to see," the doctor echoes. "But not for Laura. Laura thinks she sees something. You're uncertain, but Laura thinks she knows."

David stays silent. He knows where the doctor is headed, and he doesn't want to accompany him there. Dr. Lansing continues, "This isn't just stress. But it isn't a parasite, either. It's a textbook example of what's called a matchbox sign. From the days when patients would come in with empty matchboxes, offering them up as evidence of the bugs living under their skin. Now people use plastic bags, or Tupperware. Or take pictures on their phones. But the stuff inside's the same. Bits of dead skin. Dirt and lint. All of it nearly too small to see, except by a person whose mind is turning on her body, tearing it up and scavenging it for proof of something that's not there."

David crushes the bag in his fist. This sudden, sly reversal of meaning seems desperately unfair: that Laura should have spent so much effort trying to gather proof of what is happening to her, only to have that very effort taken as evidence that she is losing her mind.

"Dr. Lansing," David says. "If this were me. If I'd come to you complaining of an itch. Would you be so quick to dismiss it then?"

The doctor's mouth jabs downward in a frown. "Son, that's what I'm trying to tell you. I'm not dismissing it. The bugs may be imaginary, but Laura's suffering is real. Delusional parasitosis can be a symptom of depression, but it can also be an early sign of psychosis—and it's very difficult to treat, precisely because patients so rarely want to accept the help that's offered them. Right now, Laura is willing to get the treatment she needs. If you love her, don't get in the way of that. Please."

And so, Laura begins a course of medication, antidepressants mixed in with what the psychiatrist she's referred to calls one of the "milder" antipsychotics. Like the fasting regimen, in some ways, it seems to help. She finally gets some rest, although she begins sleeping eight hours a night, then nine, then ten, and adding on long naps in the afternoon. David often comes home from work to find her on that lotion-stained couch. She gains weight, and her beautiful dark hair thins. But she is no longer scratching the way she once was, and the wound on her face begins to close. The hives on her body do keep rising—despite himself, David continues to think of them as bites—but she resists the urge to dig at them, and after a day or so, they deflate and fade. David tells himself that it's enough, she's healing, but every so often, he looks at the dull-eyed, slow-moving woman on the couch, and almost hates her for stealing the person he loved away.

They sink into a kind of stasis, and David is forced to confront the possibility that this is the new normal, as good as things will ever be. Late at night, as Laura sleeps, David finds himself returning to the idea of a parasite, one more corporeal than unhappiness. It is true, after all, that Laura seems not just depressed, but drained of something fundamental. What if she really is hosting some kind of exotic infestation, and because of David's poorly timed outburst, the doctor wrongly consigned her to the realm of the mentally ill, drugging her into a mute endurance of her pain?

For all that the possibility damns him, once he latches on to it,

David cannot let it go. He loves Laura, the real Laura, that electric disaster whom he first saw spilling beer all over herself at the bar. But this Laura—he can't remember when this Laura last wore red lipstick. This Laura grooms herself very carefully, so as not to let her inner disorder show through.

And so he sits Laura down one morning. Brings her favorite blanket, makes her tea. When he asks her how she's feeling, she says the same thing she always does: "I'm okay." But the whites of her eyes are an eggy, unhealthy yellow, and there's a rim of red around her nostrils, like they've been singed.

"I've been thinking," he says, settling himself on the couch beside her. "I'm worried about you. And I'm wondering if we gave up too quickly on the idea that there was something really wrong with you. I mean, with your skin."

She ponders the bottom of her teacup and says, slowly, "I wonder sometimes, too."

"I know the Depakote is helping. But maybe there's something else."

"Maybe. I guess."

"It couldn't hurt, could it, to get a second opinion?"

"Like, another psychiatrist?"

"I was thinking a dermatologist. A good one." He opens a folder, shows her a carefully arranged stack of paper: articles, from peer-reviewed journals, that he printed out at work. "There's a lot of evidence that real—I mean, physically real—skin diseases get misdiagnosed as psychiatric problems all the time. Especially in women. Dr. Lansing is *old*. His generation, they call everything psychosomatic: fibromyalgia, chronic fatigue. If we want real answers, we need to see good doctors. Not just good. The best."

"That sounds expensive," she says.

"Laura. I don't care."

Her eyes flicker with an unexpected light, and her mouth twists in a familiar smile. "We could put it on the spreadsheet."

"*Fuck* the spreadsheet," he says. "Laura. I love you. I'll take care of you. It's going to be okay."

They drive with the windows down to the new doctor David has found, cool wind whipping past them as they review their plan. They've decided not to bring the baggie of evidence, which still lives in the refrigerator, untouched, and to avoid talking about the meds she's on unless directly asked. They want to go in clean, free of the suspicion they inadvertently triggered when Laura handed over the baggie, when David brought up her stress. Instead, she will start fresh: I'm otherwise healthy. I itch.

The new dermatologist's office is spacious, painted in pastels, and smells reassuringly clean. Though David volunteers to go with them, the doctor, more professional than Dr. Lansing, asks to see Laura alone. Twenty minutes stretches into thirty, forty-five, and when Laura emerges, David jumps out of his chair.

"What did she say?"

"She says yeah, hives, stress, et cetera. She pushed me about medications, I told her about the Depakote. I shouldn't have. You were right, I could see her mind change. Like, instantly. She offered me a chemical peel for the scar."

David shakes his head in disappointment, but now Laura is the one to comfort him. "We knew this would be hard. This is just a start."

It's true. They did; it is. They've connected online with a whole network of sufferers of difficult-to-diagnose diseases, supporters who've given them a list of sympathetic doctors twelve pages long. They'll find answers, even if it takes a lifetime. David believes it, and he can see in Laura's eyes, and in her bright, lipsticked smile, that she believes it, too.

As many times as he's imagined this moment, he's never pictured it happening here: the drab parking lot of a doctor's office, the sky gray with clouds that are flying quickly overhead. And yet once the words begin rising in him, he cannot stop them and has no wish to:

"Laura," he says. "Will you marry me?"

They wed a week later, at the courthouse. They tell no one—not their parents, not their San Francisco acquaintances, not their New York friends. Laura buys a new dress, because none of her old ones fit her, and she finds a pretty vintage hat that she decorates with a little snippet of veil. They ask another eloping couple to serve as witnesses, and pose for a handful of photos taken by strangers. Laura looks a little sad when she sees the pictures, and David can guess why: these pictures will never end up on a mantelpiece, cooed over by admiring grandchildren; in them, Laura is shockingly pale, the garish scar on her cheek clearly visible beneath the veil. But they can do it again, do it better next time. That's the point: they have infinite chances, now, to figure out how to love each other. They have their whole lives to get it right.

The night of the wedding, David is lying next to Laura when a shaft of moonlight falls across her arm. The original bite, the one that started it all, has long ago healed into a glossy ridge of scar. It's hard to believe that something so small could have caused so much damage—a bullet would have scarcely left more pain in its wake.

An inch above the scar, a new welt has formed in a soft puff of flesh, and David runs his finger over it. The welt feels warm, feverish almost, although the rest of Laura's skin is chilled. As he strokes it, he feels it throb suddenly beneath his touch: an eyelid's flicker, a watch's *tickticktick*.

David snatches his hand back, rubbing his fingers together to clear them of the lively, unnerving sensation. He wants to think he imagined it, except that his eyes continue to feed him evidence: the drum-taut skin over the welt is deformed and trembling, as though something inside is beating against it, trying to fight its way out.

"Laura," he whispers. "Laura, wake up." But she is deep in some drugged dream and cannot be woken. He squints into the darkness as the skin on her arm ripples like an unquiet sea. And then, before his eyes, the circle of flesh swells, and a dark pinprick appears at its center. A translucent bubble of blood rises slowly from the hole, and bursts in a spatter of red, as the parasite that has fed on Laura all these months pierces through her flesh and wriggles free.

David grabs for it. He clenches it in his fist and pulls, and it unravels like a living string. He drags it from her skin and casts it, damp and twitching, on the sheets between them: this impossible, this unbelievable thing.

The parasite slaps wetly on the bed, a six-inch-long tube of knobbed white flesh, lined with a thousand shivering legs that wave like seaweed in the unfamiliar air. This is proof too big for a matchbox, too strong for a plastic bag; they will return to the doctor tomorrow with this unequivocal evidence trapped in a thick glass jar. She was right all along, and he was right to believe in her; he'd come close, so close, to losing everything.

They are safe now. He will no longer be the only one who believes her. Laura's body may still teem with a thousand swarming hatchlings, but their mother is dying and tomorrow, all of medical science will be on Laura's side, helping her fight the infestation until her blood is her own again, until the day when she is once again light and free and clean.

The parasite twists itself in one last, violent spasm, and as David peers at it, the worm rears up, blind and hungry, and one of its legs brushes against his face. He clutches at it, but he is too late: it hooks into him and plunges, forcing itself through the tender spot between eye and bone in a blinding white explosion of pain.

David can feel its thousand prickling legs dancing along the inside of his cheek, scratching at his skull, stroking and teasing at the edges of his brain. Then the sensation dims and vanishes, leaving him with nothing but an itch at the site of entry, and a puffed welt, as small as a mosquito bite, at the bottom of his eye. Beside him, Laura rolls over, and moans, and scratches in her sleep, and David collapses next to her as the monster that was born beneath his lover's skin pulses through his bloodstream, swimming with unerring instinct toward his heart.

# DEATH WISH

Okay, so this was a while ago, back when I was living in Baltimore and I was really fucking lonely. That's my only excuse, to the extent I even have one: I was unemployed and renting a motel room week-to-week, on the other side of the country from everyone I knew, living off my credit cards and trying to "figure myself out." By which I mean, getting high and drunk all the time and sleeping like eighteen hours out of the twenty-four.

Pretty much the only people I talked to on a regular basis at that point in time were the girls I met on Tinder. I'd be in my room, drinking and watching porn and playing video games, and then it would occur to me that I hadn't spoken to a living person in a week or two, never mind left my room or changed my clothes or eaten something that hadn't come in a box. I'd start swiping, to try and find a girl who could help me feel like a human being for a while. When I did, we'd meet at a bar and talk for an hour, and then the girl would come back to my place to fuck. I never saw any individual girl more than a handful of times. Not on purpose, really. It was just how things played out.

This thing I'm telling you about happened with one of those girls.

She was cute—little, blonde, from the Midwest somewhere I think. I could tell from her profile we didn't have anything in common. Not that it was her fault—I didn't really have anything in common with anyone back then. My divorce was still going through, and I wasn't talking to anyone in my family except for my brother like once every two weeks . . . Look. I knew I wasn't in any state to have a relationship, and I wasn't trying to inflict myself on anybody long-term. I had that much self-awareness at least.

So me and this girl are messaging each other, and I'm telling her a little bit about myself, my circumstances, nothing deep. She seems reasonably into me, so I ask her if she wants to meet up for a drink. She says she doesn't drink, and I say, okay, we can get dessert or something, no worries. And then she says, actually, if it's okay with you, maybe I can just come over?

That level of directness happened sometimes on Tinder. Not often, but it did. I was always down with it, but internally, I'd always be like, wow, that's brave. Because I know I'm not going to rape you and murder you, but how do *you* know that? Obviously, it wasn't something I could actually ask them about. I'd just wonder.

So now this girl is coming over, and I'm rushing around trying to clean the place up, because the room is a sty and I'm the pig that lives in it. I'm showering and shaving and shoving things in the closet, trying to create the impression that I'm the kind of person who changes his underwear on a regular basis, when really, if it wasn't for Tinder, I probably would have worn the same shit-encrusted boxer shorts for so long that I'd have developed a fatal infection.

I'm still doing what I can to make myself marginally less disgusting when someone knocks on my door. Before I open it, I look through the peephole, just to make sure it's her. Who else would it be, right? But I had a kind of paranoiac streak going, no doubt because of all the drugs. There she is: this adorable girl, her hair in a high ponytail like a cheerleader, and she's got on a little pink T-shirt and jeans, and my first thought is, *hell yeah*. Because you never know, when these girls appear in real life, what they're going to look like. You can do some serious magic these days with filters and shit. But the second thing I notice is that she's got a suitcase with her. Not a big one—it's one of those roller bags, the kind you can carry onto a plane. Weird, right?

I open the door, and the first thing I do is make a joke about the suitcase: Wow, how long are you planning on staying? She laughs, and I say, no, seriously, what do you have in there? Makeup or something? She smirks, like she's got a secret, and then she winks at me and says, maybe if you're lucky, you'll find out.

There was always this moment, when I had girls over, when they'd realize I really did live in a motel room, I wasn't just passing through. I always told them beforehand—warned them, really—but sometimes, they couldn't quite believe it until they saw it with their own eyes. Even when I did a decent job cleaning up, I couldn't hide the fact that the circumstances were pretty fucking grim. If they looked seriously shattered, I'd always offer to take them somewhere else, but no one ever took me up on it. I think after the initial shock, they mostly just felt bad for me.

But this girl—if she gives a fuck about my living situation, she doesn't show it. She strolls in the door with her suitcase behind her like a flight attendant, and then she goes over to the bed and hops right on it, like—here we go! She doesn't even take off her goddamned shoes. And I know this is kind of ridiculous, after everything I said before about the state of decrepitude I'm living in, but it pisses me off. We've known each other all of thirty seconds, and here you come in with your suitcase and your dirty-ass shoes on my bed, maybe slow your roll a little, you know? The shoes are fine as far as they go—Keds, maybe?—but they're kind of scuffed up, and there's a brown smear of what I hope to God is mud on the bottom of one of the soles.

Probably, if I'd been in a different mental place, I'd have said something like, Hey, do you mind taking your shoes off before you get on the bed? And it would have been no big deal. But I guess that was the whole problem, at that point, my inability to deal with normal human interaction. I knew I was overreacting—in all likelihood, the comforter had seen way worse. I used to think about it sometimes, when I couldn't fall asleep, how the bedspread would've glowed under a black light, all the streaks of shit and blood and pus and cum that were all over it, and, by extension, all over my skin. Now I'm like, why didn't I just take the bedspread to the dry cleaners, if it bothered me so much? But I didn't. That was the life I was living, then.

Back to this girl. She's on my bed. I offer her a drink before I remember that she doesn't do that. She says, I'd like a drink of water, and I ask her if she wants ice before I realize I don't have any, so she has to settle for lukewarm tap water in a paper cup. Truly, I'm killing it here. But again, she doesn't seem to care. I ask her if she wants to watch a movie, and she says sure, but in this way that's like, *You and I both know there won't be any movie-watching happening tonight.* Which, fair enough. Some girls know what they want, and sometimes what they want is random sex in a motel room with a decent-looking guy they met on the internet. People who exaggerate the differences between what men and women want in bed don't know what they're talking about, in my opinion. Maybe your average woman is a little more conservative than your average guy, but there's always going to be some seriously crazy shit happening out at the far end of the bell curve. That's just statistics, right?

Soon, we're making out, and then we're more than making out, and then I'm making the move to get a condom, and she says, "Wait."

Okay, I think, she doesn't want to have sex, she just wants to hook up. That's pretty common. Honestly I don't even mind it. I'll take an enthusiastic blow job over lukewarm sex any day of the week.

But instead she says, "There's something about me you should know."

I say, "What?"

She says, "The thing about me is, I have really specific tastes about what I like in bed. And the only way I can enjoy myself, sexually, is if you do exactly what I tell you to do, in exactly the way that I like it."

Remember, these are more words in a row than she's said to me in the entire time we've known each other. I'm a little taken aback. But I say, "Okay, sure. No problem. Tell me."

She says, "I want you to agree that you'll respect my wishes, and do what I ask you to do, because it's really important to me."

I say, "I mean, sure, I'll respect you, obviously, but I'm not going to say that I'll do something until I know what it is."

That seems reasonable, right? But she gets a little prickly. I can see it in her face, like she wanted me to agree straightaway, no questions asked. And she was cute and everything, but come on.

In this kind of low, breathy, phone-sex voice, like she's about to suggest the hottest, dirtiest thing ever, she says, "I want us to get in the shower, together. And I want us to be, like, kissing and touching and making out a little. Normal stuff. And then, after a little while— and this is very important—when I'm not expecting it, I want you to punch me in the face as hard as you can. After you've punched me, when I've fallen down, I want you to kick me in the stomach. And then we can have sex."

What would you do in that situation? Seriously, I'm asking you. Because what I do is: I laugh at her. I laugh right in her face. Not because it's funny, but just because—I don't even know why. I laugh and laugh, and when she doesn't laugh, too, I just blink at her, until at last she says, slowly, "That's what I want. Punch me, and kick me, and then, once you do, we can have sex."

In my head, I'm like, okay, this is a crazy person.

Or she is messing with me.

Or it's like a test, and we're on reality television or something.

But I'm trying to be polite, so all I say is, "I'm sorry, I respect your desires and everything, but I'm not really into that."

And she says, "It doesn't matter if you're into it. *I'm* into it. And that's what I need to happen if we're gonna fuck."

It was the most uncomfortable goddamned thing. She's just staring at me, waiting, expecting me to agree to do this thing that obviously I'm not going to do, and I don't know what to say, but she's not giving me any hints, and it seems insane to just be like, well I guess that's it, check ya later, sister. So finally, I say, "Do you mind if we keep making out for a while, and I can think about it?"

She says yes, so that's what we do. The whole time, my brain is just fucking racing. I'm thinking, no, absolutely not, I'm not here to punch some random girl, uh-uh no way. The truth is, she didn't even know what she was asking. She couldn't have. She was a small girl, maybe a hundred pounds if I had to guess, and I'm stronger than I look. If I punched her as hard as I could, there was a legitimate chance she would actually fucking die. Even if it was some kind of setup, like the plan was that afterward she'd threaten to turn me in to the police and blackmail me, or her boyfriend would come in and rescue her and beat me up because that's what *he* gets off on, she still didn't know what she was doing, asking me to punch her that hard.

But of course, because she's cute and we're still making out and I'm into it, eventually my brain starts trying to figure out a way of thinking about it that will make this absurd request seem not quite so completely insane. Maybe she's mistaken about the amount of force she's telling me to use, but other than that, she knows what she wants. Like, there are degrees of punching, and what she wants is to be punched in a way that doesn't *actually* put her life at risk. Maybe getting caught on the phrase *as hard as you can* is just getting tripped up by semantics. The girl wants me to punch her, because that's what gets her going, and if you think about it, it's not *that* much different than a girl wanting to be slapped or spanked or choked, all of which I've done before, with various degrees of enthusiasm and success.

Okay, I'm telling myself, the girl has a kink, and it's a scary one. Who knows where she got it—I mean, I can imagine, and there are a lot of dark possibilities, I don't want to go too far down that path. But for whatever reason, she's got it now, and she can't help it, necessarily—it's like a foot fetishist or even a pedophile—we don't have control over what we want; all we can control is how we act on it. This girl acted on her desires in a perfectly mature and responsible way; she told you about it, right up front, she didn't wait until you'd gone on three dates and were like head over heels for each other; she was straightforward and she gave you a choice. In a way, she's making herself vulnerable to you, asking you to do this thing that a lot of people would judge her for. Yes, she came off as kind of bossy and rigid about it, but the truth is she was honest and open and direct, and in a way, you've got to admire that.

So then I'm at the point where I'm asking myself: *Can* I punch her? Not as hard as I can, but just kind of . . . symbolically? Assuming that afterward she'd be wildly turned on and we'd have amazing sex. Why not, right? But still I'm like—who does this? What kind of a person goes to meet a guy she doesn't know and asks him to punch her as hard as he can? Someone with a death wish, that's who. And even setting aside my own natural aversion to introducing punching into a sexual situation, what am I doing, fucking a girl with a death wish? What does that make me?

The thing is, I have that thought *now*. I wish I could say I didn't have it then: that I was too wrapped up in a depressive haze for it to occur to me. But it *did* occur to me. I thought about it but then I just . . . let it slide by. Like my conscience was a set of brakes that had worn thin. I didn't want to punch this girl, but the situation had its own momentum, and yeah, she was fucked up, but the truth was, all these girls on Tinder who were meeting up with me and banging me in my motel room, they were all fucked up to some degree. Girls with *any* kind of functional self-preservational instincts—they could smell me coming from a mile away. I guess all girls could, in one way or another. Some of them were just drawn to the stink. Because let's be honest, this girl wouldn't have asked some fucking real-estate agent to punch her, or some college kid. She'd recognized me as someone who would give her what she wanted. I'd opened the door and she'd thought, yup, that looks like a guy who might enjoy punching me in the face. To be seen that way—it was unsettling. But what was even more unsettling was that for all I knew, she was right. Maybe that desire was in me, even though I couldn't see it. And maybe by doing what she asked, I could either purge it, or prove it wasn't there.

So I ask her, one last time: "Are you *sure* you want to do this?"

She says, "I'm sure."

I say, "You don't want to just cuddle and watch a movie?"

She giggles, and says, kind of teasing, "What, are you scared or something?"

I'm about to deny it, but then I think, why not just tell the truth? So I say, "Yes, I am, actually."

She puts her hand over my hand, like she's comforting me. "I know it's strange," she says. "I don't mean to freak you out."

"I think I just need a little while to wrap my head around it," I tell her. "I've never punched a girl in the face before."

In fact, I've never punched anyone in the face before, but I'm not saying that; I don't want to sound like an amateur.

She laughs. "No experience necessary!" she says. "I'd be honored to be your first."

Looking at her smiling at me like that, I have this impulse to ask her a million questions, like, how in God's name did you end up like this, and where are you from, and do you have any brothers or sisters, and what do you do for work, and what's the first thing you remember, and what's your favorite color, and oh, by the way, what's in that suitcase that you brought?

But before I can say anything else, she squeezes my hand again. "You don't have anything to worry about," she says. "You'll be great, I promise."

"I'm not really sure what that says about me."

"It means I trust you," she says, and she kisses me on the cheek.

I don't know if that's true, but it's what I need to hear. I say, "Okay. If you're sure it's what you want, then I'll do it."

Her face lights up like a fucking Christmas tree. She kisses me again and jumps off the bed and runs into the shower to check it out. Now, this probably doesn't even bear explaining, but we are not talking about some romantic getaway bathroom with fancy soaps and a rain shower; it's a cruddy little motel stall, with mildew in the tiles and stains on the walls of mysterious provenance. At least part of me was expecting her to see it and change her mind. But nope—she turns on the water and gets right in.

She looks great naked, even in the fluorescent bathroom lights— she's got that little spinner body type that I like a lot—but at the same time, I'm covertly scoping her for bruises, wondering if I'm like the third guy she's asked to punch her this week. She doesn't have any marks on her, though. No cuts or anything. She's a perfectly normal-looking girl.

I get in the shower with her, and we kiss, and she goes down on me a little, but I'm not exactly responding because of the pressure of what's coming. Pretty soon it's clear the blow job isn't happening, so I say, hey, let's just make out, and we do, but after a few minutes she steps away and starts soaping herself, looking over my shoulder like there's something super interesting up there. I figure this is her way of signaling that she's not paying attention and now would be a good time for a punch.

So I punch her. But not really. It's just the lightest, most delicate tap. Like I'm going "boop" on her nose with my fist.

*Please let that be enough*, I'm thinking.

It's not. For a second there's this look on her face of total disdain. She says, "I need you to take this seriously, Ryan. That is *not* as hard as you can. Punch me for real. Okay?"

She starts shampooing her hair, which buys me a little more time, but I can tell that, like, the clock is ticking, and now I have this fear in me, in my body, that I can feel as a weakness in my arms, a tightness in my chest. There's a threshold in between where it's fun, and where it's real; I have to land in a space where it's not enough to truly hurt her, but it *is* enough to satisfy her, and that's a danger-ously small band; the possibility of miscalculation is high. Of course, a small piece of my brain is telling me, dude, you don't need to do this, you don't need to go down this path. But there's another part of me that's thinking about how she apologized for freaking me out, and how I'd promised her that she wasn't that weird for asking. I don't want to take that back. I want to be able to give her what she asked me for, I do.

So then we're in this absurd situation, where she keeps glancing at me more and more sharply, like, come on, dude, just do it, just punch me in the face, and the water is getting cold and she starts to get truly annoyed, but since she has to pretend not to know it's coming for it to work, she keeps endlessly shampooing her hair and sighing, and I'm clenching my fist and yelling at myself, do it, do it, do it—

And I do. I haul back and punch her, for real.

She collapses. As she's falling, she lets out this long, melodramatic "*oooooof*," and when she hits the floor, there's a little runnel of blood trickling from her nose down into the drain. Just a small one. But still.

I go, "Shit! Are you okay?!"

Immediately, I just feel sick. I'm thinking, oh my God, what if she's dead? I'm imagining my arrest, my court date, my mom crying as I'm shuffled off to prison in chains. I'm thinking: I'm going to have to dispose of her body, because no one will ever believe me if I tell them the truth.

I bend down to feel her pulse. She opens her eyes, and, like I'm her idiot partner in a high school play who's forgotten his lines, she hisses, "I'm *fine*, but you're supposed to *kick* me now."

She closes her eyes again, and let me tell you, in that moment, I hated that girl, and I'm pretty sure she hated me, too. I knew exactly what she was thinking: she'd been on the hunt for some badass dude who'd go down with her into whatever dark place she was trapped in, but instead she'd ended up with this lame-ass coward, a guy who's too fucked up to tell her to get lost, but also too scared to do what he said he would do.

I hadn't even thought that much about the kicking before, because I'd been all hung up on the punch, but now it seems even worse, kicking her while she's lying there with her eyes closed, defenseless, all curled up in the fetal position, as if she's trying to protect herself from me. There's a saying about that, even, about how wrong it is to kick someone who's already down. I'm standing over her, in this icy mildewed motel shower, trying to move my leg, and I can't, I can't do it. But I know that until I do, it won't end. Maybe in an alternative universe a version of me is picking her up and wrapping her in a towel and saying, "Honey, I respect you but you deserve better, we both deserve better," or some nonsense like that. But if I lived in that universe she wouldn't be here, I wouldn't live in this motel; at the very least, that version of me would've dry-cleaned his fucking comforter, he would've told her to get her shoes off his bed. That would have been a world that made sense. But in this world, I'm looking down at this girl, and I'm thinking, wow, fuck you, lady, because I knew my life was shit . . . but I didn't quite realize *how* shit until you came along.

In recovery, they talk about what's it like to hit rock bottom, and I want to say that was my bottom, standing over that naked girl and getting ready to kick her in the gut. That combination of responsibility and powerlessness—truly, standing over her, I saw with absolute clarity how I had no one else to blame, how I was the one who'd let my life spin completely out of control. Everything I'd ever done had brought me to that point; all my choices had led me right here, to this.

But if that *had* been my rock bottom, I'd have changed, right? Seeing the light would've done something to me, helped me somehow. But it didn't. It only made me feel worse.

So, finally, I do it. I kick her in the stomach, just like she asked. And that's when I realize why this whole thing had to happen in the shower, because she vomits. This beige oatmeal puke pours out of her mouth and mixes with the water and swirls around my ankles, and at that point my memory kind of fizzes out, like a broken television, but I can tell you it was so much worse than I thought it would be, it was so so so so bad.

Afterward, she barely rinses off. She doesn't even touch the soap, she just gets to the bed and gestures to me, and that little voice in my head is practically *screaming*, it's just like, Ryan, stop stop stop, please, but I don't, I fuck her, right there on that motel comforter, and I'm holding my breath so I can't smell the puke and there's this layer of crusted blood inside her nostrils between her nose and upper lip that's the worst goddamn thing I've ever seen.

I don't know.

When I try to reconstruct the place that I was, at that point in my life, to figure out how I got there, to that punch, to that bed, to that girl—I can't. I can see where some bad decisions led to some other bad decisions, but I can't get all the way there; it's like I imagine a curve, where I'm dropping lower and lower down, and then I'm off the radar screen, invisible, and then, after some time goes by, the line is rising, visible again, and I don't know what happened in between. Because the worst thing wasn't punching her, or fucking her afterward, or getting on my knees in the bathroom, heaving into the toilet, when it was done. It was how I felt after, when it was over, when she was gone, and I was alone.

I never found out what was in that suitcase. Maybe it was sex toys or lingerie. Maybe it was fetish gear. Maybe it was boxing gloves. Maybe it was a bomb: some sicko was like, go to this room and ask a dude to punch you, because if you don't I'll blow you both straight to kingdom come. Maybe it was empty. Maybe she was homeless, and it was everything she owned. She unmatched me on Tinder right after she left—seriously, it happened so quick I think she must've done it in the parking lot—so I'll never know.

She was a girl with a lot of problems, obviously. We both had is-sues, but I can honestly say she was the only person I've ever met who, without question, was as fucked up as me, so I guess we had that in common, at least?

Not too long after all this went down, my brother showed up in Baltimore and ran an intervention on me; my divorce went through, and eventually I got a job and moved out of the city, started going to the occasional meeting, though I could never really commit to the steps. The line of my life didn't begin ticking upward until I made sense to myself again; I could graph my decisions: even when I made bad choices, I could give you reasons for them; I could say, I did $x$ because of $y$.

It's been years, but I still think about her. Jacquelyn, her name was. I wonder about her, about how she ended up like that, about the contents of her fucking suitcase, about what she's doing now. In the end, I always come to the same conclusion, which is: She must be dead, right? The way she talked to me, how carefully she explained what she needed—I wasn't the first person she'd asked to hit her like that. I know I wasn't. And there's a natural outcome to those kind of decisions. Insert $x$, get $y$. You can't keep meeting guys in motel rooms and asking them to punch you without ending up dead sooner or later, can you?

But who knows.

Maybe you can.

# BITER

Ellie was a biter. She bit other kids in preschool, bit her cousins, bit her mom. By the time she was four years old, she was going to a special doctor twice a week to "work on" biting. At the doctor's, Ellie made two dolls bite each other, and then the dolls talked about how biting and being bitten made them feel. ("Ouch," one said. "Sorry," said the other. "I feel sad about that," said the one. "I feel happy," said the other. "But . . . sorry again.") She brainstormed lists of things she could do instead of biting, like raise her hand and ask for help, or take a deep breath and count to ten. At the doctor's suggestion, Ellie's parents put a chart on Ellie's bedroom door, and Ellie's mom put a gold star on it for every day Ellie didn't bite.

But Ellie loved biting, even more than she loved gold stars, and she kept on biting, joyfully and fiercely, until one day, after preschool, pretty Katie Davis pointed at Ellie and whispered loudly to her dad: "That one's Ellie. No one likes her. She *bites* people," and Ellie felt so sick with shame she didn't bite anyone again for more than twenty years.

———

As an adult, though her active biting days were behind her, Ellie still indulged in daydreams in which she stalked her coworkers around the office, biting them. For example, she imagined sneaking into the copy room where Thomas Widdicomb was collating reports, so engrossed in his task that he didn't notice Ellie creeping up behind him on all fours. *Ellie, what on Earth*, Thomas Widdicomb would cry, in the final seconds before Ellie sunk her teeth into his plump and hairy calf.

For while the world had succeeded in shaming Ellie out of biting, it couldn't make her forget the joy of tiptoeing behind Robbie Kettrick while he was standing at the craft table, smugly stacking blocks. Everything is normal, quiet, boring, and then here comes Ellie—*CHOMP!* Now Robbie Kettrick is screaming like a baby and everybody is scrambling and yelling, and Ellie is no longer just a little girl but a wild creature pacing the halls of the preschool, sowing chaos and destruction in her wake.

The difference between children and adults is that adults understand the consequences of their actions, and Ellie, as an adult, understood that if she wanted to pay her rent and keep her health insurance, she could not run around biting people at work. Therefore, for a long time, Ellie did not seriously consider biting her coworkers—not until the office manager died of a heart attack at lunch, in front of everyone, and the temp agency sent Corey Allen to replace him.

Corey Allen! Later, Ellie's coworkers would ask each other: What on Earth had the people at the temp agency been thinking, sending him? Green-eyed, blond-haired, pink-cheeked Corey Allen did not belong in an office environment. Corey Allen, like a faun or a satyr, belonged in a sunlit field surrounded by happy naked nymphs, making love and drinking wine. As Michelle in Accounting put it, Corey Allen gave off the impression that he might, at any second, decide to quit being an office manager and run off to live in a tree. Ellie, who was something of an outcast at work, often walked in on hushed conversations about Corey Allen that presumably centered around how much the other women in the office wanted to sleep with him. Corey Allen was beautiful and fey.

Ellie didn't want to have sex with Corey Allen. Ellie wanted to bite him, hard.

She'd discovered this while watching Corey Allen place glazed donuts on a platter before the Monday morning meeting. When he had finished arranging the donuts, he turned around and, noticing her staring at him, winked. "Why, Ellie, you look hungry," he said with a leer.

Ellie had not been checking out Corey Allen, the way he seemed to be implying; she hadn't even been thinking about the donuts. But suddenly she found herself imagining what it would be like to lock her jaws onto the soft part of Corey Allen's neck. Corey Allen would yelp and sink to his knees, that entitled look wiped right off his face. He'd slap weakly at her and cry, "Oh no, Ellie! Stop! Please! What is going on?" But Ellie wouldn't answer, because her mouth would be too full of Corey Allen's sweet and gamy flesh. Not that it had to be his neck. She wasn't picky about location. She could bite Corey Allen on his hand, or his face. Or his elbow. Or his ass. Each would have a different taste, a different mouthfeel; a different proportion of bone to fat to skin; each would be, in its own way, delectable.

Maybe I *will* bite Corey Allen, Ellie thought after the meeting. Ellie worked in communications, which meant that she spent 90 percent of her time crafting emails that no one ever read. She had a savings account and life insurance, but no lover, no ambition, no close friends. Her entire existence, she sometimes felt, was premised on the idea that pursuing pleasure was less important than avoiding pain. Perhaps the problem with adulthood was that you weighed the consequences of your actions too carefully, in a way that left you with a life you despised. What if Ellie did bite Corey Allen? What if she did? What then?

That night, Ellie changed into her nicest pajamas, lit a candle, and poured herself a glass of Cabernet. Then, she uncapped a pen, opened her favorite notebook, and turned to a fresh page.

Reasons not to bite Corey Allen
1. It is wrong.
2. I could get in trouble.

She nibbled on the tip of her pen, then added two subsidiary points.

Reasons not to bite Corey Allen
1. It is wrong.
2. I could get in trouble.
   a. I could get fired
   b. I could get arrested/fined

Ellie thought: If it meant that I could bite Corey, I would not mind getting fired. For the past year and a half, she'd spent most of her lunch hour, most days, on her phone, swiping through job postings on Monster.com. She was ready for a new position, and felt perfectly well qualified for one. However, finding a new job after quitting your old one was not the same as finding a new job after you'd been fired from your old job for biting. Would it be impossible to get a new job in those circumstances, or merely very difficult? It was hard to know.

Ellie sipped her wine and turned her attention to *b. I could get arrested/fined.* Well, that was certainly a possibility. But the truth was that if a woman bit a man in an office environment, there would be a strong assumption that the man had done something to deserve it. If, for example, she went up to Corey and bit him, in full view of everyone at Monday Morning Meeting, and then later, when they asked her why she'd done it, she answered, "Sexual gratification," then yes, she'd probably be arrested. But if, instead, she bit Corey in private, say, in the copy room, and when they asked her why she'd done it, she said, "He tried to touch me inappropriately," or even, so as not to mar his reputation, "He came up behind me and scared me; I bit him instinctively, I'm so sorry," then people would probably give her the benefit of the doubt. When you got right down to it, as a young white woman without a criminal record, Ellie probably had at least one get-out-of-jail-free card. As long as she spun some semi-reasonable story, she would be believed.

In fact, Ellie thought, as she stretched out her legs and refilled her glass of wine, there was another possibility for how this could all play out. What if she went up to Corey, in private, and bit him, and the experience was so bizarre that he didn't tell anyone about it, because he had trouble believing it himself?

Imagine. It's late in the afternoon, past five. Dark already. The office is empty. Everyone but Corey and Ellie has gone home. Corey is loading paper into the Xerox machine when Ellie enters the room. She stands behind him, inappropriately close. He thinks he knows what is coming. He stiffens, preparing to politely reject her, not because he has standards for workplace propriety, but because he's already hooking up with Rachel in HR. "Ellie . . ." he begins, apologetically, as she grabs his forearm and lifts it to her mouth.

Corey's lovely face contorts first in shock, then pain. "Stop it, Ellie!" he cries out, but no one hears him. The tendons of his arm roll and snap beneath Ellie's jaws. Finally, Corey gathers his wits enough to shove Ellie away. She stumbles backward, lands against the stacks of copy paper, and slides to the ground. Corey stares at her in horror, clutching his bleeding arm. He's waiting for her explanation, but she gives him none. Instead, she stands up calmly, straightens her skirt, and wipes the blood from her mouth before she leaves the room.

What does Corey do? Of course, he could run straight to HR and say, "Ellie bit me!" but after all, it was an office, not a preschool. Everything about the conversation would be ridiculous. "Ellie, did you bite Corey?" they would ask, and Ellie would raise her eyebrows and say, "Uh . . . no? What a weird question." If the HR people tried to push, and said, "Ellie, these are serious allegations," all Ellie would have to say was, "Yeah, seriously insane. Of course I did not bite the office manager and I don't know why he's saying that I did."

Really, the odds were high Corey wouldn't say anything at all. He would stay in the copy room for a while, contemplating the situation, and then the next day, he'd decide that the easiest thing to do would be to pretend it hadn't happened. He'd show up to work in a long-sleeved shirt, to cover the ugly bruise on his arm, the little half-moon where she'd marked him with her teeth. And then part of Corey Allen's brain would be reserved for keeping track of where, exactly, Ellie was. She'd catch him looking at her in meetings, and when they were at office parties together, he'd continually be moving, trying to keep as far as possible from her; in a way, it'd be like they were always dancing, even if he never spoke to her again. Months later, when no one else was watching, she'd grin and snap her jaws at him, and he'd turn ghost-pale, and hurry from the room. He would remember her for the rest of his life; they'd be joined by the glistening strands of his fear.

Later that night, the sweat drying on her body, her legs tangled in the sheets, Ellie forced herself to go back out to the living room and get her notebook. Fantasies were fantasies, but it was important to keep at least one foot in the realm of the real. She got back in bed and opened the notebook, and rewrote her list:

Reasons Not to Bite Corey Allen
1. It is wrong
2. It is wrong
3. It is wrong
4. It is wrong

Ellie took her notebook into work, where she put the list at the bottom of her drawer, and looked at it every time the temptation to bite Corey Allen grew too great. She invented a game, a game called Opportunity. Ellie *wasn't* going to bite Corey, even though she wanted to, and she thought she deserved some credit for that. So whenever she found herself in a situation where she *could* have bitten him, and didn't, she awarded herself a point. She recorded the time and place in her notebook, next to a little star. One point for passing him in an empty stairwell. One point for noticing when he went into a single-occupancy bathroom and didn't immediately lock the door. One point when, just like in her fantasy, she spotted him going into the copy room, by himself, after everyone else had gone home. When she reached ten points, she took herself out for ice cream, and while she ate, she allowed herself to fantasize about biting Corey Allen to her heart's content.

After a few weeks, Ellie noticed something interesting about her Opportunities. If you drew a graph illustrating the number of Opportunities she'd achieved across time, it would have started out low at first, then grown steadily as she started learning Corey Allen's schedule and identifying the prime locations in the office where you could bite someone unobserved. But then, in mid-December, there was a dramatic drop-off: Corey Allen's schedule became unpredictable, and when he entered those prime locations, they were rarely empty. There was some noise in the data, so it took Ellie a little while to realize that the person who was most often in these locations was Michelle from Accounting. Who was married.

Hmmm.

By the time the annual holiday party rolled around, playing Opportunity wasn't very much fun anymore. Ellie didn't want to fantasize about biting Corey Allen; she wanted to bite him, and the fact that she couldn't made her mad. Yes, sometimes you wanted something and couldn't have it. But it was also true that sometimes people knew what they wanted was unethical, but they went ahead and did it anyway. Like, sleeping with a married person: that was wrong, but people did it every day. Right over there, for example, was poor Michelle from Accounting's husband, wearing a Christmas sweater covered in holly berries. Imagine that guy lying awake at night, trying to figure out why his wife had become so distant. Imagine the hurt and shame he'd feel if he went through her text messages and discovered a series of romantic exchanges between his wife and Corey Allen, the very person she'd once described as "a creepy little elf." Surely, the emotional pain Michelle from Accounting's husband would feel under those circumstances would *dwarf* the physical pain from one tiny little bite. Especially if Ellie bit Corey somewhere without that many nerve endings—his back, say, or his upper arm.

Stop it, Ellie, she told herself firmly. Two wrongs don't make a right. Corey Allen is responsible for his own behavior, and you are responsible for yours.

Still, she couldn't help glaring as he mingled flirtatiously, distributing goblets of punch. He really was making some intense eye contact with Rachel from HR. Michelle from Accounting was probably feeling pretty jealous right now. But then, most likely Corey Allen was feeling jealous of Michelle from Accounting's husband, so maybe that was the whole point. It really wasn't nice of Corey Allen to flirt with Rachel like that, just to make Michelle jealous. Corey Allen was pretty much the worst.

Ellie stood around, wondering if Corey Allen would notice her. The dress she was wearing was tight, black velvet, floor-length: sexier than what she usually wore in the office, but possibly also funereal, not quite the thing to attract the attention of a person as playful as Corey Allen. Now Corey Allen was on the far side of the party, chatting up someone Ellie didn't recognize, probably a coworker's wife. Maybe Corey Allen played his own version of Opportunity, awarding himself points for every woman he could make giggle and blush.

Ellie felt overwhelmed with despair, close to suicidal. What was the point of anything? Maybe she should bite Corey Allen and then throw herself off a cliff.

Go home, Ellie, she thought. You're drunk.

She left her emptied glass on the table beside her and headed to the single-occupancy bathroom to splash some water on her face. When she emerged, there he was, alone in the otherwise empty hallway, waiting for her: Corey Allen.

A point to Ellie! Here was a golden Opportunity. Which meant, if she didn't want to do anything she'd regret, she needed to leave.

"Hello, Ellie!" Corey Allen said brightly. "I thought you were leaving! I didn't want to let you escape without saying good-bye!"

"I was just peeing," Ellie said, and tried to brush past him.

Corey Allen threw his head back and laughed, and Ellie imagined sinking her teeth into his Adam's apple like it was a Granny Smith. Goddamnit, Corey Allen, she thought. I'm trying to exert self-control here. Let me pass.

"Wait, Ellie," Corey Allen said, taking hold of her arm. "Do you see that up there? On the ceiling?"

"Huh?" Ellie said, reflexively looking up. And as she did, Corey Allen grabbed her, sealing his lips over hers, and shoving his tongue in her mouth. She tried to push him away, but he was able to restrain her with one hand while using the other to grab hold of her ass. He was remarkably strong for an elf.

When he finally released her, after what felt like an eternity, she fell back, gasping, certain she was going to puke.

"What the fuck, Corey?" she said.

Corey Allen giggled. "I thought I saw mistletoe!" he cried. "Whoops! My mistake!"

That was awful, Ellie thought. Worse than being bitten. Truly grotesque.

But then, she thought, oh right. Here's my chance.

Though she was twenty years out of practice, Ellie's nerve was steady and her aim was true. She opened her mouth like a lamprey and lunged for the mound of his cheekbone, which crunched spectacularly beneath her teeth. The bite was everything she'd dreamed of. Corey shrieked, and flailed, and clawed at her, but she did not let go; instead, she snapped her head back and forth, three times, like a dog inflicting a death shake, and bit off a chunk of his face.

Corey Allen collapsed at her feet, clutching himself and screaming.

Ellie spat a wad of his skin from her mouth, wiping his blood from her lips with the back of her hand.

Oh dear.

She'd gone too far.

He'd be disfigured.

She was going to go to jail.

At least she'd have this memory for the rest of her life. She'd use her hours of imprisonment to sketch loving pictures of Corey Allen's contorted face in the seconds after she bit him, and she'd tape them to the walls of her cell.

From behind her came an accusing voice: "I saw what happened. I saw the whole thing." It was Michelle from Accounting. Before Ellie could say anything, Michelle from Accounting wrapped her in a hug.

"Are you okay?" Michelle asked. "I'm so sorry."

"Huh?" Ellie said.

"That was assault," Michelle said. "He *assaulted* you."

"Oh yeah!" Ellie said, remembering. "He did!"

"He did the same to me. He followed me into the stairwell and grabbed me. More than once. He's a total predator. I came out here to warn you. Thank God you were able to defend yourself. You're such a fighter, Ellie. Are you sure you're okay?"

"I'm okay," said Ellie.

And she was.

Because it turned out that Corey Allen had groped not only Ellie, and not only Michelle, but several other women. The response from HR was quick and severe. Corey left, and Ellie didn't even get a letter in her file; in fact, she ended up with many more friends in the office than she'd had before.

Even so, she left within six months, in search of a fresh start, and after that, she changed jobs regularly every year. Because, as Ellie quickly learned, there was one in every office: the man everyone whispered about. All she had to do was listen, and wait, and give him an Opportunity, and, soon enough, he would find her.

# ACKNOWLEDGMENTS

Lalise Melillo. Marc Shell. Biodun Jeyifo. Glenda Carpio. Bret Anthony Johnston. Jeff VanderMeer. Ann VanderMeer. Claire Vaye Watkins. Laura Kasischke. Peter Ho Davies. Eileen Pollack. Doug Trevor. Petra Kuppers. Helen Zell. The Hopwood Foundation. Clarion Class of 2014. Michigan MFA Class of 2017. Jenni Ferrari-Adler. Taylor Curtin. Sally Wofford-Girand. Deborah Treisman. Alison Callahan. Meagan Harris. Brita Lundberg. Jennifer Bergstrom. Jennifer Robinson. Carolyn Reidy. Jon Karp. Michal Shavit. Ana Fletcher. Emma Paterson. Joe Pickering. Carly Wray. Lila Byock. Michelle Kroes. Darian Lanzetta. Olivia Blaustein. Marion Grice. Jill Kenrick. Alison Grice. Carol Roupenian. Gary Gazzaniga. Armen Roupenian. Alex Roupenian. Elisa Roupenian Toha. Martin Toha. Vivian Toha. Jenn Liddiard. Melissa Urann Hilley. Liz Maynes-Aminzade. Lesley Goodman. Andrew Jacobs. James Brandt. Nick Donofrio. Schuyler Senft-Grupp. Christin Lee. Lucy Eazer. Ashley Whitaker. Ingrid Hammond. Callie Collins.

Thank you.